New York Times bestseller Jill Shalvis is the author of many romance novels including her acclaimed Lucky Harbor, Animal Magnetism and Cedar Ridge series. The RITA winner and three-time National Readers Choice winner makes her home near Lake Tahoe.

Visit her website at www.jillshalvis.com for a complete book list and daily blog, and www.facebook.com/JillShalvis for other news, or follow her on Twitter @JillShalvis.

Jill Shalvis. Delightfully addictive:

'Packed with the trademark Shalvis humor and intense intimacy, it is definitely a must-read . . . If love, laughter and passion are the keys to any great romance, then this novel hits every note' *Romantic Times*

'Heart-warming and sexy . . . an abundance of chemistry, smoldering romance, and hilarious antics' *Publishers Weekly*

'[Shalvis] has quickly become one of my go-to authors of contemporary romance. Her writing is smart, fun, and sexy, and her books never fail to leave a smile on my face long after I've closed the last page . . . Jill Shalvis is an author not to be missed!' *The Romance Dish*

'Jill Shalvis is such a talented author that she brings to life characters who make you laugh, cry, and are a joy to read' *Romance Reviews Today*

'What I love about Jill Shalvis's books is that she writes sexy, adorable heroes . . . the sexual tension is out of this world. And of course, in true Shalvis fashion, she expertly mixes in humor that has you laughing out loud' *Heroes and Heartbreakers*

'I always enjoy reading a Jill Shalvis book. She's a consistently elegant, bold, clever writer . . . Very witty – I laughed out loud countless times and these scenes are sizzling' *All About Romance*

'If you have not read a Jill Shalvis novel yet, then you really have not read a re_____ *Reviews*

'E_____

By Jill Shalvis

Heartbreaker Bay Series
Sweet Little Lies
The Trouble With Mistletoe
One Snowy Night (e-novella)
Accidentally On Purpose

Cedar Ridge Series
Second Chance Summer
My Kind Of Wonderful
Nobody But You

Animal Magnetism Series
Animal Magnetism
Animal Attraction
Rescue My Heart
Rumour Has It
Then Came You
Still The One
All I Want

Lucky Harbor Series
Simply Irresistible
The Sweetest Thing
Head Over Heels
Lucky In Love
At Last
Forever And A Day
It Had To Be You
Always On My Mind
Once In A Lifetime
It's In His Kiss
He's So Fine
One In A Million
Merry Christmas, Baby and Under
The Mistletoe Omnibus (e-novella)

JILL SHALVIS

accidentally
on *purpose*

HEADLINE
ETERNAL

Published by arrangement with Avon Books,
an imprint of HarperCollins Publishers

First published in Great Britain in 2017
by HEADLINE ETERNAL
An imprint of HEADLINE PUBLISHING GROUP

1

Cataloguing in Publication Data is available from the British Library

ISBN 978 1 4722 4483 3

Offset in 12.54/16 pt TimesLtStd by Jouve (UK)

Printed and bound in Great Britain by CPI Group (UK) Ltd, Croydon, CR0 4YY

Headline's policy is to use papers that are natural, renewable and recyclable products
and made from wood grown in well-managed forests and other
controlled sources. The logging and manufacturing processes are expected
to conform to the environmental regulations of the country of origin.

HEADLINE PUBLISHING GROUP
An Hachette UK Company
Carmelite House
50 Victoria Embankment
London EC4Y 0DZ

www.headlineeternal.com
www.headline.co.uk
www.hachette.co.uk

Laura Reeth and Sarah Morgan
for the unfailing friendship.
Always in my heart . . .

Chapter 1

#TakeMeToYourLeader

It was a good thing Elle Wheaton loved being in charge and ordering people around, because if it wasn't for the thrill of having both those things in her job description, she absolutely didn't get paid enough to handle all the idiots in her world. "Last night was a disaster," she said.

Her boss, not looking nearly as concerned as she, shrugged. He was many things and one of them was the owner of the Pacific Pier Building in which they stood, located in the Cow Hollow district of San Francisco. A detail he preferred to keep to himself.

In fact, only one person besides herself knew his identity, but as the building's general manager, Elle alone handled everything and was always his go-between. The calm, *kickass* go-between, if she said so herself, although what had happened last night had momentarily shaken some of her calm.

"I have faith in you," he said.

She slid him a look. "In other words, 'Fix it, Elle, because I don't want to be bothered about it.'"

"Well, and that," he said with a smile as he pushed his glasses further up on his nose.

She refused to be charmed. Yes, he was sexy in that utterly oblivious way of smart geeks and, yes, they were best friends and she loved him, but in her world, love had limits. "Maybe I should recap the disaster for you," she said. "First, the little lights in every emergency exit sign in the entire building died at midnight. So when Mrs. Winslowe in 3D went to take her geriatric dog to do his business, she couldn't see the stairwell. Cut to Mr. Nottingham from 4A—whom, it should be noted, was sneaking out of his mistress's apartment in 3F— slipping and falling in dog poo."

"You can't make this stuff up," he said, still smiling.

Elle crossed her arms. "Mr. Nottingham broke his ankle and very nearly his ass, requiring an ambulance ride and a possible lawsuit. And you're amused."

"Come on, Elle. You and I both know life sucks golf balls if you let it. Gotta find the fun somewhere. We'll pay the hospital bill and buy Mr. Nottingham new pants. I'll throw in a weekend getaway and he can take his girlfriend or his wife—or both if he wants. We'll make it right." Spence smiled at her snort. "Get yourself some caffeine. You look like you're down a pint."

"My life isn't normal," she said with a shake of her head.

"Forget normal. Normal's overrated. Now drink that gross green stuff you can't survive without."

"It's just tea, you weirdo. And I could totally survive without it if I needed to." She paused. "I just can't guarantee anyone else's safety."

"Exactly, so why take chances?"

Elle rolled her eyes. She was still taking what had happened last night personally. She knew everyone in this building, each and every business on the first and second floor and every tenant on the third and fourth floor, and she felt responsible for all of them.

And someone had been hurt on her watch. Unacceptable. "You do realize that the emergency exit system falls under security's jurisdiction," she said. "Which means the security company you hired failed us."

Spence, following her line of thought, stopped looking so amused. He put down his coffee. "No, Elle."

"Spence, a year ago now you sought me out for the general manager job. You put me in charge of covering your ass, which we both know I'm very good at. So I'm going to go discuss this matter with Archer, your head of security."

He grimaced. "At least let me clear the building before you two go at each other."

"There won't be a fight." At least not that she'd tell him about. "I'm simply doing my job and that includes managing one Archer Hunt."

"Yes, technically," Spence allowed. "But we both

know that he answers to no one but himself and he certainly doesn't consider you his boss. He doesn't consider *anyone* his boss."

Elle smiled and mainlined some more tea, the nectar of the gods as far as she was concerned. "His problem, not mine."

Looking pained, Spence stood. "He's not going to enjoy you going off on him this early half-cocked, Elle."

"Ask me if I care."

"*I* care," Spence said. "It's too early to help you bury his body."

Elle let out a short laugh. Her and Archer's antagonistic attitude toward each other had been well documented. The thing was, Archer thought he ran the world, including her.

But no one ran her world except her. "If everyone would just do what they were supposed to and stay out of my way . . ." she said, trailing off because Spence was no longer listening to her. Instead he was staring out the window, his leanly muscled body suddenly tense, prompting her to his side to see what had caught his interest.

A woman was coming out of the coffee shop and Spence was staring at her. It was his ex, who had once upon a time done her best to rip out his heart.

"Want me to have her kicked off the premises?" Elle asked. "Or I could have her investigated and found guilty of a crime." She was just kidding. Mostly.

"I don't need you to handle my damn dates."

Given that he was a walking Fortune 500 company and also that he'd been badly burned, he actually did need his women investigated, but Elle didn't argue with him. Arguing with Spence was like arguing with a brick wall. But he hadn't dated since his ex and it had been months and months, and her heart squeezed because he was gun-shy now. "Hey, in case you haven't heard, hot genius mechanical engineers slash geeks are in. You'll find someone better." Much better, if she had her say . . .

He still didn't respond and Elle rolled her eyes. "How come men are idiots?"

"Because women don't come with instruction manuals." He pushed away from the window. "I've gotta go. No killing anyone today, Elle."

"Sure."

He took the time to give her a long look.

She sighed. "Fine. I won't kill Archer."

When she was alone, she applied some lip gloss—for herself, mind you, not for Archer—and left her office, taking her time walking the open hallway. She loved this building and never got tired of admiring the unique architecture of the old place; the corbeled brick and exposed iron trusses, the long picture windows in each unit, the cobblestone courtyard below with the huge fountain where idiots came from all over San Francisco and beyond to toss their money and wish for love.

She was on the second floor in the far north corner, from which if she pressed her nose up against her office window and if there wasn't any fog, she could see down the hill to the Marina Green and the bay with a very tiny slice of the Golden Gate Bridge as well.

She tried to play it cool, but even after a whole year it was a thrill to live in the heart of the city. Although she hadn't grown up far from here, it'd been a world away and at least ten rungs down on the social ladder.

It was still early enough that the place was quiet. As she passed the elevator, the doors opened and the woman in charge of housekeeping services came through pushing a large cart.

"Hey, honey," Trudy said in her been-smoking-for-three-decades voice. "Need anything?"

"Nope, I'm good." Good plus mad, but although she adored Trudy, the woman couldn't keep a secret to save her life. "Just taking in the nice morning."

"Oh, that's a disappointment," Trudy said. "I thought maybe you were looking for that hottie with the nice package, the one who runs the investigation firm down the hall."

Elle nearly choked on her tea. "Nice *package?*"

"Well I'm old, not dead." And with a wink, Trudy pushed her cart down the hall.

It was true that Archer was annoyingly hot, not that she cared. Hot was useless to her. She'd much rather have the things that had eluded her for most of her life—safety, security . . . stability.

Three things Archer had never been accused of.

At the other end of the hall, she stopped in front of the door with a discreet sign: HUNT INVESTIGATIONS.

The investigative and elite security firm was carried on Archer's reputation alone, no ads or marketing required. Basically Archer and the men he employed were finders and fixers, independent contractors for hire, and not necessarily tied by the same red tape as the law.

Which worked for Archer. Rules had never been his thing.

She opened the door and let herself into the reception area, which was much bigger than hers. Clean, masculine lines. Large furniture. Wide open space. A glass partition separated the front from the inner offices.

The check-in counter was empty. The receptionist wasn't in yet—it was too early for Mollie. But not for the other employees. Past the glass Elle could see part of the inner office. A group of men, five of them, entered by a private door. They'd clearly just come back from some sort of job that had required them to be locked and loaded since they currently looked like a SWAT team.

Elle literally stopped short. And if she was being honest, her heart stopped too because sweet baby Jesus. The lot of them stood there stripping off weapons and shirts so that all she could see was a mass of mind-blowing bodies, sweaty and tatted and in all varieties of skin colors.

It was a cornucopia of smutty goodness and she couldn't tear her eyes away. In fact, she couldn't speak either, mostly because her tongue had hit the floor. Her feet took advantage of her frozen brain, taking her to the interior door, where she wanted to press her face up against the glass.

Luckily, someone buzzed her in before she could. They all knew her. After all, her job required her to work closely with the security firm, and therein lay her deepest, darkest problem.

Working closely with Archer Hunt was dangerous in oh so many, *many* ways, not the least of which was their history, something she did her best to never think about.

She was greeted with variations on "Hey, Elle" and "Mornin'" and then they all went their separate ways, leaving her alone with their fearless leader.

Archer.

It'd been a long time since they'd let themselves be alone. In fact, she always actively sought out ways to *not* be alone with him, and given how successful she'd been, she could only figure he'd been doing the same.

Not looking particularly bothered by this unexpected development, Archer met her gaze straight on. He hadn't unloaded his weapons or his shirt and stood there in full utility combat gear, complete with a Glock on one hip, a stun gun on the other, and a pistol strapped to a thigh. His Army hat was backward on his head. The handle of a butterfly knife stuck out of a pocket in his cargoes and he had two sets of cuffs strapped to his belt. An urban warrior, wired for sound with a two-way and a Kevlar vest strapped across his chest and back, telling Elle that wherever they'd been, he hadn't just come back from Disneyland.

She managed to be both horrified and turned on at the same time. But if life had taught her one thing the hard way, it was how to hide her thoughts and emotions, so she carefully rolled up her tongue.

The corner of Archer's mouth quirked, like maybe he could read her mind. But he didn't say a word, instead seeming perfectly content to stand there all badass and wait her out. And she knew from experience that he *could* wait her out, until the end of time if need be.

So of course, she caved and spoke first. "Long morning already?"

"Long night," he said.

He was big and tough, and frustrating beyond measure for so many reasons, not the least of which was her very secret crush on him, uncomfortably balanced on the fact that she owed him her life.

Unconcerned with any of that, he began to unload his weapons. Most of the jobs he took on were routine: criminal, corporate, and insurance investigations along with elite security contracts, surveillance, fraud, and corporate background checks. But some weren't routine at all, like the forensic investigations, the occasional big bond bounty hunting, government contract work . . . all with the potential to be dangerous if not life threatening.

In contrast, the security contract he held on this building surely seemed tame and mild in comparison, but she knew it was a favor to Spence.

"We have a problem," she said.

He arched a brow, the equivalent of a long-winded query from anyone else.

She rolled her eyes and found herself in a defensive pose, hands on hips. "The emergency exit signs—"

"Already taken care of," he said.

"Okay, but Mr. Nottingham—"

"Also taken care of."

She took a deep, purposefully calming breath. It was hard to look right at him because he was very tall. At five foot seven, she was nowhere close to petite but even she barely came up to his shoulders. She hated that he had such a height advantage during their arguments. And this *was* going to be an argument.

"So what happened?" she asked. "Why did the lights go out like that, all at once?"

"Squirrels."

"Excuse me?"

At her tone, his piercing eyes flashed a disturbingly intense combination of green and light brown, reflecting the fact that he'd seen the worst of the worst and was capable of fighting it with his bare hands. She got that the edge of danger and testosterone coming off him in waves attracted the opposite sex like bees to honey but at the moment she'd like to stomp on his size thirteen Bates. Especially since he didn't repeat himself, and tired of the macho show, she poked him in the chest with her finger. His pec didn't give at all. *Stupid muscles.* "Listen," she said. "I've got pissed-off tenants, a man in the hospital, and a signed contract from you guaranteeing the safety of the people in this building. So I'm going to need you to do more than stand there all tall, dark, and silently brooding on this one, Archer, and tell me what the hell is going on, preferably using more than one word at a time."

"You want to be careful how you speak to me, Elle," he said.

The man was impenetrable. A virtual island. And he didn't like being questioned, she knew that much. But she also knew the only way to deal with him was to hold her own. He didn't respect cowards. "Fine," she said. "Will you *pretty please* tell me what the hell is going on?"

At that he looked very slightly amused, probably because she was the only one who ever dared to push him. "Last fall I told you that you had a squirrel colony going on in the roof," he said. "I said that you needed to hire someone to block off the holes left behind by woodpeckers from the year before or you were going to have problems. You assured me you'd handled it."

"Because the landscapers assured me they'd take care of it."

He shrugged a broad shoulder. "Either they blew you off or they didn't do it correctly. An entire colony of squirrels moved into the walls and had a party. Last night they hit the electrical room, where they ate through some wires."

Well, hell. No wonder he was giving her bad 'tude. He was right. This wasn't on him at all.

It was on *her*. "What happened to the squirrels?" she asked.

"Probably dead in the walls."

She blinked. "Are you telling me I killed a bunch of squirrels?"

His mouth quirked. "What do you think the landscapers would've done? Sent them on a vacay to the Bahamas?"

"Okay," she said, letting out a long exhale. "Thanks for the explanation." She turned to go.

His hand caught her, long fingers wrapping around her elbow and causing all sorts of unwelcome sensations as he pulled her back around.

"What?" she asked.

"Waiting for my apology."

"Sure," she said agreeably. "When hell freezes over." She lifted her chin, grateful for her four-inch heels so that she could almost, kind of, not quite look him in the eyes. "I'm in charge of this building, Archer, which means I'm in charge of everything that happens in it. I'm also in charge of everyone who works *for* this building."

He cocked his head, looking amused again. "You want to be the boss of me, Elle?" he asked softly.

"I *am* the boss of you."

Now he outright smiled and her breath caught. Damn, stupid, sexy smile. And then there was The Body. Yes, she thought of it in capital letters, it deserved the respect. "If you don't want to be walking funny tomorrow," she said, "you'll stop invading my personal-space bubble."

Complete bravado and they both knew it. She'd only been at this job for a year and it'd come as a surprise to her that he'd been in the building at all. An unfortunate coincidence. Before that it'd been years since they'd had any contact, but she still knew enough to get that no one got the better of him.

He was quick, light on his feet, and physically strong. But that wasn't what made him so dangerous to her. No, it was his sharp intelligence, his quick wit, how he was willing to go as dark as he needed to in order to do what he thought was right.

And then there was the biggie—the way he had of making her feel shockingly alive.

He did as she asked and stepped back but not before pausing to make sure they both knew who was in control here, and it most definitely wasn't her.

No one did intimidation like Archer, and in his line of work he could be in a coma and still intimidate everyone in the room. He had muscles on top of muscles but didn't look beefed up like a body builder might.

Instead his body seemed lean and seriously badass, with caramel skin that strayed from light to golden to mocha latte depending on what the season was, giving him a look of indeterminable origin.

And sexiness.

It worked for him, allowing him to fit in to just about any situation. Handy on the job, she imagined. But with her he was careful. Distant. And yet she'd seen the way he sometimes looked at her, and on the rare occasion when he'd touched her, like when he guided her through a door with his hand low on her back, he let himself linger. There was always a shocking and baffling yearning beyond both the glances and the touches.

That, or it was all just wishful thinking.

Not that it mattered since he still held back with her. The problem was she yearned too. Yearned for him to see her as a woman, strong and capable enough to stand at his side.

But after what they'd been through, she knew that would never happen. She turned away, annoyed by how her entire body had gone on high alert as always, every inch of her seeming to hum beneath the surface.

She should have just emailed him.

He waited until she got to the door before he spoke, "I've got a job I need your help on."

"No," she said.

He just looked at her.

She took online college classes at the crack of dawn.

Her job was demanding and took up a solid eight hours a day. At night she studied, fighting for her ever elusive accounting degree. Someday she was going to run her own accounting firm and be badass too, just in a different way than Archer. She was going to be a stable, respectable badass—in great shoes. But in the meantime, she worked herself half into the grave just to keep her head above water.

Problem was, school was expensive, very expensive. As was living in San Francisco. As were great shoes. Plus good jobs didn't grow on trees. The one she'd had before this had turned out to be a nightmare. She felt lucky here, and although she was paid very decently, college was breaking her bank. To help fund herself, she took the occasional job with Archer when he needed a woman on a job. A distraction usually, but sometimes he prevailed on her other skills, skills she'd honed a lifetime ago.

"It's a challenging job," he said, knowing exactly how to pique her interest, damn him. "Need an ID on a guy, and if it's our man, we need a distraction while we . . . *borrow* his laptop, the one he never lets out of his sight."

Hmm. Definitely a challenge. "I don't suppose he's the type you could just walk up to and ask his name," she said.

His mouth curved in a small smile. "Let's just say I'm not someone who would interest him."

"No? So who would?" she asked.

"A hot blonde with legs for days in a short, tight dress."

Heat pooled in her belly and spread outward. Dammit.

"One with the stickiest pickpocket fingers I've ever met," he added.

With a low laugh—dammit, was there anything sexier than a man who knew you to the bone?—she made it to the outer reception area. She'd just reached for the front door when it opened and she collided with someone.

The man caught her, keeping her upright. "I'm so sorry. Are you alright?"

"I'm fine," she said. In his early thirties, he was about her height, medium build, and in a very nice suit. He also had a nice smile, a *kind* smile, and more than a little male interest in his expression.

"Mike Penham," he said, offering her a hand. "I'm a client of Archer's."

"Elle Wheaton." She smiled. "Not a client."

"Ah, a mysterious woman," he said with a smile.

"No, just a busy one." She shot one last look at Archer—a mistake because his gaze was inscrutable and on her as always, and she felt her stupid heart do a stupid somersault in her chest as he came into the front room, moving with his usual liquid grace in spite of still being armed for a third-world skirmish.

"Mike," he said in greeting to the man who'd just arrived. "Come on back." He looked at Elle. "Tonight then?"

Since she'd never yet figured out how to say no to the hot bastard, she nodded. And for a single beat, the mask fell from his eyes and his golden green gaze warmed as he nodded back.

And then she shut the door between them.

Chapter 2

#AccidentallyOnPurpose

"Damn, she's smokin' hot. Is she available?"

Archer heard Mike's question about Elle but he didn't take his gaze off her as she walked her sweet ass out of his office. "No."

Mike slapped his hand dramatically to his own chest. "Right through the heart, man. You've cut me right through the heart. She's got some serious fire, that one. Love that in a woman."

Yeah Elle had fire. She was like the sun. Get too close and you'd burn up . . . With a shake of his head at himself, Archer turned away, heading for his office.

"No, but seriously," Mike said, following along after him. "I've got a shot at her, right?"

"No."

Mike laughed. The guy was a walking conglomerate and a solid client who brought in business, a lot of it in fact, but that didn't mean Archer wanted him within fifty feet of Elle.

Granted, the vulnerable, scared, isolated sixteen-year-old street rat he'd once saved when he'd been a twenty-two-year-old rookie cop was not a street rat anymore. Nor alone, scared, or vulnerable. She was outspoken and tough as nails.

But she wasn't available. Hell no.

Not that she was his.

He wanted her. And he wanted her bad too. But she'd worked her ass off to become the woman she was now. He knew he reminded her of bad times, and there was no way he'd risk setting her back or damaging her in any way. She'd been through enough without him muddying the waters. So they were friends.

Or maybe the more accurate description was that they *pretended* to be friends.

He entered his office and he gestured for Mike to have a seat. "Your message said you have a security problem."

"A big one," Mike said. "I think our digital division's got a leak."

"What makes you think so?"

"We had two new high-tech communication products that no one else even had a bead on. We had a scheduled presentation to a very selective, confidential client—"

"How selective?" Archer asked. "How confidential?"

Mike rolled his lips inward. "Let's just say *very*."

The US government, Archer figured, reading between the lines. "And let me guess, someone beat you to the punch."

"Our number one competitor," Mike said grimly. "But there's no way in hell that they beat us. Someone gave them the intel. From the inside."

"That's ugly."

"Yes. And now I need to stop the leak. You in?"

Archer nodded. "I'm in, but—"

"I know, I know," Mike said. "No guarantees, blah blah. I've heard the spiel, Hunt, but you've not failed me yet. Plus I'm going to pay you a whole helluva lot of money to make sure you don't fail me this time either."

Archer gave him a short nod. "Consider it done."

When Mike left, Archer set some plans into motion to get that job up and running, and then he got to work going over the plan for the night's distraction.

They'd been hired by an insurance company. Some of their clients were up in arms, claiming that they'd paid for additional services that had never been received.

It turned out that the insurance company didn't even provide those services and had no records of receiving the premiums.

Enter Hunt Investigations. Archer had dug in and found it all came down to one freelance insurance agent who'd quietly offered select—read: *rich*—clients some opportunities to upgrade. All that had been required were additional "premiums." The agent had then pocketed those additional premiums—of course without upgrading the policies.

With help from Archer's resident computer specialist, Joe, they'd located the "agent," a guy who had multiple aliases but was currently using the name Chuck Smithson. Some further research revealed that Chuck was a loner who trusted no one. He moved around between hotels and kept a cross-body messenger bag on him at all times, which most likely held his laptop and all his secrets. And since he lived in a state of paranoia and didn't back up anywhere that they could hack into, they needed that laptop for evidence.

During their research, they'd found that swindler Chuck had an additional habit—he enjoyed trolling Internet hookup sites. Archer had gotten an email earlier from Elle that she was in on the job, so they'd set up a profile for bait. Chuck had taken that bait hook, line, and sinker, and was in fact expecting to meet "Candy Cunningham" tonight for a drink.

All Archer needed Elle to do was ID Chuck and then keep him busy while they took a look in the briefcase and copied his hard drive. The evidence wouldn't be admissible in court but the insurance company didn't want to take it that far and risk the public hearing about their humiliatingly heavy losses. They just wanted Hunt Investigations to confirm their suspicions before figuring out their next step.

Archer texted his team and waited as they began to file back in, fresh from showers, various forms of caffeine in one hand, breakfast in the other.

Max was head of the pack and since he'd been with his girlfriend, Rory, for two months now—a record for him—there was a definite pep to his step. He sat across the conference table from Archer with Carl, his Doberman, at his side. Carl was a huge asset to their team but at the moment all he had on his brain was the massive donut in his master's hand.

Max shoved a huge bite of said donut into his mouth. "All set for tonight, boss," he said to Archer. "We've got entrances and exits covered and Finn's going to have all eyes on deck for us."

Finn was the owner and bartender at O'Riley's, the pub on the ground floor of the building where the distraction would take place. He also happened to be a close friend.

Archer didn't usually bring work so close to his home base but he never took chances when it came to Elle.

Never.

She was a great asset when he needed a distraction because she had a way of making a man forget he had a brain. He'd been a victim of this himself, more than once. Thing was, too many times to count she'd managed to get him information that had closed a case for him, info he couldn't have gotten without bloodshed.

She claimed to do these jobs because she loved the money. He knew that wasn't strictly true. She did love money, in the way that only someone who'd grown up without any could. But he knew that wasn't why she did it. Nope, she worked for him when he asked because she thought she owed him.

But the truth was, he owed her.

The rest of the guys got comfortable. Joe, who besides being his IT guy was also his right-hand man. Then there was Lucas, Trev, and Reyes. Their conference room was big, but so were they and the room seemed to shrink in their presence.

"Why do you smell like maple and bacon?" Joe asked Max.

"Because I'm eating a maple and bacon donut," Max said.

"No shit?"

"No shit."

Joe's stomach growled loud enough to echo off the walls.

Max blew out a sigh and tossed him a white paper bag. "You gotta share with Carl though—I promised him some."

Carl gave one sharp bark in agreement.

The rest of the guys protested, loudly.

"I want it."

"Shit, man, I'll even pay for it."

But Joe held tight to the bag, fighting the others off. When he was in the clear, he pulled out the donut, broke off a corner, and tossed it to Carl, who caught it in midair with an audible snap of his huge jaws.

"Dude," Max chided his dog, "you didn't even taste that."

Carl licked his massive chops but didn't take his eyes off Joe, his new BFF.

Joe bit into the rest of the donut. Closing his eyes, he leaned his head back and moaned.

"Maybe you need a moment alone with that thing," Archer said dryly.

"Yes. *Jesus*."

"Right?" Max said with a smile. "I wanna marry this donut and have its babies."

This started an explicit, filthy conversation that had everyone laughing until Archer opened his laptop. Immediately all conversation and amusement faded away.

Time to get to work.

Thirty minutes before the night's gig, Archer heard the outer door to his offices open and close and then soft voices.

His receptionist, Mollie, greeting someone.

A few seconds later he heard the soft *click, click, click* of heels heading his way.

Mollie wore heels. So did some of his clients. But he knew the sound of these. Even if there hadn't been attitude in every single step he would've recognized Elle's smooth, confident stride anywhere.

And if that didn't clue him in, the fact that his dick stirred was a dead giveaway.

A text from Mollie came through announcing Elle's arrival just as the woman herself knocked once on his door. She leaned against the wood, saying nothing.

She looked . . . heart-stopping. That was the thing about Elle, she was always one hundred percent put together. He'd had plenty of women in his life. He knew the effort that they put in and the mind-boggling time they took, so he had no idea how Elle did it day in and day out. But whether on the job or in her personal life, it didn't matter, she dressed like a million bucks and she never had so much as a single strand of her shoulder length blonde hair out of place. In fact, there'd only been one time in the eleven years he'd known her when she hadn't been on her game and she sure as hell wouldn't thank him for the reminder of that long ago, fateful night.

Earlier this morning she'd been in a power-red suit dress that had screamed success, even at the crack of dawn. She'd changed into a killer little black dress, emphasis on *little*. Her heels defied gravity with sexy little straps around her ankles and bows at the back, and her expression said she ate men for breakfast, lunch, and dinner.

She did a slow twirl and he stopped breathing as he slowly rose from his chair. "Holy shit, Elle."

"I wasn't going for holy shit. I was going for sophisticated sexy."

"Copy that," he said. "But you're also one hundred percent holy shit. You're also a walking heart attack and aneurism—an all-in-one special."

"Good. I was worried that maybe I look a little bit too much like I belong on Post Street."

He looked her over again, enjoying the view way too much. "Post Street's looking good."

She rolled her eyes. "You should check out the corner of Post and *Kiss My Ass*."

He grinned and strolled over to her. She smelled like a million bucks, making him want to press his face into her hair, or better yet her neck so he could inhale her like she was his own maple and bacon donut. Instead, he handed her an earpiece. "Comms. We'll all be connected. There'll be constant eyes on you too. The guys are already in place. Our mark isn't known to be dangerous or armed but—"

"You're not taking any chances with me yadda yadda," she said impatiently, taking the earpiece. "I've heard the spiel before. I'm not a special snowflake, Archer. If I was, I wouldn't be here—you wouldn't allow it."

All true. But he could no more curb his insane need to keep her protected and safe than he could stop breathing. It'd always been like that for him with her.

She put in the earpiece and give him a little nod.

"Okay," he said. "So—"

"I've read the file you emailed me," she interrupted. "I'm going in as Candy Cunningham, the girl Chuck swiped for and thinks is tonight's hookup. I'm to get in, ID him, hold his attention until you guys do your thing with the laptop that's hopefully in his briefcase, and then get out."

"And get out fast, Elle. I don't want him to know you're—"

"Not Candy," she said. "I think I know what I'm

doing by now. You ready to do this or do you need to freshen up your lipstick?"

Since she was now wired for sound and so was Archer, he heard the snickers and snorts from his men in his ear. He didn't bother to respond. He could and did demand their respect. But he was under no such illusions when it came to controlling Elle.

They took the elevator in silence. Elle stared at the doors. Archer stared at Elle. He had no idea how the dress was containing her full breasts with that low, plunging vee. Every move she made, they strained to escape.

What felt like a year later, the elevator doors finally opened. He caught Elle's hand and waited until she met his gaze. "You've got fifteen minutes to gain his attention or walk out," he said. "After that we go to Plan B."

"Which is?"

"A plan that doesn't involve you."

"In that dress, she's only going to need one minute," Joe said in Archer's ear from his vantage point in the courtyard.

"I'd put money down on fifteen seconds," Reyes said.

"Shut it," Archer said.

Radio silence followed this directive.

Elle snorted and walked off, her heels clicking over the cobblestones as she passed the fountain in the center of the courtyard and entered the pub.

Archer took a moment to shake it off—around her he had to do that a helluva lot—and followed. He

was going in as a patron and would be guarding her
sexy ass.

O'Riley's was one-half bar, one-half seated dining.
The walls were dark wood that gave an old-world feel to
the place. Brass lanterns hung from the rafters and rustic
baseboards finished the look that said *sit your tired ass
down, order good food and spirits, and be merry.*

Catching sight of Elle heading toward the bar wasn't
difficult, people parted like the Red Sea for her, making
room. She settled herself on a barstool right next to
Chuck Smithson and nodded to the bartender.

Finn.

"Nonalcoholic," Archer murmured.

Finn, also wired, nodded even though they'd already
gone through all this. On the job there was never any
alcohol allowed.

Elle waited for her drink and then took a sip, all
without looking at their guy.

Chuck sat on the stool next to her. He was five foot
four, wiry, and with his wrinkled academic-looking
clothes and thick black-rimmed glasses he was either
a hipster wannabe or making a play for imitating a
slightly grown-up Harry Potter. His feet didn't touch
the floor, instead they were hooked into a rung of
the barstool, his messenger bag settled between his
boots. He'd swiveled to watch, actually stare, at Elle,
and when she slowly turned as if eyeing the room, he
straightened, pushed his glasses higher on the bridge of
his nose and sent her a hopeful smile.

She gave him one in return, a sugary sweet smile that Archer sure as hell had never seen aimed his way before and which had Chuck nearly falling off his stool.

"Man, she's something," Joe whispered in their ears.

"You're drooling," Max said.

"We're all drooling," Lucas said. "She's a walking boner."

"Silence," Archer ordered quietly and they all shut the hell up.

Still looking sweet and somehow demure despite the sexy-as-hell getup, Elle leaned into Chuck. Archer watched closely, fascinated because he knew she could pick a pocket in a few seconds flat right in front of his eyes and he wouldn't even see it.

"Chuck?" Elle whispered.

Her pic had been on her bio but the guy swallowed hard and nodded, his eyes lit like he'd just discovered it was Christmas morning. "Candy?"

Elle bit her lower lip, managing to look a little shy. "Would you mind showing me your ID?" she asked. "You wouldn't believe the number of creepers I have to weed through."

"I bet," Chuck said sympathetically. "It's because you're so beautiful."

This guy was eating out of the palm of her hand. She wasn't even going to have to use her skills. Archer found himself smiling at her cleverness and shaking his head in awe. He loved watching her in action, which he didn't get to see often.

She hadn't made a secret of the fact that she didn't like him all that much. Not that he blamed her. She associated him with a very bad part of her past, plus he knew she thought he was too bossy and a control freak—both of which happened to be true.

But it took one to know one.

Chuck hopped of his stool and pulled a wallet from his back pocket.

Elle, smart enough to kick off her high heels to cut her own height down before standing up too, gathered her shoes by the strap, hanging them off a finger. She then leaned into Chuck to look at his ID, letting her hair fall into his face and, Archer was pretty sure, also letting her breast brush against the guy's arm.

Chuck swallowed hard, blinking when Elle lifted her beaming face to his. "Nice to meet you, Chuck Smithson," she said.

"ID confirmation," Max said into his comms from where he sat at the bar two spots over, appearing to be lost in the basketball game on the TV behind the bar. "I'm in place to move in."

Now all Elle had to do was keep Chuck distracted from his messenger bag while he did.

"Can we dance?" Elle asked, shy. Timid.

Archer didn't have a type when it came to women. He liked them in all shapes and sizes and in a wide variety of personalities. But shy and timid had never done much for him.

Until right that minute. Even knowing it was a damn act, knowing that Elle didn't have a shy or timid bone in her body, he wanted to go over there, haul her in tight, and comfort her. It was such a shocking urge he nearly missed what came next.

"Uh." Chuck blinked up at Elle, still several inches shorter than she. "I'm not much of a dancer—"

"Oh, no worries," she said sweetly, "everyone's got a dancer deep inside him."

"But—"

"Please?" she asked softly, batting those baby blues.

Chuck downed his drink. "For liquid courage," he said, gesturing to Finn for another.

"Make it a double," Archer instructed Finn.

"I'll lead," Elle promised Chuck as he tossed back the second drink. Winding an arm in one of his, she pulled him away from the bar.

"But my stuff . . ." Twisting back, he eyed his messenger bag on the floor.

"It's safe here." Elle looked at Finn behind the bar. "Right?"

"Absolutely," Finn said.

"But—"

But nothing. The poor dumb fucker never knew what hit him. As Elle led him by the balls to the dance floor, keeping Chuck's back to the bar, Joe moved in, smoothly grabbed the briefcase, and vanished.

On the small, crowded dance floor, Elle began to move, shimmying that body of hers, dazzling Chuck— and every other man in the place—into an open-mouthed stupor.

Not Archer. No, he was in heart failure because if

she wasn't careful she was going to come right out of that dress. "Joe, report," he said, rubbing his left eye, which had started to twitch.

"We're an inch from a nipple-gate situation," Max said in a reverent, hopeful whisper.

Archer made a mental note to kill him later. *"Joe."*

"Need three more minutes."

Shit. The seconds crawled by, while on the dance floor Chuck had moved up against Elle and was grinning ear to ear as he tried to keep up with her.

As if anyone could.

"Done," Joe finally said, and Archer breathed for the first time in the longest three minutes of his life.

"Copied the hard drive," Joe said, and then in the next beat Archer watched as he smoothly replaced the messenger bag beneath Chuck's barstool.

Not two seconds later Chuck turned from the dance floor, his gaze seeking and finding his messenger bag, still under his barstool.

"All done, boss," Joe said. "Oh and the guy's got a handful of different IDs on him as well as the laptop. Scanned everything."

Score. "Elle," Archer said. "Make your exit."

The music was loud, so was the pub. People were having a great time. And apparently Chuck was one of them because his liquid courage had clearly kicked in. Some confidence too because he kept trying to get his hands all over Elle as they moved together to the beat.

"You're so pretty!" Chuck yelled up to Elle's face.

She smiled.

"No, I mean like . . . porn pretty!" He was still yelling. "I'm kind of a connoisseur, so I'd know! Have you ever thought about it? You'd make millions!" He grinned. "Usually when I get drunk, I talk loud, like *really* loud! But I'm not doing that now because you don't even look scared!"

"You ever miss being a cop in moments like this?" Max asked conversationally in Archer's ear. "Cuz then you could go arrest that fucker."

No, Archer didn't miss being a cop. As for what he *did* miss from that old life—his dad for one, no matter how hard-assed the guy had been—he'd shoved it deep and moved on. The real question was *why the hell was Elle still dancing?* He'd given her orders to move out. Making his way through the crowd, he hit the dance floor and tapped Chuck on the shoulder.

The guy turned and looked up, up, up into Archer's face. "Erm—" he squeaked out. With a gulp, he relinquished his hold on Elle like she was a hot potato and scampered off like a rat into the night. After stopping for his messenger bag, of course.

Elle bent to slip back into her heels.

Apparently she needed the armor with Archer. Slipping an arm around her waist to give her the support she needed to buckle herself into the FMPs, he waited until she straightened then said, "What the fuck was that?"

"Me doing my job," she said in a *duh* voice.

"Since when is dirty dancing with a felon your job?"

She narrowed her fierce eyes. "You told me to get close to him. You told me to ID him and then keep him distracted, whatever it takes."

"Okay, *no*," he said. "I absolutely did not say *whatever it takes*."

She glared up at him.

"What?" he asked.

"Nothing." Her voice was ice.

"Oh boy," Joe muttered in Archer's ear. "When a woman says 'nothing' in that tone, it most definitely means something and you should be wearing a cup to finish that conversation. Just sayin'."

Archer put a finger to his eye before it twitched right out of his head. "I told you to make your exit," he said to Elle with what he thought was remarkable calm while ignoring Joe, who was a dead man walking anyway. "When I tell you something, Elle, I expect you to listen."

He heard a collective sucking in of air through his comms and ignored that too.

"Wow," Elle finally said.

"Okay," Max piped up. "I have a girlfriend now so I know this one. When Rory says 'wow' like that, it's not a compliment. It means she's thinking long and hard on how and when I'll pay for my stupidity."

"Agreed," Joe said. "She's simply expressing amazement that a man can be such an idiot. Abort mission, boss. I repeat. *Abort. Mission.*"

Shit. Archer ripped out his earpiece and then did the same to Elle's, stuffing both in his pocket.

She shrugged and walked away, leaving him on the dance floor. Watching her go, an odd feeling cranked over in his chest. Irritation, he decided. Frustration. The woman got to him like no one else.

And yet he'd kept tabs on her, watching her back. He couldn't explain why, but apparently old habits died hard.

Did she ever think about that night? She'd never made a single reference to it, not once. And he'd never brought it up, not wanting to bring her back to a bad place.

When he walked off the dance floor and headed toward the bar, she was there, right there, picking up the wrap she'd left. Something fell from it and hit the floor.

They both crouched low at the same time but Archer beat her to it. When he realized what he held, he lifted his head and stared at her in shock.

It was the small pocket knife he'd given her all those years ago.

Which meant she *did* think about that night.

Chapter 3

#TrainWreck

Elle made a move to snatch the knife from Archer's fingers but the bastard held firm. She started a tug-of-war with him before remembering that she no longer let anyone see her sweat and forced herself to go still.

Not that Archer let go. "You still have it," he said, a whisper of surprise in his voice.

The equivalent of a full-on double take from the man who was all but impossible to shock.

And yes, of course she still had the knife. Did he really think she wouldn't? She didn't blush very often but she felt heat rush to her face now. Regret, partly.

Mostly full-blown mortification.

She'd very carefully taught herself to be strong and confident and to never look back.

Ever.

Sentimentality didn't have a place in her life. Or so

she told herself. So why then had she been carrying the small pocket knife Archer had given her the night he'd saved her all those years ago? Especially since the thought of how she'd tried to repay him—and God, the humility of how she'd actually offered him the only thing she'd had, that being her body, which he'd turned down flat—still made her face flame. The worst part had been when he'd vanished like it'd been nothing to him, when to her it'd been everything.

She might not know why he'd done what he had but she still wasn't leaving here without that knife. It was a badge. A reminder of who she'd been and who she was now.

Neither of them had moved. Around them the night life in the pub went on. Laughter, conversations, more dancing . . . all oblivious to this tight, little cocoon of just the two of them crouched in front of the bar. They might as well have been completely alone for all the attention anyone paid them.

Balanced with apparent ease on the balls of his feet, Archer leaned in even closer if that was possible, close enough that his knees touched hers. Close enough that she could see every single gold spec in his hazel eyes. Every single black-as-ink eyelash framing those eyes. He was hours past a five o'clock shadow and a muscle ticked in his square jaw.

A rare tell from a man who could be a stone when he wanted.

The rest of him was as big and bad and intimidating

as ever. His large body blocked out everything behind him and although he could be terrifyingly scary when he wanted to be, he never was with her. With her he was careful. Cautious.

Distant.

And she hated that most of all.

This time when she tried to tug the knife from his long fingers, he let her. Rising, she stared down at him. "We done here?"

He rose to his feet too. And just looked at her.

"Well?" she asked.

"We're never done," he said.

No kidding. But since she had no witty retort for him, she turned on her heel and headed for the doors. She pushed out into the blissfully cool night and strode across the courtyard, which was lit with strings of tiny, beautiful white lights threaded across the shops and small trees that lined the way. San Francisco in February could be just about anything: icy, wet, powder dry, even warm . . . Tonight the sky was a blanket of black velvet, scattered with diamonds. The air was cold and crisp, and it showed in the white puffy clouds she exhaled, hoping for some inner calm.

It didn't come.

She strode to the fountain in the center of the courtyard and stopped to take a minute. And actually, she probably needed more than one.

In her life she'd very carefully and purposely gone after the things she'd missed out on in her childhood and she'd gone after those things hard. She was carefully put together, tough to the core, and, she liked to think, loyal to a fault. And the fact was, she felt incredibly loyal to Archer. After all, he'd gotten her out of a bad situation and she was grateful to him for that. He'd changed the course of her life. But she could admit to herself that deep down she was also a little pissy that he'd never seemed to want more from her. Not that this was a surprise, not when she'd cost him so much. Such as his first career.

And his family . . .

The water in the fountain fell in soft streams into the copper base, which was lined with coins. The thing had been standing here for fifty years longer than the 1928 building around it, dating back to the days when there'd actually been cows in Cow Hollow. The myth went that if you made a wish with a true heart, true love would find you.

God forbid, Elle thought with a shudder.

But it'd worked enough times over the past century that people believed the legend. And in fact, two of her good friends had found love thanks to this very fountain.

As far as Elle was concerned, only a damn fool would make a wish for love. Love brought nothing but complicated problems and she could do without more complications or problems, thank you very much.

"Aren't you going to toss some money in and wish for true love to find you?" came a raspy voice. "That's what everyone else does."

It was Old Man Eddie, who lived in the alley. By

choice, mind you. Several of the building regulars, including herself, had tried to help him more than once, but Eddie said he lived an alternative lifestyle and he wanted to be left alone to do it.

He flashed a smile that went with his shock of white Christopher Lloyd-circa-*Back-to-the-Future* hair, board shorts, rain boots, and a Cal Berkeley sweatshirt that said *Don't Panic, It's Organic* over an image of a weed leaf. Since he'd actually gone to Cal Berkeley in the seventies after previously frying his brain at Woodstock, she flashed a smile back. "I'm most definitely not going to wish for true love," she said. A warm deserted island, maybe. World peace, definitely.

But never love.

"Pru found Finn by wishing," he reminded her. "And Willa found Keane."

"And I'm happy for them," she said. "But I'm not wishing."

"Bummer, dudette, because I was thinking if you were planning on throwing any money away, you might find a better use for it instead."

"Let me guess," she said. "You'd be happy to take it off my hands?"

"Couldn't have said it better myself."

"For the record, I never throw money away," she said, but she slid her hand into the hidden pocket of her wrap, pulling out her emergency twenty, which hadn't fallen out in the bar. Of course not. It'd had to have been the knife. She gave a mental grimace and handed Eddie the cash.

"Thanks, darlin'." He slipped the twenty away before kissing her on each cheek. "I've got today's newspaper, can I repay you by giving you your horoscope?"

"Don't bother. I'm sure mine says 'please just don't kill anyone today.'"

He laughed softly. "And it's no secret who you'd kill either. He's smart as hell, our boy. Intuitive too and a gifted investigator. He takes care of his own. He'd take a bullet for you—we both know that. But one thing he's not good at is admitting his feelings."

"Who?"

He gave her a don't-be-stupid look.

"Archer?" she asked.

"Well who else do you let drive you crazy?" he asked.

Good point.

He patted her on the arm. "Just remember, there's not a lot of softness in his life, or room for weakness—of which you're definitely one. He has absolutely no idea what to do with you, and as an action guy, that's confusing to him. So maybe think about taking it easy on him. Even just a little bit."

She sighed and then opened her mouth to say that she and Archer never went *easy* on each other but the old man had vanished back down his alley, leaving her alone in the night.

The theme song of her life.

She went to pull out her phone to call an Uber and then remembered she'd handed her cell to Spence to hold for her during the distraction. Spence, who was in all likelihood still sitting at the bar. "Dammit." She headed back across the courtyard and let herself into the pub again.

Spence was indeed at the far right side of the bar, at the area Finn always held open for their gang. But that wasn't what caught and held her attention. Nope, that honor went to the other side where Archer sat talking to some beautiful woman who was clearly coming on to him, leaning in, a perfectly manicured hand on his biceps. She was smiling with lots of white, straight teeth, her hair carefully tousled in a way that said it was possible she'd just gotten out of bed and wasn't all that opposed to going back.

Rolling her eyes, Elle headed toward Spence. Pru was with him, as were Willa and Haley. Willa ran South Bark, a one-stop pet shop across the courtyard from the pub. Haley worked at the second-floor optometrist's office and was currently single, but she and one of Finn's waitresses had been flirting for several weeks now and everyone had fingers crossed that it'd turn into something good.

Spence slid Elle's phone across the bar top toward her and then, when he caught the look on her face, passed his glass over as well.

"Jameson?" she asked.

"Only the best for you," he said, watching with quiet amusement as she tossed it back and then coughed. "Easy, tiger."

Turning her back on the sight of Archer and the woman, the both of them flirting freely now, she nodded a thanks to Finn, who brought her another drink.

"She came on to him if it helps any," Willa said, always the peacemaker of the group. Willa had the heart of a saint.

Elle did not. "I couldn't care less."

"Uh-huh," Spence said.

Why were all men assholes? "You know what?" she asked, setting her glass down. "I'm out."

"Aw, come on." Spence grabbed her hand. "Stay. I'll even let you try to kick my ass in darts."

She pointed at him. "I *own* you in darts. But no. Not tonight."

"It's only ten o'clock."

"I have to get up early for class and work."

"Adulting means you get to do whatever you want," Spence said.

He only said that because he'd sold his start-up two years back for an undisclosed sum, a.k.a. big bucks, and he no longer had to be on the hamster wheel. Instead he bought shit to amuse himself—like this building—and did whatever suited him, which lately had been walking dogs for Willa's shop. Elle knew he only did so because women were suckers for a man walking their pet. "No, adulting is like"—she searched for the right words—"looking both ways before you cross the street and then getting hit by an airplane."

He laughed and she started to walk off, but at the last minute she couldn't help herself. She once again glanced at the other end of the bar where Archer and the woman sat laughing, and she knew she wasn't smart enough to "go easy" on him or leave well enough alone.

"Elle," Willa said from behind her. "Honey, maybe whatever you're planning isn't a great idea."

No kidding. "I'm not *planning* anything," she said. "I'm being . . . spontaneous."

"But you're never spontaneous," Pru said. "You make a Pinterest board before you change your lip gloss color."

Dammit. True story. "Hey, that was a secret board that I let you on because you wanted to compare colors. And I know what I'm doing here."

"But do you really though?" Spence asked.

Ignoring them, Elle headed toward Archer, unsure of exactly what was bothering her so much about the way he was letting that woman come on to him. Okay, that was a lie. She knew exactly what was bothering her and it was the fact that he never flirted with *her*. Absurd. Ridiculous. *Asinine* . . .

And yet did she stop? No, she did not. She kept heading right for them, leaning in between them to pat Archer on the shoulder. "Hey, nice to see you out and about," she said, all friendly-like. "Your full body rash must be all cleared up then . . . ?" She trailed off, letting her gaze run over him from head to toe, lingering quite by accident on his crotch because as it turned out, Trudy was right. He did indeed have an impressive-looking package.

Archer gave a slow shake of his head, a small almost smile playing about his lips. "Nice to see you, Candy," he said calmly, the jackass.

She sent him an eat-shit-and-die look, and in return he smiled a full two hundred watts.

Damn him. She wished she'd said *cock rot* instead of rash. Rash wasn't bad enough. With her fuse fully lit now, she turned on her heel and stormed out into the night. Ignoring the chill, she got an Uber and headed home, which was one side of a postage-stamp-sized duplex in Russian Hill.

She loved her place almost more than she loved her shoes, even if she couldn't turn around in it without bumping her elbows on the walls. It was cozy, quaint, warm . . . everything her life had never been before.

She made herself some hot tea and sat at her tiny kitchen table in her tiny kitchen and stayed up late into the night doing homework for her two accounting classes.

And absolutely not thinking about one irritating, infuriating, smug, arrogant Archer Hunt.

Chapter 4

#OffTheDeepEnd

Archer lived in an old converted warehouse in the Marina. He had a gym on the ground floor and in the early mornings he always hit that first, beating the crap out of a punching bag. He did this to keep his body in lean, mean, fighting shape. He also did it to clear his mind.

But his mind wasn't having it today.

Elle had kept his knife. She literally carried a piece of him around with her wherever she went and he had no idea what to make of that. Especially in the day since she'd done her best to ignore him. And when she wasn't ignoring him, she was treating him like a bug on her windshield.

He got it. She deserved far better than he could ever come up with. And plus no way would he ever risk her being with him because she felt she owed him. So he'd put up walls, trying to be disciplined when it came to her. For her sake.

But she'd kept his knife . . .

Reaching into his pocket, he pulled out an agate worry stone. The very one she'd given him in return for the knife in that run-down park the night when everything had gone to shit for the both of them. Pounding the punching bag until his muscles quivered pleasantly, he reminded himself that Elle had changed.

They'd both changed.

And neither was interested in going back. Convinced of that, he showered and headed to work.

The morning's light was just hitting the courtyard of the Pacific Pier Building as he walked through. The cobblestones beneath his feet glinted from the middle of the night's light mist. Heading past the fountain, he took the stairs to his second-floor office but instead of turning right at the top, he went left.

And ended up in front of the door that read ELLE WHEATON, GENERAL MANAGER.

Spence came out of her office and went brows up at the sight of him.

And the weirdest thing happened. Archer's gut tightened and a seed of some unnamed emotion barreled through him.

He'd been the one who'd talked Spence into hiring Elle for the job. But then something unexpected had happened—over the past year she and Spence had become unexpectedly tight.

While she'd kept her distance from Archer.

He had no business giving a single shit about it but he did. It was a hell of a thing to realize he was actually jealous. It pissed him off that he felt that way, but it was fact. He was pretty sure if anything was going to happen between Elle and Spence that it would've already happened, but ridiculously he still felt bitten by the green monster.

"What's up?" Spence asked.

"Nothing."

Spence looked him over for a long beat and then smiled. "She's eating you up and spitting you out."

"Bullshit," Archer said, and then he paused. "But if she was, why is that amusing?"

Spence clapped him on the shoulder. "Going to be fun to watch, that's all."

"What's going to be fun to watch?"

"You on your ass." And with that enigmatic statement, Spence walked off, hands in his pockets, still looking vastly amused, the fucker.

Archer shook it off and reached for Elle's office door. It was locked, but given that Spence had just come out, she was obviously in there. She was always in this early. She was one of the hardest working people he knew. He wasn't sure what her endgame was but he suspected world domination, and to get there she took online college classes from six to eight a.m. several mornings a week. She came here to do them because her Internet at home was unreliable.

She'd be furious to hear just how much he knew about her, not that he ever intended to tell her. After all, he valued his life. "Elle," he said with a knock on the door.

Nothing.

She was being cautious after last night's stunt at the bar. Smart woman. But it didn't matter. As head of the building's security, he had keys to everything, although he didn't pull them out now because he wasn't stupid.

Elle was on the other side of that door. He could hear her breathing and chances were she'd shoot him on sight if he let himself in. After the "body rash" thing, he was feeling the same desire in return, except his weapon of choice would be his hands. He'd put them around her pretty throat and squeeze.

This wasn't a new urge, but he could resist.

Just as he'd resisted his other more troubling urge—to haul her into him and kiss them both stupid. Or at least more stupid than he was in this very moment.

That wasn't a new feeling either but he had no intention of following it through. On either.

"What do you want?" she asked through the door.

"Should I give you the long or the short list?"

Nothing but a loaded silence.

"You," he said. "You're my problem."

"You're mad about last night."

"You mean when you implied to everyone in the pub that I had a sexually transmitted disease?"

There was a gasp behind him. He turned and found

Trudy standing there with her ever present cleaning cart. Her gaze dropped to his crotch and he barely resisted the urge to cup himself.

"The clinic on Post is really good," the woman actually whispered to him. "And, um . . . discreet."

Archer heard Elle snort and ground his teeth together. "It's a joke," he said.

"Sure it is, honey." Trudy patted him on the arm sympathetically. "I gotta say though, my fantasy life just took a big hit." And then she rolled off with her cart.

Archer turned back to the still closed door.

"For the record," Elle said through it, sounding like she might be laughing. "I never said *sexually transmitted* anything. Not that I'm surprised your mind went there."

He closed his eyes and inhaled deep for calm.

No calm came.

"Fine," Elle said. "I suck at apologies, but I suppose I could've handled last night better."

"You're right," he said. "You suck at apologies."

He could almost feel her smile. He felt when it faded too as well as her hesitation to open the door. She had good reason for that.

"You know you're going to pay," he said softly. "Right?"

"What are you going to do? Cuff me and drag me off to the pub to announce that I was just messing with you?"

He nearly said *If I were to cuff you, babe, the pub*

would be the last place I'd take you . . . but he kept his big trap shut tight. No need to muddy the waters with his own confusing emotions since they weren't going to ever go there. "You can't hide forever, Elle. I will find you."

A small thump sounded and then came a muffled oath. "Dammit, you made me spill my tea!"

For some reason this improved his mood greatly, and with his first smile of the morning, he turned and headed to his office.

"Hey, boss." Mollie, his receptionist and also Joe's baby sister, waved cheerfully at him. "Just dumped a bunch of stuff on your desk including yesterday's mail, which you never opened."

Archer was good at solving mysteries and rooting out the asshats and the douches of the world. Real good. But he wasn't all that into the paperwork that went with it.

He strode into his office and eyeballed the pile on his desk like it was a ticking bomb. On top of the stack sat a small, neat envelope with writing he unfortunately recognized. Picking it up, he felt the change in air pressure, like maybe his police captain father was suddenly standing right here in the room watching him.

Judging him.

The urge to stand up straighter and salute irritated the shit out of him.

"It's an invite to a retirement party," Mollie said, coming into the office behind him to set some more paperwork on his desk.

He lifted his head and looked at her. "How do you know?"

She shrugged. "It's your second invite. You must've not answered the first and when they sent another, I got curious."

"You opened my mail?"

"It's my job," she said. "He added a note this time. It says 'get your ass home.'"

Archer tossed the envelope to his desk and strode to his corner windows. He'd chosen this office because from here he could see the courtyard and also the street. He liked to have all angles open. A bonus was that beyond the streets of Cow Hollow down the hill, he could see straight to the bay.

"You want me to RSVP for you?" Mollie asked.

"The phone's ringing."

"Oh!" She froze, ear cocked. "Oh shit, you're right!" And with that, she rushed out of the room.

Archer tossed the invite into the trash can.

When a second set of heels clicked into the room, he craned his neck, watching as Elle walked to the trash can and scooped out the invite, homing in on it like a beacon. Given that she did some side work for him with decent frequency, she wasn't a stranger to his office. In fact, she made herself at home with a 'tude that spurred on his. "Feeling brave?" he asked.

"Your dad's retiring next month?" she asked, reading the invite.

He closed his eyes and resisted the urge to bash his

head against the window. "Why do you always answer a question with another question?"

"You should go to this," she said softly, lifting her gaze to his.

Archer was pretty sure that was a very bad idea. He hadn't been home much. It was easier to stay away. Eleven years ago he'd been a rookie fast-tracked cop on a joint task force. When it'd all gone bad and he'd had the blink of an eye to jeopardize the entire sting to get a girl out safely, he hadn't hesitated.

This hadn't been out of character for him. He'd always followed his own inner moral code on what he thought was right and wrong. The problem was that those codes didn't always line up exactly with the letter of the law.

The girl had been underage, trying to return something her sister had stolen. Not that it mattered. She'd been in the wrong place at the wrong time—which was not to say she'd been unaware of the danger she'd put herself in. She'd known. And she'd done it anyway. And it had been that show of bravery and loyalty and desperation to do the right thing that had gone straight to Archer's heart.

Yeah. He'd still had one back then.

He'd met Elle's eyes. They were the same baby blue as they'd been that night. Deep and filled with secrets.

"When was the last time you saw him?" she asked.

"Christmas. We had dinner."

She nodded. "And the time before that?"

Stubborn as hell to the end, like a terrier on a bone. "The Christmas before that," he admitted.

She didn't chastise him. She didn't judge. She just nodded, her gaze hooded now. "I'm sorry," she said quietly.

"No need."

She shook her head. "It's sweet of you to try to shield me but I know it's my fault."

This caught him completely off guard, something else only she tended to accomplish with any regularity. "Two things," he said. "One, I'm not sweet. I don't have a single sweet bone in my body. And two, this is *not* your fault. It's mine."

She just stared at him, holding his gaze prisoner in her own. He knew she believed herself to be a fortress. Locked up tight, never giving herself away.

But he also knew *her,* maybe better than anyone else, which meant he'd catalogued her tells a long time ago. She was worried about him, which for the record he hated. "Look, just forget about it, okay?"

"If you promise to go to the retirement party," she said.

Had he just likened her to a terrier? Make it a pit bull.

"Promise me," she said softly.

He was human. He made mistakes. But he tried very hard to not repeat any of those mistakes. And yet he kept looking right into her eyes and falling into them. Every time.

"Archer."

He knew she wouldn't give up or shut up until he agreed, so it might as well be on his terms. "Fine. If you promise to not talk about it again, I'll go."

She gave a slow nod and turned and walked out of his office.

"Hey," he called after her. "You never said what you wanted."

"Since you made me spill my tea, I came for some of the coffee Mollie makes you guys every morning."

Shaking his head, he turned back to the windows but he didn't see the view. He saw the events of that long-ago night flipping through his brain like a slide show— specifically what had happened after the bust had gone bad. Elle, huddled into herself in torn clothes, bleeding from various scrapes and cuts, eyes flashing with false bravado, body trembling. She'd run further into that run-down park and he'd really had to work at finding her.

She'd been on a swing, sitting very still. Very alone.

He'd told himself he'd done enough just letting her escape the scene, that he needed to walk away, but he couldn't, even though his own ass had been toast in a very large way. After all, he'd just detonated his entire life and yet there he stood worrying about the girl who'd been the accelerant on the fire he'd bombed his career with.

He'd wanted to take her to a doctor but she'd refused to go anywhere with him. So he'd given her his own pocket knife and told her she could use it to protect herself against him if she felt the need.

Then he'd taken her to an urgent care clinic and had her checked out. She'd needed stitches on her cheek where she'd been hit hard enough to split the skin but that had thankfully been the worst of her injuries. He'd then taken her home and put her to bed on his couch, where she'd slept like the dead.

Or like a girl who'd not been safe in so long she'd forgotten what real sleep felt like.

He'd known this because he watched over her for hours. In the morning he'd made her breakfast and then gone to take a shower. When he'd come out, she'd been gone, the agate stone sitting on top of the folded blankets he'd given her to sleep with.

He'd been suspended from the force, and rightfully so. He'd fucked up big-time on multiple levels and his father had just barely managed to keep him on the force at all.

But Archer had quit. He'd realized he wasn't cut out for having his hands tied just because his idea of right and wrong didn't match up with someone else's.

This hadn't gone over so well. In fact, his dad had been so furious they hadn't spoken for several years afterward, not aided by the fact that since his mom had died of cancer ten years ago, they'd never been able to see eye-to-eye. Without the sweet, loving peacemaker of the family around, there'd been no one to mediate.

Eventually they'd managed to be in the same room again without the inevitable fight over Archer's habit of making bad choices. They even spoke on occasion now. Holidays. Birthdays. That time a few years back when his dad had been shot in the leg on the job that was still the guy's entire life. And Archer got that. Just as he got that his hardcore cop dad was never going to understand that Archer had done what he'd had to.

Or why.

And yet he'd just promised Elle he'd go to the retirement party, where he'd likely have to face much of the entire force.

One of these days he was really going to have to figure out this strange hold and power Elle had over him.

But not today.

Chapter 5

#EverythingIsBetterWithChocolate

That weekend Archer and some of the guys went camping. It was something they tried to do every few months when they all had a few days off at the same time. It involved four-wheeling, fishing, and usually some form of stupidity since they were all so competitive. But hey, no one had died yet and they'd only needed an ER trip that one time back when someone had dared Joe to climb a tree and he'd fallen out of it, breaking his collarbone.

Archer drove. Spence rode shotgun with Joe and Finn in the backseat. It was an hour and a half drive to Big Basin Redwoods State Park and they stopped along the way for supplies.

Beer and bait.

When they got there, Archer got out of the truck and inhaled deep. The city was gone. They were in the mountains now, surrounded by ancient three-hundred-foot trees and enough nature to quiet even the busiest of minds.

The reason he came . . .

They spent the day hiking, fishing, and making increasingly ridiculous bets, the latest being that whoever caught the least amount of fish had to take a dip in the river. It was February. The river was an ice bath.

Highly motivated to stay dry, Archer caught three fish. Spence and Joe caught two each.

Finn only managed one and grumbled the entire time he was stripping down to his birthday suit, muttering dire warnings about hypothermia.

The rest of them just grinned, toasting themselves and their brilliance while Finn climbed into and out of the water in record time.

"Maybe you should get better at fishing," Spence said to a teeth-chattering Finn.

Finn yanked his clothes back on and flipped Spence the bird.

Archer tossed more wood on the fire and shoved Finn close to it. Watching Finn lose had been fun. So was the righteous knowledge that he was the best fisherman out of all of them. But that didn't mean he wanted Finn to die of hypothermia.

"If *you'd* lost," Finn said to Spence. "You wouldn't have had the stones to go in."

"Oh I've got the stones," Spence said. "The stones to walk over there and discover an algae on the surface. A skin-eating algae." He smiled. "One that makes swimming unsafe."

Finn blinked. "Huh. I didn't think of that."

Spence tapped his temple with a finger. "Not just a hat rack."

The sun went down fast up here. One minute it was daylight and in the next breath, inky black night. They got more serious about the fire, drinking the beer while Archer cooked the fish. As he was doing that, Spence went through their stuff and said "what the ever loving fuck?"

Everyone turned to look at him.

"Where's the junk food?" he asked.

"In the gray bin," Finn said. "I personally loaded it up with chocolate, graham crackers, and macro marshmallows because last time I got the minis you guys bitched about it for two days."

"There's no gray bin," Spence said. "Where is the gray bin?"

"Shit," Finn said. "It must not have gotten in the truck."

"We can't go on without the s'mores," Joe said, looking stricken. "I've been looking forward to them all day."

Archer agreed. They needed s'mores. But the nearest store was thirty minutes out and they'd all had a few beers. "Too bad Google Express doesn't deliver to Timbuktu."

"If I'd known Finn was going to be stupid," Spence said, "I'd have programmed my latest drone to drop the supplies right to us."

"It's Finn's fault," Joe said. "He should have to fix it."

"How?" Finn asked. "How in the holy hell do you expect me to fix this?"

"Call Pru," Spence suggested.

"Call her what?"

"Call her out here to bring us s'more supplies."

Finn let out a rough laugh. "I can't do that."

"But you can FaceTime her from the grocery store to make sure you're buying her the correct brand of tampons like you did last week?" Archer asked.

"Hey," Finn said, pointing at him. "That was supposed to be our secret."

"Call her," Spence said.

"She'll laugh at me and tell me to suck it up."

"See that's the thing," Joe said logically. "*We're* all single. We don't have anyone to call without looking like a complete pussy. But you, you already have Pru, so who cares if she laughs at you?"

Spence nodded at this logic. So did Archer.

"Okay, but for the record," Finn said, launching into defense mode, "*I* care."

Spence pulled out his phone.

"What are you doing?" Finn asked him, sounding nervous.

"Wait for it," Spence said, and then spoke into the phone. "Pru? Finn needs you."

"Oh my God," Finn protested, trying unsuccessfully to grab Spence's phone away. "Give that to me."

Spence covered the speaker piece on his phone and flexed his muscles as he avoided Finn's reach. "Been working out," he whispered proudly.

"At least tell her I didn't break my collarbone falling out of a tree," Finn demanded.

"One time," Joe muttered. "I only did that one time."

"Finn needs you to bring the makings for s'mores," Spence said to Pru. "Big marshmallows. The biggest, Pru. Enough to feed"—he looked around at the guys, counting the four of them—"*eight.*"

They all nodded. Double sounded good.

The last thing Elle had planned on doing Saturday night was driving up to Big Basin in the dark with Pru and Kylie to bring Finn some mysterious item he had to have. They'd tried to get Willa to come too but she and Keane had turned off their phones.

They were smart.

And probably going at it like bunnies.

Elle didn't blame them. In fact, she was a little envious of them.

"Thanks for coming with me," Pru said. "I'm sure you were both busy."

Kylie laughed. "If by busy you mean staying home and trying to beat my Lumosity score, then yes, I was very busy."

Elle was driving Finn's vehicle because Pru didn't have one, and also because she couldn't find her glasses. Elle wasn't a camper. In fact, she'd never camped. She didn't see the appeal of sleeping on the ground or having to use the wild frontier as a bathroom. Nope, she required electricity and a flushable toilet.

They'd left the city behind long ago and she'd never seen such darkness. She leaned closer to the windshield, squinting into the black night. The road was a bitch and she didn't want to miss the turnoff. "I can't believe we're doing this. You so owe us. And what are we delivering anyway?"

"It's complicated," Pru said noncommittally, a very large brown bag at her feet.

"Complicated how?"

Something in Pru's silence sent impending doom through Elle's gut. She slid another look at Pru. "He's camping alone, right? Because that's what you said. Even though camping alone is stupid and selfish because of the danger, and Finn isn't either of those things."

"Turn right!" Kylie called from the backseat. Their resident navigator had her nose practically pressed to her cell phone screen. "In twenty-five feet."

Elle turned right and the road went from asphalt to gravel. Bumpy, rutted gravel that took every bit of her concentration for the half mile until they came to the campgrounds.

"I think half my fillings just fell out," Kylie said.

"Campsite twenty-four," Pru said.

Five minutes later they rounded a tight corner and came upon the correct campsite. Elle calmly parked, turned off the engine, and stared out at the rip-roaring campfire, around which sat one, two, three . . . *four* men-sized shapes, one of them looking suspiciously like Archer. She felt the righteous annoyance that always hit her in his presence, for him simply being a breathing human being. "Dammit, Pru."

"It's not what you think," Pru said quickly.

"No? Because what I think is that you're a big fibber," Elle said.

"Okay, so it's a little what you think," Pru said, sagging in defeat. "But mostly I didn't want to drive up here alone. I knew you wouldn't come if I told you that Archer was here, and I really needed to deliver the s'more supplies. They were desperate."

Even as she said it, the guys all stood up and turned toward them with varying degrees of expressivity. Finn was out-and-out grinning, clearly excited to see Pru. Spence was looking hopeful, which made sense now that Elle knew their true mission. Spence had never met a dessert he didn't love.

Archer had never been one to give anything away, but his expression was relaxed, far more so than Elle had ever seen.

The wilderness agreed with him.

That is until his sharp gaze beamed in through the windshield—which he wouldn't have been able to see through if Kylie hadn't chosen that moment to open her door so that the interior light lit them up like they were in a fish tank.

Archer stilled for a single beat and his carefree smile vanished.

Terrific. She'd ruined his evening. Just as she'd ruined his life once upon a time—it was good to know she still had it. "Let's just get this over with." She said it calmly but she was having an inner and private moment of panic and anxiety, feeling a whole lot like that stupid sixteen-year-old daughter of a grifter, who'd continuously put Elle and her sister, Morgan, into desperate situations, using them as pawns, making them all live like thieves in the night.

Finn and Joe rushed forward like eager puppies, grabbing the brown bag. Well, Joe grabbed the bag and Finn grabbed Pru, the two of them in a tight lip lock like they hadn't just seen each other earlier in the day. In fact, given how they were busy eating each other's face, it was as if they hadn't seen each other in years.

Leaving the lovebirds at the car, Joe smiled at Kylie and Elle. "Ladies, welcome. Come to the fire and get warm."

"We're not staying," Elle said.

"Oh just for a few minutes?" Pru asked, tearing her mouth from Finn's to do so. "Please?"

Elle looked down at her heels. She'd assumed they were doing a quick turn and burn. It was Saturday but she'd worked regardless and had left straight from the office. And since she hadn't expected to stay, she hadn't bothered to change.

Joe took in the problem with one sweep of his observant gaze. "Hold on," he said, and running to the fire, he shoved the bag into Spence's arms and then ran back for Elle.

Before she could stop him, he'd scooped her up and

carried her to the fire. "I know how you feel about camping," he said earnestly.

"Joe," she said on a laugh. "Put me down."

"Do I have to?"

"Yes!" Under any other circumstances, she might've enjoyed the physical contact of being up against a man. Joe was tall and built and sexy as hell. He had a trouble-filled smile that promised a girl a good time, and she knew thanks to gossip that he had the moves to back up that unspoken promise.

But the only thing she had backing up was the air in her lungs because she could feel Archer's gaze on her. Dark. Assessing.

"It's not that Elle doesn't do camping or bears," he said dryly. "She doesn't do hiking shoes. Or, apparently, jackets." With that, he shrugged out of his down parka and came toward her.

The initial buzz of warmth at the realization of how well he knew her vanished when she saw his intention. "Not necessary," she said, eyes glued to the midnight blue flannel shirt he wore beneath, opened over a matching T-shirt, both stretching to accommodate his broad shoulders.

"Your lips are blue," he said. He wrapped her up in his jacket, which was deliciously warm from his body heat and, adding to the torture, also smelled like him. Which was to say delicious.

She opened her mouth to say something, she had no idea what, but it didn't matter because the minute he'd finished tucking her into his jacket, he turned away from her and headed back to the fire.

"I'm not cold," Pru said. "I'm wearing my new camping jeans. They're fleece lined." She executed a little twirl. "They're thick, so as a bonus, I won't get any splinters sitting on that log in front of the fire." She stilled and then twisted around, trying to see her own ass. "Wait. Are they too thick? Do they make me look fat?"

The look of panic on Finn's face did improve Elle's mood very slightly.

Pru gave him the big eyes. "Do they?"

"No." Finn looked a little like a deer in the head-lights. "*No*. Of course not."

Joe nudged him. "Man, when a woman asks if she looks fat, it's not enough to say no. You gotta look and act surprised by the question. Leap backward if necessary."

Finn grabbed Pru and pulled her down into his lap and sank his fists in her hair, staring into her eyes. "I don't think you look fat in those jeans. I don't think you look fat in anything. Or in nothing at all. I love every inch of you."

Pru grinned. "Thanks, babe. I love you too."

He narrowed his eyes. "That was a test."

"Yes." She kissed him. "But don't worry. You passed."

Elle felt another little tug of envy and wondered if she'd ever feel so comfortable with someone that she could open herself up like Pru had, in front of an audience no less, as if she didn't care if the entire world knew how much she loved Finn. Elle had always assumed that kind of love made one weak. But nothing about what Pru and Finn had felt weak to her.

They roasted marshmallows. Elle was trying hard not to rush Pru, but she really wanted to get out of there before she did something stupid. Like melt a marshmallow over Archer's hot bod and lick it up.

"Truth or dare!" Joe decided, handing out beers to everyone.

"What, are we twelve?" Elle asked.

Joe just grinned, looking very relaxed, reminding her that the guys had a head start on the beer. An all-day head start.

"Chicken?"

This came from Archer, uttered in his low, sexy voice, and her stomach executed a free fall. She risked a peek at him and caught sight of a predatory smile barely curving his lips. She shifted a bit. Was it hotter all of a sudden? Or was that only her internal temperature that had skyrocketed? "I just think that games are dumb—"

"Me first!" Pru said happily, clasping her hands. "Spence! Truth or dare?"

He thought about it until Pru gave him a hurry-up gesture.

"Give me a minute," he said. "I'm trying to decide how evil you're going to be if I choose dare."

Pru smiled, and Spence swore. "Okay," he said, "so *very* evil. Truth."

"Well that's no fun." She pouted.

"What's no fun is taking a dip in the river in February. *Truth,*" he repeated firmly.

"Hmm." Pru stared at him intently. "What do you want out of life?"

He stroked his chin, giving it serious thought. "Tacos. What?" he said when she rolled her eyes. "We had fish but I'm still hungry. Did you bring anything besides s'mores stuff?"

Spence was always hungry. They all ignored him.

"Me next!" Kylie called out, bouncing on the log on which she sat, clapping her hands. "Elle. Truth or dare?"

Elle narrowed her eyes. "Why me?"

"Truth or dare?" Kylie repeated.

She sighed. "Truth. But only because I'm not leaving this log for any stupid dare."

"Okay," Kylie said so happily that Elle knew she'd walked right into Kylie's plans, whatever they might be. "You always look so fantastic and perfectly put together."

"Thanks but that wasn't a question," Elle said.

"Do you ever let anyone see you when you're not . . . perfect?"

Archer snorted but turned it into a cough when Elle glared at him.

"No," she said to Kylie. "My turn." She looked at Archer. "Truth or dare?"

"Truth," he said warily.

"What's the biggest risk you've ever taken?"

"Playing this game with you," he said.

Everyone but Elle laughed their fool heads off. Idiots, all of them.

"That one didn't count," Pru said in Elle's defense. "She gets to go again."

"Okay," she said, looking once more to Archer. "Truth or dare?"

"You really want to come after me again? Oh and two isn't going to look good on your resume."

"Now who's chicken?" she asked. Baited really, because they all knew that Archer was a lot of things but chicken wasn't one of them.

"Well to be fair," Finn said. "The last person to lose had to strip naked and get into the water. Which I know because it was me."

"And the water was cold," Spence added helpfully.

"How do you know?" Finn asked. "You didn't have to get in."

Spence raised an eyebrow at him. "We could tell."

Finn narrowed his eyes. "Hey, shrinkage is a real thing!"

"Truth," Archer answered Elle.

She mentally cracked her knuckles. "What's your most embarrassing moment?" she asked.

He didn't say anything, just looked at her.

"Come on," she taunted, having no idea why she was poking the bear. "I'll tell you mine if you tell me yours."

His voice dropped to a pitch that sent tingles down her spine. "I already know yours."

Actually he didn't, but she refused to discuss it here. "Fine. I'll adjust the question. What's your biggest regret?"

Again he just looked at her. Mr. Talkative.

"Are you refusing to answer?" she asked. "Because you know what the dare is."

"Watch out for shrinkage," Spence muttered.

"Yes," Archer said without hesitation, his gaze holding hers prisoner. "I'm refusing to answer."

One hundred percent certain he'd choose to change his mind about talking if he thought he had to go for a dunk, she pointed to the river.

But she should've known better. There was no budging Archer when he'd made up his mind about something. Just as he'd clearly decided long ago that she was still a young, vulnerable street rat to be protected and nothing more, he wasn't going to be pushed into answering a question he didn't want to answer. Instead, he stood and walked to the water's edge. The shadows shielded most of him from view but she could still see his general outline. And although he undeniably annoyed her by just breathing, there was also no denying that even just his outline affected *her* pulse.

Not twenty feet away, and apparently completely unconcerned by having an audience, he began to pull off his clothes. He did this quickly and efficiently, dropping both of his shirts to the ground, kicking off his boots and socks, shucking his jeans, all without looking back.

"Where's your gun?" Joe called out.

"Locked in the truck," he said. "To keep me from killing anyone who pisses me off tonight."

Around the campfire, the others were talking amongst themselves, laughing and having a great time, but Elle couldn't tear her gaze away from Archer.

He was stripped down to nothing but boxer briefs now. And then those were gone too and he walked out into the water a few steps before diving in and vanishing beneath the gleaming black surface of the rushing current.

Chapter 6

#CarpeDiem

Elle strained to stare at the spot where Archer had vanished. "He's in the water!" she told everyone in horror.

"Yeah," Finn said. "You dared him."

"But . . . that's crazy. He'll get hypothermia."

"I didn't," Finn said.

"Just shrinkage," Spence said with a smirk.

Finn threw an empty beer can at him, which Spence easily dodged.

And still Archer didn't surface.

Elle stood up. Waited. And then when she couldn't stand it anymore, she started toward the river's edge.

"You going to strip too?" Joe asked hopefully.

She turned back to glare at him.

He blinked and pointed at Spence. Spence gave him a shove that had Joe falling off his log.

"Hey, man," Joe said from the dirt. "You really *have* been working out."

"Told you."

Elle kept walking toward the water.

"Elle, he's fine, stay warm by the fire," Finn said.

She stopped her forward motion but didn't sit down.

"It's okay, he's a great swimmer," Joe assured her. "One time I watched him dive off a thirty-foot embankment into the bay to save a jumper in a raging storm. He didn't even blink an eye."

In the river, which had to be freezing as it was winter for God's sake, a dark head finally emerged. And then a body. Like an Adonis, Archer walked casually out of the water. On the shore, he ran his hands over the length of himself, sluicing off the water before bending to pick up his clothes and shoes. Then, still buck naked, he moved back to the fire and stood in front of it, letting it dry him.

"Truth," Finn said to Pru.

Pru was staring at Archer, mouth open. "Huh?"

"Truth," Finn repeated and then waved a hand in front of her face. "Hello? Woman, I said truth."

"Sorry." Pru grinned a little sheepishly. "I got distracted by the Greek god statue in front of the fire."

"I thought *I* was your Greek god statue."

"You totally are," Pru said, still not taking her eyes off Archer as she patted Finn on the leg.

Kylie appeared to be having the same problem as Pru. Wow, she mouthed.

Archer began to pull on his clothes before taking

a seat next to Elle on the log. He shook his head and water flew from his hair.

"Hey," she said. "Not all of us are insane." She glanced at him and realized he had to be freezing. "Here, let me give your jacket back—"

"I'm good."

Well, fine. If he wanted to be stubborn, that worked for her because she wanted to be warm.

Pru was smiling at Finn. "I was hoping you'd say truth. So how did you get to be the poor sap who had to coax someone out here tonight? Why not Spence, Joe, or Archer?"

Finn smiled back. "None of them have a hottie to call."

She laughed and Finn turned to Archer, sitting next to him. "Truth or dare?"

"Dare," Archer said.

"Seriously?" Finn asked. "You don't want to re-evaluate and say truth to possibly spare yourself another dip?"

"Fine. Truth."

Finn smiled, like *gotcha*. "What's up with you and Elle?"

Elle sucked in a breath and did her best to look neutral. Switzerland.

Archer never took his eyes off Finn. "Nothing."

"That's not the truth," Finn said.

But it was, Elle thought. There was nothing up with her and Archer.

And wasn't that just her problem.

She wanted there to be. She had no idea why but she wanted it badly. Well, okay, so she did know. She suspected it was because he'd once been her hero, acting on her behalf for no other reason than he believed it the right thing to do. There'd been no ulterior motives, he hadn't wanted a damn thing from her.

And that had been a shocking first for her. She'd never forgotten it. The only reason she even knew what it'd cost him was because she'd kept tabs on him the best she could. Which admittedly hadn't been very well. She'd lost track of him years ago. Until she'd come to work in the Pacific Pier Building, that is.

"If you don't think it's the truth," Archer said calmly to Finn. "Then give me a dare."

Finn's mouth curved. "Okay, I dare you to get Elle to say that there's nothing going on between the two of you."

Archer sighed. "We'll need a moment to discuss."

"No we won't," Elle said.

"Take as many moments as you need," Finn said as if she hadn't spoken, and he waggled his brow.

Archer pointed at Finn and made the motion of shooting a gun, but he gamely stood. The next thing Elle knew, he'd wrapped his big hand around one of hers and was dragging her away from the fire and into the woods.

"Hey," she said, having to run to keep up with him. "My shoes—"

He slowed and without turning to her, reached back, hooked a hand around her thigh and hoisted her up so that he was carrying her piggy back.

It momentarily stunned her. Or, more accurately, the

feel of his broad back to her chest stunned her. As did the feel of his arms now hooked around her legs. "Put me down!"

"The terrain's uneven and God forbid but it's dirty out here," he said. "You really want to ruin your Guccis?"

"They're Kate Spade." And no, dammit, she didn't want to ruin them. She blew out a sigh and dropped her forehead to his beefy shoulder.

But this wasn't helpful as it put his neck within an inch or two of her mouth. He had a really great throat and damn if even after a day in the woods fishing and hiking and God knew what, he still smelled sexy as hell.

"Are you . . . sniffing me?" he asked.

She froze, her nose pressed to the back of his neck. "No."

"Yes you are." He sounded amused. "You just inhaled me like I was one of Tina's muffins from the coffee shop—"

Later she would swear she had no idea what came over her, but she bit him. Not a hard bite, more like a nibble. With a lot of teeth.

"What the—" He stopped and let her slide down his body.

And at the shockingly intimate contact and slow glide of his parts against hers, she felt herself tremble.

He whipped around to face her before she could find her sea legs, his expression dark and unreadable. "What was that?" he demanded.

Planting her feet—or rather, her heels—she went hands on hips. That was the only way to deal with him, just like one would when faced with an animal in the wild. Make herself as big and tall as she could and refuse to back down.

But as for what had come over her, honestly, she had absolutely zero idea. Maybe temper that he could read her like a map. Definitely frustration because he wound her up so tight that she sometimes fantasized about him deep in the night. Or all the time. And the hardest one to admit—embarrassment that she felt this way at all. If he ever found out, he'd be horrified and she'd have to move to Siberia. "Oh, please," she scoffed, trying to hide her shame. Her only regret was that she hadn't bitten him harder. "Don't even try to tell me I hurt you. You're impenetrable. A rock."

"You think I can't be hurt?" he asked with a whisper of disbelief.

"I think you don't let it show if you are." She didn't realize they were literally toe-to-toe and nose-to-nose until she drew a deep breath and felt her chest brush his.

"What would you know about my feelings, Elle?" he asked very, very quietly, his warm breath brushing her temple.

And just like that, a new kind of tension came over her, something else as well, something that skittered along every single nerve ending in her body.

Bad body.

"Nothing," she said. "I know nothing of your feelings because you're an island to me."

"Yeah? Well, you're Siberia."

"What the hell does that mean?" she demanded. "Are you saying I'm cold?"

"Icy cold."

Which was funny because she was so mad she was hot and she couldn't think, couldn't speak, so she crossed her arms tight over herself, closing off, which was of course proving his words. And only because maybe way deep down she *did* want to know his feelings, wanted to know them more than anything, wanted to know that she mattered to him, that she could reach him, that she could indeed hurt him, she poked him in a hard pec.

He wrapped his fingers around her wrist. "Stop."

Yeah, that would have been the wise thing to do. Definitely. But she'd never been all that wise when it came to him so she used her free hand to tell him he was number one. With her middle finger. "How's that for icy, you overgrown, knuckle-dragging oaf—"

Swearing beneath his breath, he caught that wrist too and stepped into her, making her not only shut the hell up but also stumble back a few steps, off balance. A tree came up against her back and Archer used that to his advantage, pinning her there with lots of solid muscle.

Her breath caught. At the sound he froze, his gaze going heavy lidded as he stared at her mouth. Then he planted both hands flat on the huge tree on either side of her, framing her shoulders as he let out a long, careful exhale, resting his cheek against her hair. "You drive me crazy," he murmured, his voice reverberating through his chest and into hers.

The words were such a contrast to his actions that it took her mind a moment to catch up. "Yeah, well, right back at you," she managed, thrown off by the effortless way he was leaning into her, holding her there with his weight, completely immobilizing her.

And that wasn't her biggest problem . . .

It was turning her on. *"Move."*

He started to do just that and she would never in a million years be able to explain what she did next. She fisted her hands in his shirt, lifted her face, and . . . kissed him.

She felt his big body jerk in shock and tightened her grip, making a shockingly needy little whimper and he stilled. In the next beat he banded his arms around her and kissed her back. He kissed her slow and deep, taking his sweet-ass time about it too.

Tendrils of undeniable pleasure coursed through her, melting her bones away. She was still angry. So angry. And yet she couldn't even remember why. That, coupled with her own sexual frustration and need, God, so much need, she literally went blank. Well, her brain did.

Not her body.

Her body reacted like it'd been deprived of touch for years, which was actually true. She moved against him, writhed really, trying desperately to get even closer, winding her arms around his neck to pull him into a better position to keep kissing him. When their tongues touched, they generated so much heat she nearly went up in flames and she tried to climb his body like he was a jungle gym.

This wrenched a groan from deep in his throat.

Sexiest sound ever.

Suddenly they were pulling at each other, grappling to get even closer, their hands furiously trying to gain purchase. She couldn't get enough of him, his heat, the undeniable strength in every inch of his body. They were standing in a place not too far from the fire where anyone could come upon them and she didn't even care.

When they were finally forced apart by their need for air, they stared at each other for a long beat. Elle would have liked to have the last word by casually pushing off and walking away, but she couldn't. As in she literally couldn't because the bones in her legs had gone on vacation, leaving her clinging to him. "Don't take this the wrong way," she said shakily. "I just can't find my feet."

Archer let out a low laughing groan into her neck and the movement of his mouth on her heated flesh had her toes curling. Since her hands were still in his hair she merely fisted them and tugged, and then they were kissing again.

Or still.

It was crazy, insanity really, but it was as if she'd die if she didn't get her hands on him. Apparently he felt the same way because while she worked her fingers beneath his shirt and all over his chest and abs—and good God, those abs—he wrenched his jacket from her shoulders got his hands on her breasts, like touching her was more critical than the blood in his veins.

She'd have thought his skin would be chilled from his dip in the river but he was hot to the touch. He felt amazing and she actually got to the button fly on his Levi's before he wrenched free and took a step back from her.

Good thing the tree was still at her back or she'd have slid bonelessly to the dirt.

Not looking all that steady himself, Archer shoved a hand into his hair and fisted his fingers in the silky strands, like maybe he'd gone crazy.

She certainly had. She was . . . stunned. Shocked. And wildly out of breath. She put a hand to her racing heart to see if she could keep the organ in her chest since it was throwing itself against her ribcage with every single heartbeat. "Next time," she said unsteadily. "We do that without a potential audience."

He just looked at her and then her heart stopped beating like a drum. It stopped beating period. Because she understood what his look said—there wasn't going to be a next time. "Okay, scratch that."

"Elle—"

"No. Never mind."

"We're . . . friends," he said. "I've known you since you were a kid."

Oh hell to the no did she want to hear the rest of that speech. Because yes, maybe she had a secret thing for him, and yes, maybe she'd fallen a long time ago, but she'd hoped he'd be able to see her for the woman she was now. A damn successful, strong woman.

But clearly that wasn't going to happen. Nothing was ever going to happen and she couldn't stick it out anymore, hoping, waiting. That was just sad and desperate, and she was neither. She had given it a whole year, and what was she waiting around for anyway? Archer didn't represent any of the things she wanted, certainly not safety or security.

Or love.

Because that's what she really wanted. She knew that now.

And maybe he did love her in his own way. As a friend. As someone he'd once protected and always would. She got that, she really did, but it was time to take the reins on this. She started with straightening her blouse—when had he gotten her unbuttoned?—and carefully looked around her rather than meet his gaze, not sure what she would see. Or what she wanted to see. It'd be nice if he felt even a fraction of the crazy discombobulation she felt, but she had a feeling she'd see regret and that was going to make her even madder. Still, she risked a peek and found his default expression—the blank one that told her nothing.

Nor did he speak. The man, damn him, was as obstinate as . . . well, herself. He could outwait Job.

She, unfortunately, could not. She'd never been able to wait for anything, not a cup of tea to brew, not for slow Internet, and certainly not for Archer to speak. So she went on the offensive. "Listen, we're going to attribute that to . . ." She searched for a logical reason to explain why she'd nearly jumped his bones but logic had deserted her. "High altitude," she said. Yeah, that was it. "The high altitude makes it hard to think."

He was a dark outline in the night, not touching her but still standing close. "We're not at any significant altitude here."

Seriously? He couldn't even give her that? She went on the defensive. "Look, I get that I kissed you, but you know what? You kissed me back, with tongue. In fact, you got to second base, Mr. Cool. So feel free to help me out here and come up with something better."

When he didn't say anything, she started to retreat again and nearly fell on her ass when her heels sank into the soft ground. She didn't even care. "I'm going back to the fire before anyone gets the wrong idea," she said stiffly. "I'm going to tell them that there is absolutely *nothing* happening between us. Less than nothing—"

"It's you," he said.

"What's me?"

"My deepest, darkest regret. It's you."

Wait . . . what?

But on that stunning statement, he walked away first, heading back to the fire. She blinked and hesitated, but only for a minute before she hurried to keep up with him because although she might want to kill his sexy ass—which she wasn't even going to notice, not ever again!—it didn't mean she had any intention of being left behind as potential bear bait, thank you very much.

Chapter 7

#CalgonTakeMeAway

The girls didn't stay overnight. They took a vote and Pru was the only one who wanted to. Kylie and Elle had way more sense.

"I need my pillow," Kylie said when the three of them had huddled beneath a tree to confer.

"I need to *not* be on a mountain," Elle said, but what she really meant was that she needed to be at least a hundred miles from Archer right now.

"I know, I get it." Pru sighed. "I really do. Just give me a minute to say goodbye to Finn first."

Kylie watched Pru go and pull Finn aside. "She's going to need more than a minute."

"Yeah," Elle said but her mind wasn't on Pru and Finn. *She was Archer's biggest regret . . . ?* What did that even mean?

"I'm going to have another s'more while we're waiting," Kylie said, and she walked back to the fire.

Still reeling while pretending not to be, Elle stayed beneath the tree, looking up through the branches to the night sky, which was clear, crisp, and admittedly stunning.

She felt Archer come up beside her, felt the heat and strength of him, and as always her body stilled although she didn't take her eyes off the sky. "What did you mean?" she asked.

He didn't pretend to not understand. "That night," he said quietly. "I didn't get you out before you got hurt. That's my biggest regret."

The air backed up in her lungs at this unexpected statement and unwelcome memories flooded her. She and Morgan had left home about six months before that night, leaving their grifter mom to her business. The sisters had wanted a better life for themselves, a life free of trouble. Or at least that was what Elle had wanted, but Morgan, eighteen to Elle's sixteen, had difficulty leaving trouble behind.

Unbeknownst to Elle, Morgan had gone back to working on the side for Lars, her bad-news boyfriend, in the same field as their mom. When one of Lars's cons had involved a jewelry heist with a load of invaluable Russian antiques, Morgan had gotten scared and come clean to Elle, wanting out but having no idea how to get out.

Elle had told her she'd take care of it. And she'd tried. She'd taken the part of the loot that Morgan had in her possession back to Lars to tell him to leave her sister the hell alone or else. She had no "else" but she'd been willing to wing it in order to get Morgan out.

Unfortunately, two things had gone wrong. One, Lars hadn't been amenable to what she had to say. In fact, he'd pinned her against the wall, his plan to beat her into submission and she wasn't sure what else, but it wasn't going to be good. He'd gotten halfway through that plan when the second problem had hit and hit hard.

A police raid and drug bust. Seemed along with illegal antiques, the boyfriend had also been drug running. And there she'd been, holding evidence no less. She should've been caught up with the others and arrested, but she'd had a guardian angel looking over her that night.

Archer.

He'd been undercover and he'd blown his cover to pull her out. It'd cost him everything. His job. His relationship with his dad.

She had no idea how he'd ever forgiven her. Or maybe he hadn't, given that so many years had gone by without any contact between them. That had changed last year when she'd landed her job in the same building as Hunt Investigations, but she couldn't say they'd made much headway, since whenever they ended up in the same place at the same time they either bickered like children or were as silent and awkward as strangers.

And now she could add *or kissed like their lives depended on it* to the list.

But mostly what she remembered when she thought about that night was how alone she'd been. Alone, scared, and cornered in that old park . . . And Archer had seen her that way. No wonder he didn't want her.

To him, she was nothing but that little girl. All the maturing and growing up she'd done, the success she'd had, none of it could erase that horrifying first impression she'd made.

And as always happened when she thought about it, the bottom fell out of her stomach. She swallowed hard and shook her head. "You weren't responsible for me, Archer. I was there of my own accord. What happened was my fault. *Everything* that happened that night was my fault."

"And yet you've never forgiven me for it," he said.

Her heart squeezed so hard she had to close her eyes and take a long, deep breath and a moment to try to get herself together. She couldn't believe he thought that. "It wasn't you I had to forgive. It was myself."

When he didn't speak, she opened her eyes.

But just like that long-ago night, she was alone.

Four nights later, after several long days of work and hours and hours of homework in her office, Elle finally followed her stomach downstairs and across the courtyard, the goal being the pub for some of Finn's famous chicken wings and a tall glass of something with a good kick.

She'd gotten a text from Finn that tonight was country night. Her concession to a costume was switching out her heels for some pretty cowboy boots and adding a cowboy hat and a belt that proclaimed her a REBEL on the silver belt buckle.

She hadn't spoken to Archer since the Kiss Debacle.

And although she hadn't run into him, he'd made plenty of appearances in her dreams and he hadn't walked away from her in those. In fact, just thinking about all the things he'd done to her in the deep dark of her fantasy world always made her break out in a sweat.

She could only imagine what would happen if they were ever stupid enough to try to swallow each other's tonsils again. Her vagina might actually go up in flames . . .

But they wouldn't be stupid enough for that. Or at least he wouldn't. After all, he'd been the one to put the brakes on. And he'd not even looked back.

Which made that the second time. She didn't usually keep score but she really needed to remember that the next time he appeared behind her eyelids in the night. He wasn't right for her. And he was never going to be right for her.

Ever.

And if that thought hurt, she shoved it away, shoved it deep. She was good at that, real good. She'd shoved deep lots of bad before. Such as giving up on ever having anything that resembled a "normal" family. She'd never known her dad and she'd walked away from her mom a long time ago. She'd had to do the same with her sister, although that one had been a lot harder and still haunted her.

So Archer not wanting her? Right in her wheelhouse.

Halfway across the courtyard, she ran into Kylie standing at the fountain. She stood there in skinny jeans that emphasized her toned, petite body. She had a tear in one knee and another across her opposite thigh, was wearing a tool belt and a fleece-line leather bomber jacket, and was looking both incredibly feminine and badass at the same time.

Elle loved the look, although she thought Kylie could use a little lip gloss. Not to please a man or anything like that. Just because she seemed pale today and needed a little color.

Kylie blew out a sigh like the day had been hard and long, and shoved back her long, wavy brunette hair, leaving a streak of sawdust in it.

"Um," Elle said, pointing to it but Kylie waved her hand like she didn't care. She had her little rescue pup, Vinnie, on a bright blue leash at her side. Four months ago he'd been all head and ears, small enough to fit into her pocket.

He was still all head and ears, and might still grow up to be either a very big rat or a French Bulldog. It was anyone's guess.

In any case, Vinnie was wearing a bolo tie—clearly ready for country night at the pub. He looked up at her, his warm brown eyes dancing with the kind of excitement for life only a dog could muster.

"You look very handsome, cowboy," she told him.

Vinnie panted happily and melted to the cobblestones to expose his kibbles and bits.

"Just like a man," Elle said on a laugh but dutifully bent down to scratch his belly. She looked up at Kylie.

"You're staring down that water like it's your mortal enemy. What gives?"

Kylie shrugged. "It's going to sound pretty stupid to you."

"Try me."

"Okay," Kylie said. "I'm trying to decide if I trust love enough to actually wish for it." She revealed the quarter in her palm.

"Is that what you're doing out here?" Elle asked. "You're trying to get the balls together to wish for love?"

"Well, yeah." Kylie looked at her. "Both Pru and Willa found love as a direct result of their wishing."

"You really believe that?"

Kylie bit her lower lip, watching as Willa and Keane came out of the stairwell holding hands as they made their way through the wrought-iron gate to the street and vanished. "I want to believe." She looked at Elle. "You really don't ever feel tempted?"

Maybe for a teeny-tiny second . . . but she was over that now, not that she'd ruin someone else's dream. "I don't know. But I do know this—I wouldn't want to have to wish for it. If it were to happen, I'd want it to happen organically."

Kylie blinked at her. "Wow. I didn't see that coming from you. You're a closet romantic."

Elle hadn't seen that coming either, but it was unfortunately true. She let out a low laugh and shook her head. "In the end, it doesn't matter what I think. It's what *you* think that really matters." She took the quarter from

Kylie's hand and tossed it into the water. "Bring Kylie true love," she told the fountain. She looked at Kylie. "There. It's out of your hands now. It's done."

Kylie flashed a grin. "Because you've deemed it so?"

"That's right."

Kylie shook her head, still smiling. "Does the whole world always do exactly as you command?"

She got that question a lot. "When it knows what's good for it," she quipped.

Kylie smiled. "So are you going to laugh at me if I say I really want to believe the wish will come true?"

"Well, not to your face," Elle said. "Are you hungry? Because I need Finn's chicken wings in the worst possible way and you don't even want to know how badly I need a drink to go with them."

"Yes," Kylie said fervently.

"Okay, then. But first . . ." Elle pulled as much of the sawdust from Kylie's hair as she could.

The pub was crowded. Luckily for them, Finn always kept the far side of the bar open to the people who lived and worked in the building. Pru, Haley, Willa, and Keane were already there, in varying degrees of "cowboy" attire.

Kylie sat, but Elle remained on her feet as they dug into the chicken wings. She'd been sitting all day and she feared getting a flat ass. She wasn't ready to concede her curves just because she was working her ass off for a better life than she'd ever had before.

She wanted the good life *and* her curves, dammit.

"There's one unhappy cowboy," Pru said, gesturing

to one of the dining tables, where a family sat with two little kids wearing more barbeque sauce than their food. The two-year-old was wailing at the top of his lungs, the slightly older one grinning from ear to ear.

Elle shuddered. "Can you imagine?"

"Yes," Pru said with a soft smile.

Willa nodded, looking a little sappy. "It can't be harder than having pets. At least kids eventually learn to use the toilet."

Her boyfriend, Keane, laughed. "Such a romantic."

"Always," Willa said. "Maybe we should go practice procreation."

Keane leaned in for a kiss. "Anytime."

"You too," Finn said to Pru. "You just say the word. I could practice the shit out of procreating."

Elle watched the kids another minute. Small children tended to make her nervous. They were like little ticking time bombs just waiting to go off. "I don't know if I see myself with kids," she admitted.

"Hey, you'd make a great mother," Pru said sincerely. "You're strong and smart, and you always stick up for those you care about. Seriously, any kid would be lucky to have you as a mom."

"The whole birth thing though," Elle said. "It just seems like a poor exit strategy, doesn't it?"

Someone tapped her on the shoulder and she turned to face a guy in a very nice suit, looking like a million bucks. And his smile looked like another million. Mike, she remembered, one of Archer's clients.

"Hey," he said. "Fancy meeting you here."

Uh-huh. "You know I work in the building," she said.

He rubbed his jaw and gave a wry smile. "Okay, so I was hoping to see you here. I'd really like to ask you to dance because that's my signature move, but Archer told me very firmly that you were taken."

She put her drink down and purposefully inhaled a deep breath, letting it out slowly. "He said what?"

Mike nodded and took a few nuts out of the mixed nuts bowl on the bar. "Yeah. He was pretty clear about it, actually."

Archer, the man who didn't want her for himself, had said she was taken. She could actually feel steam coming out of her ears. She hadn't had a guy into her in . . . well, forever. In fact, she hadn't had sex in two years and her parts were threatening to mutiny. "He said I was taken," she repeated, needing to be sure before she planned Archer's death.

His slow, painful death.

"He did," Mike said. "I think his exact words were 'off-limits' and 'don't even think about it.'"

She might have growled. She certainly seethed. But honestly, a lot of the temper was at herself because when would she learn? Archer would never stop thinking of her as a responsibility, and she really did owe it to herself to move on, to find a man who could see her for more than just a scared, vulnerable girl.

"Whoa there, rebel," Spence murmured behind her, having come in during the exchange. "No sense committing murder before you've finished your drink."

"Are you sure?" she asked. "Because I see a lot of sense in it."

Spence shook his head. "I'm not in the mood to bail you out of jail today."

"Tomorrow then?" she asked, but sighed at his firm expression. "Oh forget it. I hate orange and I think jumpsuits are the work of the devil."

"That's my girl," Spence said. "Always thinking."

Mike, who'd followed the conversation closely, grinned. "So . . . you're saying Archer was mistaken."

Oh yes. Mistaken. On so many levels. And she mentally tossed in the towel. Enough was enough, it really was time to move on from him and get herself that life she wanted. Past time. "I'm saying Archer shouldn't speak for me," she said as she took a second, closer look at Mike, who was successful, sharp, and quite easy on the eyes. Sure, he didn't send her heart rate into the stratosphere, but hey, maybe she could work on that.

"I'm sitting over there, having drinks with some buddies." He gestured behind him to a table where three guys were drinking beer and watching a game on one of the big-screen TVs on the wall. "They bet me that I wouldn't be able to start a conversation with the most beautiful woman in the bar." He grinned. "Wanna prove them wrong and go out to dinner with me on their dime?"

Deciding she needed a second opinion, she glanced over at Spence who gave her a slow head shake.

"Negative," Spence said. "It's a bad idea."

Okay, never mind the second opinion. She turned back to Mike. Being impulsive had never been her thing but there was a first time for everything. "Yes," she said.

"Oh Christ," Spence muttered.

Mike grinned. "Great, let's go."

"Go?" she asked, having expected they'd stay in the pub.

"Oh, I've got something different from the pub in mind, great as it is," he said. "Trust me?"

"Hell no."

Mike just laughed. "An honest woman. I love it. And smart too. How about this. I promise you a good time, and if I fail you can sic Archer on me to kick my ass. How's that?"

"I fight my own battles," she said.

"Fine. *You* can kick my ass." He was nudging her to the front door of the pub, his hand on the small of her back when Elle felt a prickle of awareness at the nape of her neck. Turning her head, her gaze tracked to the back of the pub, where Archer had come out of the pool room, cue in hand, eyes on her.

For the briefest of seconds she hesitated there at the pub door, Mike at her side, Archer in her peripheral vision. There was no expression on his face, none. He was his usual cool, calm, impenetrable self and it was that, in the end that got to her. If he didn't want her to go out with someone else, well then he should've asked her out himself—before she'd changed her mind about him, that is.

"You okay?" Mike asked, eyes on her, seemingly unaware of Archer's presence.

She had no idea, to be honest. She suspected she wasn't but that had never stopped her from pretending to be. "Of course. I'm fine," she said, exercising her one true superpower of shoving her emotions down deep.

Thirty minutes later she found herself boarding a helicopter for a tour of the city. She'd never done anything like it in her entire life and she could feel her heart pounding in her throat excitedly as they rose straight up into the air.

Mike, sitting next to her, proved to be a great tour guide. He showed her a view of San Francisco she'd never seen from this angle before. The Golden Gate Bridge, Alcatraz Island, Fisherman's Wharf . . . They even flew above Point Reyes, where she could see the entire mountainside covered in a blanket of greens and oranges and browns, the cliffs rolling toward the sea. Sunlight glinted off the deep blue ocean.

And then halfway through their hour of flight time, the pilot spoke privately to Mike through their comms.

"What's wrong?" Elle asked as they turned back.

Mike smiled but it was a wry one. "You absolutely certain that you're not taken?"

"Of course I'm sure!"

He reached for her hand. "The heli belongs to an

influential businessman buddy of mine, one who hires Archer's company for his security."

She had a bad feeling about this. "And?"

"And suddenly this chopper is needed elsewhere. I think Archer shut us down."

Whelp, that did it. She was going to have to find a way to look good in an orange jumpsuit after all because she was indeed going up for murder one.

Mike was a good sport about it, so good that when he brought her home, she let him kiss her goodnight. She stilled at the touch of his mouth, soft yet firm on hers, willing herself to get lost in the connection. His mouth was warm and very nice as it brushed over hers. He had some serious talent, but then again, players usually did. It was lovely and even caused a few little sparks as he shifted his nice, hard body into hers.

But no wildfire.

Dammit.

When Mike pulled back, there was nothing but good humor in his gaze. "Thanks for trying," he said, and with a last brush of his mouth over her cheek, he was gone.

Elle watched him drive away and then pulled out her phone.

When Archer's phone went off he was lying flat on a four-story roof in the Mission District. He had a pair of binoculars up to his face and was watching for a high dollar skip in the building across the street—most definitely *not* needing the chopper he'd called back.

He didn't have to look at the phone to see who the text was from—it shook with the fury that could belong to only one woman.

Elle.

He ignored it while thoughts of her invaded his mind, as they'd been doing for so long now that he should've been used to it. He'd tried to train himself over the years to *not* think about her, and he'd mostly succeeded. Until last year when he'd found out she'd been let go from a job because she'd refused to sleep with her boss. That hadn't been the official reason she'd been terminated; she'd been officially fired for accessing files above her authorization level and breaching her confidentiality contract when she'd allegedly "accidentally" forwarded company emails outside the company.

Technically true, but Archer knew the real story. After Elle had refused to sleep with her scumbag boss, he'd threatened to fire her. This hadn't helped Elle's lack of trust in authority figures in the least, and instead of going to HR, she'd taken matters into her own hands. As collateral and protection, she'd forwarded emails between the scumbag and his mistress . . . to his wife.

How did Archer know all this? Because he'd been watching over her. Yes, he'd invaded her privacy, and yes, he was clearly a very sick man. He didn't care. He'd long ago realized he couldn't help himself when it came to her.

Just like when Spence had first bought the Pacific Pier Building. It'd taken little to no effort to talk him into hiring Elle for the general manager position. After all, she really was excellent at her job.

He'd never told her about his involvement, nor did he plan on ever telling her. He valued his life more than that. Besides, he'd actually believed that after all that time of keeping his distance from her, he'd have no problem keeping his hands off her once she was in the building. He told himself he was giving her a real chance at living a full, happy life, including finding a man she could relax with, a man who hadn't once seen her at her most vulnerable.

In truth, keeping his distance had been the hardest thing he'd ever done. He hated himself for desiring her as much as he did. Now *and* then. She'd been a kid for God's sake. He'd had no business wanting her at all. It'd made him work doubly hard at keeping her safe over the years. Safe for life, he'd promised himself. She deserved that after such a rough start. So yeah, the illusion of distance had become his best friend.

At least until the other night when they'd been camping and Spence had called the girls in for the s'mores mission. Because the illusion of distance had shifted the second Elle had planted her warm mouth on his. And when he'd gotten a taste of her, he'd completely lost his fucking mind as well.

Elle had been right about one thing—that couldn't happen again.

Giving in to his curiosity, he finally pulled out his phone and accessed his text.

Elle: I'm going to kiss you!
Archer: With tongue?
Elle: Kill you. I'm going to KILL you. Ducking auto-correct!

Archer found himself grinning like an idiot. He used his Bluetooth to call her and was still cracking up when she connected but didn't speak. "Looking forward to this kiss," he said.

"You really called me just to say that?" came her frosty voice. "Calls are only for when someone *dies,* Archer. And even that could come in a text."

He heard a snort in his ear, cluing him into the fact that his guys could hear her through their comms. He sighed. "Did you need something, Elle?"

"To know when you'll be home so I can kill you," she said. "And that's *k-i-l-l,* not *k-i-s-s.*"

More muffled snorts.

"Okay, great," he said. "Thanks for narrowing that down."

But she'd already disconnected.

And because their skip made an appearance just then, he did what he did best. He compartmentalized his life. He slid his phone away and got to work.

Elle told herself to just go to bed. It was ten p.m. and she could use the rest. She kicked off her boots but instead of lovingly putting them back in their place in her closet like she always did, she let them fall carelessly to the floor. She started to strip down but eyed her laptop as an idea came to her.

Maybe Archer was working, but that didn't mean she couldn't email him exactly what she thought of his butting his nose into her business and breaking up the first date she'd had in forever. She opened the laptop and went at it, her fingers working furiously, outlining in great detail what a dick he was.

At heart, she was a businesswoman. She knew the value of holding her cards close to the vest. She'd long ago taught herself patience and also the need for giving a decision a good, long thought process. Often she'd made herself sleep on especially difficult decisions before allowing herself to react. So normally she'd sit on this email until morning.

But not this time, she just couldn't do it.

She hit send.

Then she calmly finished getting ready for bed, putting everything away, including the cowboy boots. She removed her makeup and moisturized. She flossed.

Then she got under her covers and . . . stared at the ceiling going over every scathing word of her email. She'd called him more than a few choice names and she'd ended it with "Don't call me, don't email me, don't come to my office, don't anything, not ever again."

And she meant it. Nodding to herself, she turned over, punched her pillow and tried to go to sleep.

Don't anything, not ever again . . .

The words haunted her. It would mean no more working with him, and maybe no more seeing him, and *that* gave her the first small inkling of what was possibly regret. She might want to kill him half the time but the other half of the time she . . . well, she didn't know exactly, but she knew she'd miss it, whatever it was. Maybe she was giving up on a romance between them but did that mean she could or should give up their . . . friendship? Is that what they had? Elle didn't know, but she did know this—she wasn't prepared to cut him out of her life entirely.

She also had to give a fond thought to the money he paid her when she worked for him, money that funded her shoe habit. And then there were his guys, all of whom she adored.

Don't anything, not ever again . . .

Okay, Elle, she ordered herself, put it in perspective. What he'd done tonight, calling off her date with Mike, had been wrong. He'd definitely crossed a line there, but to be honest so had she, going out with someone he had to deal with as a client.

They'd both been wrong. Mostly him, but still. She could accept some of the blame.

Don't anything, not ever again . . .

And that's when it hit her, the full reality of what she'd emailed him had the air backing up in her lungs, and her eyes popped open.

What had she done?

Well, she'd let her temper get the best of her and she'd cut him out of her life instead of just making him pay. Shit. Making him pay would've been so much more satisfying. She sat up and texted Spence.

> Elle: Is there any way to delete an email once you've sent it?
> Spence: What did you do?
> Elle: It's a yes or no question!
> Spence: No. Not without being a felon. What are you up to, Elle?

Best not to bother him with an explanation, she decided. And anyway, she knew what she had to do. She had to break into Archer's office and erase that email, hopefully before he accessed it on his phone—which she assumed he wouldn't do since he was on a job.

No problem. No problem at all . . .

> Spence: Elle?
> Spence: Seriously, Elle. Answer or I'll send out SWAT.
> Elle: The person you are trying to reach pleads the fifth . . .

And then, knowing how smart Spence was, she turned off her phone so he couldn't track her and stop her. Because nothing could stop her.

Chapter 8

#BeAllYouCanBe

Elle threw back her covers and hurriedly dressed, for the first time in her life throwing on clothes without conscious, careful thought. She pulled her hair up in a ponytail and left her place.

She took a cab because she couldn't spare the time to wait for an Uber. Once at the Pacific Pier Building, she ran through the courtyard, which was completely empty at this time of night.

The pub was still going strong though and she was very lucky to find Spence in the back room playing pool with Finn and Keane. She didn't see Archer and suspected slash hoped he was still on a job, but he was a sneaky bastard so she needed to be sure. Pretending she wasn't out of breath or panicked to the gills, she strolled up to the pool table, hugging Keane hello. And then Finn. She saved Spence for last and he arched a brow at her warm greeting.

"Thought you were on a date," he said. "Pleading the fifth."

"Was. So . . . where's your fourth musketeer?"

"On a job." He looked at her for a long beat. "What are you up to, Elle?"

Dammit. This was the problem with having a genius as a BFF. He saw everything. He knew everything. And he could think ten steps ahead of her. "Nothing," she said. "Nothing at all." She added a smile because she knew what he didn't. That that big, beautiful brain of his had one fatal flaw—he lacked experience in outwitting, outlasting, and outplaying a Female on a Mission. "Okay, then, good to see you but I've gotta go."

He grabbed her by the back of her sweater and held tight. "You know to call me when you need me."

"Yes."

"Before the cops arrive."

She laughed, as he'd intended. "Yes." She hugged him. "It's late. Past my bedtime. Don't wanna turn into a pumpkin." And then she made her escape.

She didn't breathe again until she was on the second floor outside Hunt Investigations. Slowly she opened her fist and looked down at what she'd palmed from Spence's pocket.

His keys, including the master key for the building.

Yes, she was quite the felon tonight and she came by it naturally.

Her plan was simple. Get into Archer's office, access his email and erase her message—assuming he hadn't seen it already—and get out again without being detected. That she was doing all this to a security specialist did give her some pause but she had her pride at stake here as well as any future interactions with Archer. Not that there would be anything more than a simple friendship.

She got inside Hunt Investigations and hit her first snag. She didn't have a key for the interior door to the back offices. But hold on a minute . . . there was a light on in the back—

"Elle?"

She just about swallowed her own tongue when Joe appeared on the other side of the glass partition, looking at her in surprise.

"Hi," she said, mind racing. "You're working late."

"Stupid report on a takedown that went bad earlier."

Her heart stopped. "How bad?"

Joe blew out a breath. "Our guy threw a knife before we could relieve him of his weapons, and let's say he had good aim."

"Oh my God," she said, stomach jangling. "Who's hurt?"

"We got lucky. The blade would've hit our contract worker because he didn't duck as fast as the rest of us. But you know our gang, someone's always gotta play the hero."

She did know. She'd heard the stories. These guys had all at one time or another saved each other's lives. "Who dove for him and got stabbed?"

"Who do you think?" Joe asked. "Archer, of course."

Elle felt the blood rush out of her head and her vision went cobwebby.

"Hey. Hey, whoa there . . ." she heard Joe say from a million miles away. And then his hands were supporting her, bringing her into the back, pushing her into a chair.

Well, she'd accomplished getting into the interior offices if nothing else . . . "How bad?" she whispered.

"It sliced through his biceps," Joe said. "Not too bad. He tried to tell the paramedics he only needed a Band-Aid but they insisted on stitches. He's probably already done and in bed."

Elle nodded as her vision cleared. "Good to know. Thank you."

"No problem." Joe stroked a hand down her arm, clearly trying to soothe. "But if you didn't know about the incident, what are you doing here?"

Uh-oh. Good question. She stood up and didn't have to one hundred percent fake the tears in her voice when she met Joe's gaze. "I left something here."

Joe took one look into her eyes, saw the tears, and clearly panicked. "Where is it? I'll get it for you."

She wrung her hands together and let a tear fall. "I wouldn't want to bother you—"

"It's no bother." He whirled around the office and pounced on the box of tissues sitting on Mollie's desk like it was a pot of gold.

He pulled out just about every tissue in the box and

shoved the whole mess at her, the whites of his eyes showing. "Tell me what you need."

She sniffed a little dramatically and made a show of dabbing her eyes. "It's in Archer's office."

He blinked. "Uh—"

She started walking down the hall and got just inside Archer's office to flip on the light when Joe caught up to her.

"Elle—"

"It's on his computer," she said, opening it, willing it to boot up fast.

Joe reached around her and gently but firmly shut the laptop. "I'd do just about anything for you, you know that, but I love my job."

She met his gaze.

His own was apologetic and regretful, but also filled with steely resolve. "I have orders."

"Not to let me in?" she asked incredulously.

"Not to let *anyone* in his office."

"But I'm already in."

He grimaced. "I know and when he finds out, I'm going to end up right back here facing down him instead of you, and no offense cuz you're scary as shit, but he's scarier. If I let you on his computer, my ass is fired and like I said, I love this job. Don't make me get tough with you, Elle."

He was braced for her to fight him but here was the thing. He was a sweetheart and she couldn't do it to him. "You sure Archer's okay?"

"He's been through way worse."

Knowing this to be true, she sighed and strode out of the office ahead of him, cursing herself and her stupid impulses when it came to one annoying-as-shit Archer Hunt. So he would read her email, so what? She'd meant every word. Mostly.

Okay, so only parts of it.

Dammit and he'd been hurt tonight too! She got to the outer door and realized Joe wasn't right on her heels. She could hear him coming down the hallway but she couldn't see him yet. Thinking quickly, she opened and shut the office door, hard.

And then crouched down behind the reception couch to wait until he left. She was going to delete that damn email and then she was going to stop lusting after Archer no matter what. On her own terms. Terms that allowed her to go see for herself that he was really okay after being stabbed. Because if he was going to die, it would because *she* killed him, not because of some scumbag bad guy.

Archer hated hospitals. Hated the smell, hated the sound of the machines beeping and hissing, hated the pale walls that always seemed to close in on him. He hated everything about them and had ever since his mom had died after her very long, very tortured battle with cancer.

If he never stepped inside one again in his entire life he'd be perfectly happy.

A nurse popped her head in and smiled at him. "You look ready to get out of here."

"I was ready before I arrived."

"Good news then," she said. "I'm just waiting for a signature from the doctor and you're free."

Archer ground his teeth when she vanished but resigned himself to the wait. When his phone went off, he pulled it from his pocket and stared at the notification in disbelief. Someone had just tried accessing his computer. His office computer. Someone was in his office and it wasn't him.

This was immediately followed by a text from Joe, which explained the situation but not the reason.

> Joe: Elle's here. Wanted something off your computer. Per protocol, I escorted her from your office. She pretended to leave but she's hiding in reception area. Please advise.
> Archer: Remote lock all exits without revealing yourself.
> Joe: You mean lock her in? Repeat, lock her IN???
> Archer: Affirmative. My ETA's ten minutes.

He shook his head in disbelief. Elle wanted on his computer. He had no idea what the hell she could be looking for, but she didn't do anything without a reason. She was up to something and it couldn't be good.

Screw the doctor's signature. Ignoring the pain throbbing through his arm, he pulled his shirt and sweatshirt back on and strode from the ER cubicle.

He got to his offices in six minutes and came in the back entrance. Joe was standing there waiting for him, looking terrified. Earlier that night he'd faced down a crazy dude with a knife without blinking, but Elle scared him. Good to know. "I've got it from here," he said.

Joe let out a huge breath of clear relief, nodded, and then ran out of there faster than Archer had ever seen him move. He didn't blame the guy. Elle was gorgeous, wily, conniving, amazing, and truly scary as fuck.

He made his way down the hall, not bothering to hide his presence but not making a lot of noise either. His arm was aching like a son of a bitch and he was to-the-bone exhausted. He wasn't sure what he'd find, but he knew one thing.

It wasn't going to be easy.

It never was with Elle.

He got halfway down the hallway when he heard a noise in the storage room. Jesus, what the hell was she up to? He stepped into the doorway and flipped on the light.

There she was, looking like the hottest B&E expert he'd ever seen, all in black, half crouched beside a shelving unit, a stapler in her raised hand like she'd been about to throw it.

"What the hell, Archer?" she said, rising to her full height, lowering her weapon of mass destruction. "You scared the crap out of me."

"What were you going to do, attack me with the stapler?" he asked. "That'll only work if it's a heavy-duty one, and even then you don't throw it, you'll miss. You swing it with as much momentum as you can muster and hit the guy on the head. As long as it's not *my* head."

With a grimace that could have been annoyance or embarrassment, she set it back on the shelf. "All I knew was that it wasn't Joe coming down the hall. He walks with a heavier gait and also he's still slightly favoring his left foot from when he broke it last year. I thought it might be you because you walk like a wildcat stalking his prey but I couldn't be sure."

Now wasn't the time to be impressed with her skills. He already knew she was amazing, and if she wasn't bat-shit crazy, he'd have hired her a long time ago.

Hell, who was he kidding? He couldn't hire her, she'd kill him in his sleep.

Or vice versa.

Her gaze went to the bandage around his arm. "Are you okay?" she asked.

"Oh, no," he said. "You first. What the hell are you doing here in the middle of the night?"

"Well, I wouldn't say middle of the night exactly. It's only midnight."

"That's not an answer, Elle."

She hesitated and looked away. A very rare tell for a woman who seldom if ever gave herself away. He decided he was too tired for this, for these games that he didn't ever seem to have a full set of rules to. "You broke into my office."

"Technically, no," she said. "I didn't break in, there was no need."

"Yeah, because you flashed those dangerous baby blues at Joe," he said.

"Don't blame Joe."

"I don't. I blame you."

Eyes still on his arm, she took a step closer to him. Brave to the end. Always had been too. Few people dared half the shit with him that she did, but for some reason with her he allowed it. Clearly it was early onset of insanity due to misguided lust, he decided. "What did you need in my office, Elle? What's on my computer?"

"Was it deep?" she asked, very gently running a finger down his injured arm. "Did you need a lot of stitches? Are there any complications?"

He caught her hand in his. "No, no, and no." His other hand went to her ponytail, which he used to tug her face up to his. The gesture felt shockingly intimate and a vision came to him of other reasons why he might fist his hand in her hair to hold her head.

Maybe he'd hit his own head tonight and didn't know it. That would explain a lot. "Now you," he said. "What are you up to, Elle?"

"Nothing."

"A lie," he said. "Let me guess why. You were mad that I cut short your booty call. Then you sent me an email that you clearly regret sending so you broke in here with the intention of deleting it from my computer before I could read it on my phone. How am I doing?"

She was good. Really good. She didn't even wince at the realization he'd already read the email. She simply inhaled slow and deep and said, "It wasn't a booty call. It was a date."

"It was Mike," he said. "It was totally a booty call. You need to learn the difference."

She stared at him for a long time, clearly taking this in, torn between trusting him and holding on to her mad. "He seems like a nice guy," she finally said.

"He is. He's a nice guy who loves women. All of them."

She took this in as well and then hugged herself, another rare tell. "I'm single. That gives me the right to see who I want and do whatever I want with them."

Then it was his turn to draw in a slow, controlled breath, during which he tried to erase the image of her doing "whatever she wanted" with Mike.

Or any man other than him.

Christ, he had it bad.

"Look," she said. "You pissed me off with the Neanderthal act of ending my date, okay? You don't have any claim on me, Archer."

Their gazes locked and held while he bit his tongue to keep the words in. Bit it hard too. Because it hadn't been an act at all. Just the real him. "We done here?"

Her eyes narrowed. Yep, if the steam coming out of her ears meant anything, they were completely done.

Elle whirled away to leave, but her temper took over and before she could stop herself, she spun back. "And for your information, I do know the difference between a date and a booty call. A date is when two people go out and enjoy each other's company, not just falling into bed like you probably did last week with that woman from the pub after the distraction job. Because that, Archer, *that* was a booty call."

"What are you talking about?"

She gaped at him, not sure if she was surprised or pissed. "You don't even remember. Unbelievable. I hope she gave you something that makes your dick fall off."

He stared at her and then laughed.

Laughed.

"The other day you announced that I've got a full body rash and now you hope my dick falls off," he repeated, still grinning. "Priceless."

She saw red. She gave him a nudge that was maybe more of a push because he was in her personal-space bubble again, looking big, bad, and just rumpled enough to be sexy as hell. The push didn't do anything. Of course it didn't. First she'd been careful because of his arm and, second, no one could budge the stubborn ass unless he allowed it, which didn't stop her from doing it again.

"Stop," he said, eyes still flashing but not with amusement now.

She heard the danger in his voice but she couldn't heed it. She'd lost her shit. So she shoved him again and before she could blink, he'd curled his fingers into her sweater and pulled her to him, reversing their position to push her against the wall and pin her there with his hard, badass body, eyes dark as midnight.

When he spoke, his words threw her for a loop.

"You carry my knife on you," he said. "All the time."

He wasn't touching her with his hands. One was planted on the wall on the side of her face, the other was at his side, probably because it hurt to lift it. If she turned her head to the side, her mouth would brush against his forearm. It was shocking how badly she wanted to do that. "It's a righteous knife," she managed.

"You carry it," he repeated.

She realized he was surprised. Maybe even stunned. "Yes," she said while mentally battening down her inner emotional hatches. She'd been waiting all damn year for him to see her as something more than just one of the gang. She'd finally lost her shit and kissed him on that mountain. And afterward when he'd withdrawn, she'd remembered something important. She was stronger than this. She didn't want a man who didn't want her back, dammit. Maybe she'd had a very momentary lapse of good judgment, but she could recover from that.

Was recovering from that.

To prove it to herself, she slid out from between him and the wall and headed to the door because she was out. All the way out.

And he let her go.

Chapter 9

#TakesALickingAndKeepsOnTicking

The next morning, Elle had just finished her online accounting class and was making the transition from school to work, putting away her books, getting a refill of tea, and . . . shoring up her inner resolve to kick ass and forget about a certain six-foot-plus man who brought out both the best and absolute worst in her.

Mostly the absolute worst.

When the knock on her outer office door sounded, she frowned. It was eight in the morning. She had no appointments this early. Nothing until ten when she had to meet a potential tenant for one of the two available retails units downstairs.

She stood, gulping down the last of her tea for a caffeine rush before moving to the door. She figured it was Trudy or her janitor husband, Luis, with a tenant question. Or maybe Spence, who often ran in the mornings and then came to steal whatever breakfast leftovers she had.

It wasn't Trudy or Luis.

It wasn't Spence.

It was a blast from her past, and an unwelcome one at that.

"Surprise!" her visitor said.

Surprise indeed. "What are you doing here?"

"I thought it was about time we caught up." Morgan flashed a charming smile. *"Sis."*

Elle's sister had made herself scarce for years even though they both lived in the same city and followed each other on Instagram. Elle had tried to keep in touch until she was blue in the face, making sure that Morgan always knew how to find her, but Morgan tended to show up in Elle's world when she needed something. Twice for bail money and once to pay off the guy Morgan could never seem to shake—her on-again, off-again boyfriend, Lars. She'd "borrowed" money from him and even the fact that Lars and Morgan went back years hadn't stopped him from threatening to bash in her kneecaps if she didn't pay up.

That had been two years ago. The guy scared the hell out of Elle—and she didn't scare easily. Dealing with him was all too reminiscent of her entire child-hood with her mom, and she'd promised herself never again. She wouldn't let herself be dragged into that life she'd run so hard from. "Not buying the 'catch up' line," she said. "You want something."

Morgan sighed. "Is it so hard to believe that I just wanted to see you?"

"Actually, yes." Elle had learned a long time ago to listen to her instincts because they were almost always right. "I'm sorry," she said. And she really was. It'd been a long time since she'd yearned for something, anything, from Morgan. Such as a *real* sisterly relationship. But fact was fact. If Morgan was here, it was because she needed something. Something that would be costly to Elle, and she'd paid enough. "But I really can't do this with you right now."

Morgan's smile slipped. "Can't? Or won't?" She shook her head. "No, you know what? Don't answer that, I already know." And with that, she turned and slammed the door behind her.

Elle paced her office for a few minutes, her mind whirling as emotions pummeled her. Regret. Guilt. An overwhelming sense of sadness because Morgan was the only family she had, dammit. She was a crappy sister but without that tenuous connection, she felt . . . alone. Hating herself for it, she yanked the door open again but Morgan was already gone.

She went downstairs to be sure, but when there was no sight of Morgan anywhere, she headed into Tina's coffee shop and bought an entire bag of muffins, which she took to Willa's shop.

Pru was in there with Willa, and at the sight of Elle and the bag in her hands, they actually jumped up and down in excitement. Willa had Vinnie, probably babysitting him for Kylie, and the little guy got in on the action, barking so hard his back legs lifted off the ground. Willa came in for a hug and held on tight, and after a brief hesitation, Elle held on right back.

"You're the *best*," Willa said, pulling back with a smile. "You always know what I need." Her smile faded a little bit. "Hey. What a minute. What's wrong?"

"Nothing."

"Sure," Willa said. "We could go with that and talk about other stuff, like how hot Chris Evans is or the fact that it's going to rain later for the millionth time this week. Or better yet, we could discuss those amazing shoes you've got on today. But you should know that as soon as you leave, we're gonna switch the topic to you."

"Me?" Elle asked.

"Yes. We'll worry about what's wrong, if maybe you need help and you're just being too stubborn to ask. Or . . . you could just spare us the gray hair and tell us."

"Gray hair? Really?"

"Hey, family worries about family," Pru said. "And family gives family gray hair."

They loved her. They really did, and at that realization, it all spilled right out of her. "My sister's in town," she heard herself say. "And that means bad shit is coming along right behind her as always, like category five hurricane bad shit. Also, I'm never going gray, not even for you two—at least not that anyone will ever know."

Pru smiled and took her hand. "You do know that when this category five storm hits, your real sisters will be at your back, right?"

Willa took her other hand and squeezed, nodding her agreement with Pru's words, her eyes solemn. "Always," she said. "Through sickness, gray hair, and health, babe."

Elle's throat went tight, too tight to talk. Because really, she wasn't alone at all. She'd wanted family and she had it. Her friends were her family, more so than any blood relation had ever been.

For the rest of the day, Elle struggled with what she'd done, turning Morgan away crisis unheard. And yes, she was one hundred percent sure there'd been some sort of crisis. She felt like such a jerk.

She also struggled with something else. She needed to apologize to Archer. Not for the email. Oh hell, no way was she going to apologize for her feelings, especially as in the moment they'd been genuine. But she'd B&E'd his office and had used one of his men to do it.

Not cool of her.

And then there was the other thing—she'd been watching his office all day, wanting to get eyes on him and make sure he was really okay after being stabbed. Eyes only. No mouth. Under absolutely no circumstances was she going to let her mouth get involved.

She'd given him up and she was sticking by that decision.

But he'd stayed away from his office. This wasn't all that uncommon. He spent whole weeks out in the field on jobs. In his opinion, the office was an evil necessity. So she gave it up and tried to get the scoop from Mollie.

"He's doing better," Mollie said. "Not that he'd admit he wasn't in top form all this week."

"So he's on a job."

"Of course," Mollie said. "That man doesn't take time off for, and I'll quote him here, 'a little scratch.' Luckily he's just doing surveillance."

"Where?" Elle asked.

"Sorry, honey." Mollie shook her head. "I can't give out his location."

"He shouldn't be working at all, should he?"

"No. The doctor doesn't want him working for at least another week, which of course he thinks is ridiculous. The guys would've handled today's surveillance but he refused help. He's not into letting people take care of him, which is silly since the man's done nothing but take care of all of us like we're his family." She shook her head. "Anyway, I'd really like to tell you where he's at since you're probably the only one of all of us who can improve his mood, but—"

"Oh trust me," Elle said, "I don't improve his mood."

Mollie gave her a get-real look. "Are you seriously going to stand in my reception room in that amazing dress—and I'm going to need deets on where you got that—and look me right in the eyes and tell me you don't know what kind of influence you have on that man?"

Elle opened her mouth and then shut it. Her phone rang and she'd never been so happy for the excuse to step out into the hallway to answer it.

The number wasn't one she recognized and when she answered, she knew she'd never heard the voice before either.

"Morgan," a man's gruff voice said.

Elle narrowed her eyes. "No. You've got the wrong number—"

"Elle, then."

She stilled. "Who is this?"

But he'd disconnected. "Dammit." She turned to walk down the hallway and nearly plowed into Joe. "Hey," she said. "Just who I wanted to see."

"No," he said.

"Excuse me?"

He blew out a sigh and scrubbed a hand down his face, looking pained. "Look, Elle, you're hot as hell and I really like you. But on top of all that, boss man's in a bitch of a mood today, okay? I mean I know you'd improve it but—"

"Okay, you're the second person to say that to me. It's not true."

He snorted. "Yeah, right, but you're still going to have to find another stooge for today's game."

"For your information, there is no game," she said, watching as he vanished into the office. *"Chicken."* She pulled out her phone again and called Trev.

"Hell no," he answered. "You're scary, sweet thing. But Archer's scarier."

A scary man who was making it all but impossible to apologize! She called Spence.

"I knew it was going to be you," he said, distinctly not happy to hear her voice. "Thanks for returning my keys last night after you kyped them and used them to break into Archer's office."

She'd set them on his kitchen counter before going home. "How did you know it was me?"

"Because I let you take them."

Either she was losing her touch or he was just that good. She voted for the latter. "I need to know where Archer is."

"Fine but I'm only going to tell you because I think you'll actually improve his mood."

She pulled the phone from her ear and stared at it, and then shook her head. "Why does everyone keep saying that to me?"

He snorted. "Stand by," he said. "I'll text you."

And sure enough, five minutes later a text came through with an address and a note.

Spence: He's on a surveillance recon only, nothing dangerous, and he's alone. You owe me. Muffins, Elle. For a week.

Archer was on one of those rare jobs where he spent most of his time wondering why he'd taken it on in the first place. He hadn't wanted to—as a rule he turned away most domestic cases. Having to stand between a husband and a wife with proof of infidelity on one side or the other never failed to leave him with a bad taste in his mouth. Yeah, he was cynical and jaded and could be a cold bastard. He knew and accepted this about himself. But he still hated providing the final nail in the coffin on a marriage.

This case involved doing just that. His client was a wealthy socialite at the top of the food chain, the elite of the elite in San Francisco, and she suspected her city council husband was cheating on her.

Archer had taken the case only because he owed the mayor a favor, and he'd called Archer himself and asked for his help for his "dear friend."

He'd reluctantly agreed, ultimately deciding it would be good for him to clear the slate. Plus it was a job he could actually do one-handed, thankfully, as it would be at least another week before he was up to his usual speed. Getting knifed was a bitch. Worse, his men had turned into a bunch of babysitters, watching out for him, taking on the jobs they didn't think he should do.

It was something he'd have done for any one of them, but having it turned on him when he was so used to being in charge drove him nuts. He was leaning casually against the hood of his car like maybe he was waiting for someone, watching the entrance of his client's husband's town house when he heard the sound of heels coming his way.

Not Elle.

That was his first thought. The stride was neither purposeful nor effortlessly graceful enough, but it was the walk of a woman on a mission.

He turned to see Maya, his client, standing on the sidewalk. "What are you doing here?" he asked.

She smiled and came to lean against his car at his side, mocking his stance. "Just found out that Kyle's out of town tonight, left on short notice. Thought you might want to know since I'd told you he'd be here tonight with his skank."

"You could have called me with this info."

She bumped her shoulder against his. "What would the fun have been in that?"

While he processed that statement and all she meant by it, his brain processed something else. Another set of heels coming his way, these ones everything that Maya's hadn't been.

Elle.

She was holding a brown bag from his absolute favorite Thai take-out in all the land, making his mouth water. Or hell, maybe that was just Elle herself in a stark white blouse and a tight royal blue skirt hugging her sexy curves.

He had zero idea what she was doing and he'd found it best to not waste time wondering. Elle kept her own council. The question, as always, was did she come seeking a truce—or the next round of battle?

Elle slowed her steps at the sight of Archer and a woman leaning on his vehicle, standing closer than social niceties dictated. She'd learned early to be as sure and confident as she could, and if she couldn't—then to fake it.

But sometimes faking it took a minute, such as now,

when she was hit by two things. One, she shouldn't have come. She'd given him up and she needed, intended, to stay strong on that.

And two, she hadn't gone through normal social situations like a regular child. Hell, she'd never even *been* a child. Certain emotions had always had to take a backseat to survival so she'd never had to deal with them before.

Jealousy being one of them.

And it was absolutely jealousy feasting on her good sense as she took in the sight of Archer with yet another woman cozying up to him, probably in a trance under all the testosterone and pheromones that came off him in waves.

Yeah, it was a very good thing she'd given him up. She spun on a heel to walk away but Archer was faster.

He was always faster.

Snatching her by the wrist, he slowly reeled her in, taking advantage of her quick little stumble on her heels to haul her in close and wrap his arms around her.

"Hey, baby," he said gruffly, his mouth at her jaw.

She froze in shock. *Baby?*

"So glad you finally made it," he growled against her skin, causing a full body shiver. "What took you so long?"

It was a tough decision between kneeing him in the family jewels or jumping his sexy bones, but he took it out of her hands when he lifted her a little higher so that now her feet were entirely off the ground.

And then he kissed her.

At the first touch of his sexy, knowing, talented mouth on hers, all thought processes shut off. Her brain ceased to work. Not her body though. Nope, operating independently now, it wrapped itself around him as pleasure, sheer, unadulterated pleasure, infused every inch of her.

Archer tightened his grip and deepened their connection and she felt a hard tug on her heart. Somewhere far, far away, her brain clicked back on and understood that this was all for show, that for whatever reason they were in a distraction job and that worked because it meant that this wasn't real. And that was perfect since with his tongue in her mouth and her tongue now rubbing up on his like a cat in heat, she couldn't muster up a single objection. Instead she threw herself fully into her role of the protective, possessive girlfriend and wrapped her arms around him.

When the kiss ended and he pulled back, eyes hot, she smiled, hoping he couldn't feel her knees knocking together. "Brought you dinner, sugar."

He arched a brow, whether at her put-on heavy Southern accent or the nickname she had no idea. Sometimes on distractions she did this, pulled a persona out of her arsenal, and she knew damn well she was good enough at it to win an Academy Award.

"Look at you," he said, amused, "being all domesticated and . . . sweet."

Oh, he'd pay for that. She handed him the brown

bag with one hand while her other slid from low on his spine southbound and right into his back pocket, where she pinched his ass.

Hard.

He merely grinned at her. "Smells delicious. What do I owe you?"

"We'll settle up." More of a threat than a promise, and to make sure he knew it, she pinched him again. *"Later."* Then she turned to the woman. "So who's this?" she drawled.

"Maya Rodriguez," Archer said. "My client. Maya, this is—"

"Candy," Elle said. "Archer's . . . fiancée. You aren't by any chance hitting on another woman's fiancé, are you?"

Archer choked on that one and Elle helpfully pounded him on the back hard enough to nearly crack a few ribs.

Maya shook her head. "I'm sorry, I wasn't aware that he was engaged. I was just"—she glanced at Archer—"hopeful, is all. You're a lucky woman, Candy. Archer here's the full package. Smart, dedicated . . ." She smiled. "Sexy."

He smiled at her.

"Candy" resisted the urge to pinch him yet again.

"Family is very important to me," Maya said. "In fact, family's everything." Her eyes went a little misty. "My father cheated on my mom for years. And now my ratfink bastard husband is doing the same. And

I nearly . . ." She glanced at Archer, looking regretful. "Well, never mind. We have a daughter. I need to get it together for her sake." She pulled out her phone and showed them the pic on her screen—an adorable-looking little girl with a sweet smile.

Well, hell. "She's beautiful," Elle said quietly.

Maya's eyes were still misty. "I know. She's the best thing I've ever done in my entire life. I know everyone says that, but it's true. It's something you can't understand unless you have your own family, tight-knit like the two of you." She smiled a little bit bittersweetly. "Don't be like me, okay? Don't fall into the pattern. Appreciate what you've got and fight for it." She took another step back. "I've gotta go. But I sincerely hope the two of you have the real thing and that a silly, lonely woman making a play she shouldn't have made can't hurt what you have."

They both watched her walk away.

"You realize that within the hour the entire county will think I'm engaged," Archer said, not sounding particularly bothered.

"Hey," Elle said, losing the Southern accent. "*You're* the one who started that. You kissed me. Which, by the way, is confusing. You clearly don't want to be with me but you kiss me like you can't get enough. I'm over it, Archer. Keep that admittedly great mouth to yourself until you figure your shit out."

He turned his head and met her gaze.

"I mean it," she said, not liking the attitude implied

in his expression. "I deserve more. I mean I understand, I do. Once you've protected someone the way you protected me, you get . . . well, protective. But I'm no longer that sixteen-year-old girl, Archer. I'm a grown woman, and while we're at it you're welcome by the way for the save just now. By my calculations, that was the fifteenth job I've done for you."

A whisper of what she thought was surprise crossed his face. "You keep count?" he asked.

"Of course I keep count. And don't think I don't know that we're still not even. I'm working on that. I pay my debts, Archer." A wind had kicked up and she hugged herself. "All of them."

"Elle . . ." All traces of humor were gone from his face. "There is no debt."

"Yes, there is," she said, earnestly now, needing him to understand. "What you did for me all those years ago, it was everything. We're still not even, not even close. And actually, I don't know how I can ever repay you. You took me in and showed me something I didn't know—that I could walk away from a life I didn't want. That I could instead create a new life I *did* want. All I had to do was . . . well, do it."

He didn't move. He was maybe not even breathing. "I want you to listen to me very carefully," he finally said in a very serious voice. "There's no price on what we do for each other. Ever."

"But pulling me out of there was at such a huge cost to yourself, then taking me to the doctor, giving me food and shelter, stuffing that two hundred bucks in the sweatshirt you gave me, leaving it for me to find in the pocket—"

"Anyone would have tried to help you, Elle."

Not where she'd grown up. "Here. Hope it's good. I've gotta go."

"You never told me why you're here in the first place," he said to her back. "Or which one of my guys I have to talk to for giving out my location."

The wind kicked it up even more, bringing in some fast-moving clouds that matched the impending storm in her gut. She turned to face him. "None of them."

He gave her a small smile. "Now who's protecting someone?" He studied her. "My money's on Spence."

"How do you figure?"

"Because there's no way Joe fell victim to your smile again so quickly after last night," he said. "And Mollie idolizes you but she also loves me. Spence is the only one currently susceptible enough to your charms to cave. So let's cut to the chase, Elle. Why are you really here?"

No way was she going to admit to being worried about him. It would just go straight to his big, fat head. "I wanted to apologize, but I'm no longer feeling it."

"For the B&E or for using one of my men?"

She sighed. "Both."

His gaze never left hers. "There's more. You were worried about me."

"Well that would be like worrying about a lion in his

own habitat, wouldn't it? King of his jungle, always in charge, never showing weakness—"

"Yeah," he said softly. "You were worried about me."

She blew out a breath. "Maybe. Just this once." She started to move away again but he caught her.

"I'm done here," he said. "I'll give you a ride, but we're going to eat first."

He took her to the Marina Green where he made her get out and sit with him on a park bench sheltered from the wind by a thick grove of tall trees. They watched the storm move in on the water, making it shimmer and dance as it ebbed and flowed heavily against the shoreline.

She'd forgotten forks. All they had were chopsticks. Problem was that it was his right arm that had been cut and he was right-handed. Watching him try to use the chopsticks with his left hand was far more entertaining than it should be. Three times he missed his mouth by a mile and when she smiled, he slid her a look.

"I'm starving to death over here and you think it's funny," he said.

"What's funny is seeing you actually suck at something." She stood, gathered their stuff, and tossed it in a trash can. The wind was rounding the out-of-control mark and the occasional boom of thunder could be heard. Elle's hair blew around her head as she stalked back to his truck and got in.

He followed, sliding behind the wheel, his hair sexily windblown. "Thanks," he said, staring straight ahead, out the windshield. "For tonight."

"For fighting off your client for you or for the food?"

He looked at her. "You know there's not a lot of people who'd do the things you do for me."

"You mean yell at you?"

"I mean," he said patiently, refusing to be drawn into an argument. "Being there for me."

Stunned, she stared at him while he drove, and then finally she turned to look out into the night as the city went by in slashes of light from the buildings around them.

If she had been there for him, he'd certainly done the same for her. He mocked her. He teased her. He drove her nuts. But she could ask anything of him, anything at all, and she knew he'd find a way to come through, no matter what.

"Where to?" he asked.

"I was supposed to go to the pub and meet up with Willa, Pru, and Haley."

Her sisters of the heart, and Maya's words floated around in her head.

Family is family. Family is everything . . .

She thought of her sister standing on her doorstep and the look on Morgan's face just before Elle had shut the door on it. She'd looked . . . regretful. Sad.

With a sigh, Elle leaned back against the headrest and closed her eyes. It'd been haunting her. It wasn't often she let herself regret a decision she made but she was regretting that one, big-time. Why hadn't she at least heard Morgan out?

She didn't realize that Archer had parked until she felt his finger stroke a strand of hair from her temple, tucking it behind her ear.

Opening her eyes, she realized they were at the Pacific Pier Building.

"Hey," he said quietly.

"Do you think family is everything?"

He let out a long exhale. "If you're talking about the family we make and not the one we're born into, then yes."

Once in a while, he said something so profound she forgot she wanted to kill him the rest of the time.

Not true, a little voice said. Sometimes you still want to kiss him . . .

"You okay?" he asked. "I think I just lost you there for a minute."

She managed a smile as she slid out of the truck. The temp had dropped at least ten degrees. "Come on, Archer. You should know by now. I'm always okay."

Chapter 10

#LikeAGoodNeighbor

Elle didn't sleep well. She tossed and turned, and by the time she showered, she'd reaffirmed her promise to herself that she wasn't going to let her feelings for Archer, confusing as they were, hold her back.

She took her online class in her office but kept tuning out the professor. She eyed the stack of things that had to be done at work later and sighed. She loved her job, she did, but some days the best thing she could say about it was that her chair spun.

Still, she gamely transitioned from class to the job, only to be stymied when she couldn't log in on her work computer. Resetting the password only further frustrated her because the password had to include an uppercase letter, a number, a haiku, a gang sign, and the blood of a virgin.

Over it, she stood. She needed a 'tude adjustment

before she tossed her computer out the second-story window. Leaving her office, she took the elevator up, staring at her reflection in the metal doors, feeling . . . lonely.

Which was ridiculous. Her life was fine, good even. She didn't need Archer, or any man actually. But she wanted one, even if only for a night. She wanted to be held, touched. Desired.

She had to use a special keycard to get the elevator to stop on the fifth floor, which everyone thought was paid storage, authorized personnel only.

It wasn't paid storage.

It was a penthouse apartment, huge and rambling, with gorgeous, heart-stopping, three-hundred-and-sixty-degree views of the city.

Spence's.

He wasn't home so she let herself in and walked to the tall windows to look out at the city below, determined to get her life back on track. The security and safety track. Happiness would be nice as well but beggars couldn't be choosers.

She was still standing there when Spence, accompanied by his friend and former business partner Caleb, walked in. They were in running gear and all sweaty, talking about some computer program for one of their drones.

Spence looked up with a smile on his face that faded at whatever he found on hers. She had a great poker face when she wanted but at the moment she was feeling too raw to access it.

Not wanting to reveal the crazy in front of Caleb, she headed into Spence's kitchen. His fridge was usually well stocked because he was always hungry and everyone knew it. Women loved to make food for him. Trudy was the worst culprit of them all. She constantly cooked for him so he didn't have to lift a finger for himself.

Elle opened his fridge and found a container of perfect little mouth-size quiches. Setting it on the counter, she dug in.

"Help yourself," Spence said dryly.

She didn't answer; she just kept eating.

"You know, I might've been up here with a woman," Spence said. "In a compromising situation."

"Really?" Caleb asked. "Who?"

Spence shot him a dirty look. "Not the point."

Caleb sent Elle a friendly smile. She actually liked the guy. She didn't know what it was about him, but she didn't seem to scare him off like she did most people. He was good-looking in a rugged cowboy sort of way, smart as hell, and always took the time to talk to her. He'd asked her out several times now but she'd always been busy.

Maybe it was time to change that.

"What?" he asked when he realized she was staring at him.

Spence winced. "Caleb, man, what have I told you? Never approach it when it's angry. You have to wait until the steam stops coming out of her ears. And even then, you need a full-scale strategy. Never, ever, ever ask it a direct question."

Elle rolled her eyes and kept eating.

Caleb didn't look intimidated, which she realized she liked. A lot. She knew he had something like four or five older sisters. She supposed that had given him a certain immunity from the Fear of Women. "I'm not angry," she said. At least not at that moment.

Caleb held her gaze. "You're something," he said perceptively. "I mean you look beautiful as always, but . . . off." His warm chocolate brown eyes were sincere—he wasn't playing with her. "You okay?"

She stopped chewing and actually felt her heart skip a beat, but hell no, she was not going to reveal that she felt alone. And lonely . . . She'd done enough revealing of herself lately, thank you very much. Been there, bought the T-shirt, and got sunburned anyway. "I'm okay. Really," she said into his obvious doubt. "In fact . . . ask me again that thing you sometimes ask me."

Caleb looked at Spence and then back to Elle, his gaze confused.

Men. "Ask me again," she said meaningfully.

He blinked. "You mean . . ."

"*Yes.*"

He swallowed hard. "You want to go out with me?"

"Yes."

He grinned. "Sweet. Now?"

"Well, you're kind of sweaty right now so—"

"I can be showered and ready in five seconds," he said without missing a beat, already heading to the door. "We could go out to breakfast."

There was something to be said for a show of enthusiasm, but she had work. "How about dinner?" she suggested. "Tonight."

"Oh," he said and laughed a little. "Right. That's better."

Spence opened his mouth, caught Elle's glare, and wisely shut it again.

Elle took another quiche, smiled at Caleb, and went to work, feeling much better about things.

Half an hour later she got a text.

> Spence: I hope you know what you're doing.
> Elle: I do know what I'm doing. I'm working for you.
> Spence: Are you always such a smartass?
> Elle: No, sometimes I'm sleeping.

Archer and some of his guys went to the pub for lunch. He'd been told by his doctor to stay home but the hell with that. He needed the distraction of work. For years he'd so carefully squelched his desire for Elle. Or at least pretended to squelch it, but suddenly, or not so suddenly at all, he was losing the battle, miserably. He'd actually thought he could keep his hands off her, never mind her mouth, but he'd failed at that too.

When Caleb showed up at their table, Archer nodded and gestured to their platter of hot wings and fries. "There's plenty."

"Thanks but I'm not staying." Caleb was as smart as Spence, meaning that he was smarter than anyone in the entire place, but unlike Spence who could be equally comfortable walking a dog or designing a drone or addressing an entire board of directors, Caleb didn't seem comfortable at all. "I just wanted to tell you that I'm taking Elle out tonight."

The chatter at the table came to a complete and abrupt stop.

Caleb never took his gaze off Archer. "Just wanted you to know."

"Why?" Archer asked.

Something crossed Caleb's face at that. "I guess because if our situations were reversed, I'd want to know. Anyway, have a good lunch."

And then he was gone.

"If Caleb gets to go out with her, I can too, right?" Joe asked.

"No," Archer said.

"But—"

Trev grabbed a chicken wing and stuffed it in Joe's mouth. "You're welcome," he muttered under his breath, and if there was more conversation, Archer didn't hear it over the heavy thudding of his heartbeat in his ears.

On the one hand, he was proud of Elle for actively seeking out the life she wanted and certainly deserved. On the other hand, watching her go get it sliced right through him in a way that made breathing nearly impossible and hurt more than being stabbed.

Caleb came for Elle after work. They walked the Embarcadero, something she hadn't done in a long time. It was fun. And okay, maybe some of that sense of adventure and excitement came from the fact that she knew Caleb was active on several different dating sites—which meant that she wouldn't be able to break his heart.

"Have to admit," he said as they walked along the water toward Fisherman's Wharf, winding in and out amongst a good-sized crowd, "I was surprised when you agreed to come out with me tonight."

"And I was surprised you had room in your busy social schedule."

He laughed, not insulted. "You can't believe everything you hear."

She cocked her head. "So what percentage of what I hear would you say I should believe?"

He flashed an easy grin. "Fifty. Sixty tops."

When they got to Pier 39, they stood in the west marina under a setting sun and watched the sea lions doze on the docks. "Sure has been nice having you around ever since Archer got Spence to hire you as building manager last year," Caleb said.

Elle took her eyes off the water and stared at him. "What?"

Caleb smiled. "Yeah, we all like having you around. You soften the boss up—not that he'd ever admit it."

It was difficult to speak evenly with the blood rushing through her ears. "I got my job through a headhunter," she said with what she felt was remarkable restraint. "Not Archer."

"Uh . . ." Caleb finally clued in and read her expression. Whatever he saw in her face clearly tipped him off to the fact that he'd screwed up in a very large way because he swallowed hard and backed up a step. "How about some food, yeah? We could get—"

"Caleb, what did Archer have to do with me getting the job?"

"I don't know."

"*Caleb.*"

"Christ, Elle," he said, shoving his fingers through his hair, looking pained. "Can we please forget that I said anything? I overheard Spence and Archer talking about it once a long time ago and I was just looking to make conversation with the hot chick instead of staring at you like a dumbass."

She did her best to let it go but failed utterly. Because here was the thing. Spence owned the Pacific Pier Building. Spence and Archer were very close friends. It didn't take her nearly complete accounting degree to do the math here. Somehow Archer had known she needed work and he'd had Spence hire her—for the job she'd so carefully sought out, the one she'd assumed she'd gotten on her own.

Caleb was tense now and she did feel bad about that because it wasn't his fault. Archer was a dead man walking. She laid a hand on his arm and his muscles jerked.

He laughed in soft apology. "You know," he said, "I thought I wanted you to touch me. I thought that a whole helluva lot. But right now I'm just scared." He turned to face her. "I shouldn't have said that about your job. It was thoughtless."

"You said it because you thought I knew," she said, capable of placing blame where it was due, and that wasn't on him. "Not your fault, Caleb."

Not looking like he felt any better about it, he nodded. And then his phone went off with a text.

"Shit," he said, reading it. "This wasn't supposed to happen but I've got some work stuff going on with Spence and he needs me."

"It's okay," Elle said, sensing a rat. A very cute, sexy geeky rat in glasses named Spence.

"I'm sorry," Caleb said with genuine regret. "Let me drive you home."

She glanced over his shoulder and felt her back teeth grind together. "No, it's okay. I'm going to stay. Don't worry about me, Caleb. I have a feeling something's going to come up for me too."

Like committing murder . . .

Caleb pulled her in for a quick hug and a kiss on her cheek. "Rain check," he said.

She smiled and watched him walk away before turning to Archer, standing on the other side of the pier.

He pushed off the beam he'd been lazily leaning against and walked toward her.

"Two for two," she said. "You know, if you're not careful, I'm going to think you're into me."

"I am into you," he said.

"Because I'm suddenly unavailable to you and dating others?"

"I told you," he said. "Mike's a player. I did you a favor."

"And Caleb?"

"A good guy," he allowed. "But you're off-limits to him."

She crossed her arms. "And why is that? And it better not be because seeing others date me suddenly made you want to do the same."

His gaze never left her. "I don't want to do the same as Mike or Caleb."

"No?" she asked.

He gave a slow head shake. "No. Because dating isn't all I want to do to you."

Not amused, she crossed her arms and glared at him. "Correct me if I'm wrong but you've had an entire year to act like a jealous idiot, Archer."

"Well, I'm dyslexic, so . . ."

She was so mad that she actually couldn't access most of her vocabulary. "You're insane" was the best she could do.

"In a good way, right?"

"Oh my God." Tossing up her hands, she turned to go anywhere but here.

"You wanted a date tonight," he said to her back. "Go out with me."

She faced him again. "Tell me one good reason why I would do that."

"Because we've never gone out on a date and that's on me. I should have taken you out."

"You don't date," she reminded him. "You charm—when you're in the mood. You play." And ooze sex appeal . . . "But you don't date, at least not like normal men."

"I do tonight," he said. "Dinner, Elle. Or whatever you want."

She didn't believe him, but she had questions, and she wanted answers. Here was an opportunity to grill him, and she did love a good opportunity. "Fine," she said. "A hot dog."

"What?"

She pointed to the hot dog stand.

"That's what you want for dinner on our first date," he said. "A hot dog from a street vendor."

"Yep. Problem?"

"Not at all," he said. "But you're letting me off easy and you don't do easy. What's the catch?"

"No catch." *Liar, liar, pants on fire.* She walked to the hot dog stand. She ordered two for herself and then piled them high with ketchup, mustard, and pickles. And then, just to be mean, she added onions.

Archer watched her in silence, although she was pretty sure he shuddered at her plate. He also ordered two hot dogs, mustard only.

"Boring," she said.

He looked surprised. Probably a woman had never called him boring before in his life.

They found a bench facing the water where Archer proceeded to watch as she demolished her hot dogs. She might have bothered with a smidgeon of embarrassment but, one, it turned out being mad made her hungry, and two, his eyes were lit with genuine amusement.

"What?" she asked testily.

"I'm just impressed. I like a woman who can enjoy her food."

"Hmm," she said, waiting until he took a big bite. "So. You got me my job?"

He choked on the hot dog. It was greatly satisfying. She slapped him on the back a few times, probably harder than necessary. "You can use sign language if you need to but I want an answer."

"You got yourself the job," he managed. "On your own merits. I just recommended you for it. That's all."

So it was true. He'd interfered. The implications boggled her brain. "Wow," she finally said. "Just wow."

"You can't be mad," he said. "It was all you."

"You know," she said with a quiet she absolutely did not feel. The calm before the storm that was brewing inside her. A category five storm at that . . . "I'm not even sure where to start."

"Maybe you want to sleep on it," he suggested.

She opened her mouth and then closed it, sincerely having trouble finding the right words for the first time in her life. "I need . . . I don't know." She stood up, shaking her head when he tried to follow.

"You need a minute," he said. "I get that."

"Oh, I'm going to need more than a minute." She drew a deep breath. "You know what, Archer? My needs are simple. All I've ever wanted was to be independent and strong. I thought I was doing both of those things but you just pulled the rug out from underneath me."

He grimaced. "Elle, listen to me. You are independent and strong. Christ, you're the most independent, strong woman I know. You're incredible. I hope you know that. I didn't tell you because there was no reason to. You got the job because of you. Not me."

Fed up with him, she shook her head. "Don't follow me." And then she walked away, getting into the first cab she came to.

Chapter 11

#ThatsWhatSheSaid

By some miracle, Archer managed to get into his truck and follow Elle's cab back to the Pacific Pier Building. When she got out, so did he, and while she was looking in her purse for her wallet, he paid her driver.

She chewed on her back teeth over that but didn't argue. Mostly, he knew, because she was being polite in front of the cab driver. "Thanks," she said begrudgingly. "But to be clear, I'm fine. You don't need to watch out for me. You've done your time, a whole year apparently. I already owe you more than I can repay so please stop. I'm moving on and so should you."

He watched her walk off but she didn't enter the pub as he'd expected. Instead she slowed at the fountain and stared pensively into the water, arms wrapped around herself as if cold. He waited, not wanting to intrude but also not wanting to walk away in case she needed him—a thought that was laughable because she'd made herself clear. She didn't need anyone, and most certainly not him.

She thought she still owed him. His worst nightmare, because as long as she truly believed that, he couldn't even fantasize about having her as his someday. Because every time they were together, he'd worry it was in repayment.

Which reminded him of something he was ashamed to realize he'd forgotten until right this very moment.

Tonight was his dad's retirement party and he hadn't even RSVP'd. He hadn't called. He hadn't anything. With guilt and self-loathing rolling over him in waves, he pulled out his phone and accessed his contacts. He scrolled to his dad and stared at the number.

Call or text? No, texting would be the chicken-shit route. He shoved the phone back into his pocket. Then he swore and tugged it out again, called, and . . . got his dad's voice mail. "Dad," he said at the beep. "Hey. Look, I know it's last minute and I should've called you long before now and at least RSVP'd to your party tonight." He ran a hand over his face. "I'm sorry but I'd like to still come by, if that's okay with you. You can text if you'd rather just . . . Let me know." *Shit*. He disconnected and stood there for a long beat, not sure what to do with himself. Finally he swore some more and then looked up at the odd prickling at the base of his neck.

Elle was no longer by the fountain. She'd moved closer and stood right there, watching him.

"Hey," she said quietly, her expression softer than he was used to seeing when she looked at him. *She felt sorry for him.*

And if that didn't suck big-time. "Don't," he said.

"Don't what?"

Pity me. But he couldn't even say it. "I've gotta go," he said instead and headed to the stairs. He had a damn suit in his damn office closet for the very occasional meetings that required it. He needed to change into it and get to his dad's retirement party, hoping that late was better than never.

"So we're back to you being silent and brooding because I overheard your message to your dad?" she asked, hugging herself in the cold night air. "Kinda rude, don't you think?"

"Go to the pub, Elle." But he should've known better. Telling her what to do never worked out for him but he just shook his head. "It's warmer in there." Then he jogged up the stairs and let himself into his office. Five minutes later he'd changed and was back outside.

Elle stood there waiting for him. And something deep inside him tightened. In spite of his being a dick, she cared about him. He'd been doing his damnedest since that insane kiss they'd shared to not give out the wrong signals, but that was hard when he no longer knew wrong from right when it came to her. He was completely upside down. He shrugged out of his jacket and wrapped her up in it. "I told you to go inside, it's too cold out here for that dress." Which, just a side note, was hot as hell on her.

"You're not going to your dad's retirement party alone," she said.

"Yes, I am." It was his penance, and besides that, he didn't want anyone witnessing what promised to be an incredibly awkward reunion. Archer hated awkward. Hated an audience to it even more.

"I've texted Spence," she said. "He's on his way."

Shit. "I'm not bringing Spence. He'll talk too much."

"You need to bring someone," she insisted. "Finn's working. How about Willa?"

"She talks more than Spence."

Elle didn't look particularly moved. "Okay then, one of your guys. Joe or Trev—"

"Read my lips, Elle. *No.*"

She crossed her arms, the stubborn look on her face said that she wasn't going to let this go. He blew out a breath. "Fine. If you want someone to come with me so badly, then I vote for you. Get in the damn truck."

She arched a brow. "Out of all the people you know, you want to take the one person who drives you the most nuts? The one who's mad at you? *Really* mad?"

"I want the one person I trust to have my back for this."

That seemed to shock her. It certainly shut her up. And it had the added benefit of dissolving a whole lot of her resentment and anger too.

But not all. Of course not. It was Elle, after all.

"Fine," she said, heading to his truck, heels clicking, hips moving in that innately sexy graceful way she had. "But don't forget—this isn't a date *or* a booty call."

He laughed. *Laughed.* Only she could do that to him,

bring him out of a mood. Make his day. And maybe sometime he'd sit down and analyze that but it wouldn't be today. "Can we just go?"

"Oh by all means," she said, "let's get this over with."

He shook his head but had to admit that he loved her smartass mouth. In truth, he was crazy to bring her with him. Being around people right now was a bad idea. But being around Elle, the one person on the planet who knew the road map to getting beneath his skin? Insanity. There was a storm brewing big-time, which actually suited his mood. A big gust nearly knocked him on his ass as he opened the passenger door for her and she slid her warm, curvy body in past him, giving him a zing of awareness that rocked him from head to toe. Letting out a long, slow breath, he walked around and slid in behind the wheel. "You ready?"

"I was born ready."

Yeah. That's what he was afraid of.

Elle watched Archer drive, his face as dark as the thunderclouds churning overhead. She knew the feeling of having so much going on inside that you felt like the storm was also raging inside your gut.

"I can't believe I almost forgot," he said quietly, almost to himself.

This shouldn't have pierced her Archer-proof shield but it did. Archer spent a lot of his life being as tough and badass as possible. He had to be that way. But it was in moments like these that she realized he was human, just a flesh-and-blood man who made mistakes like everyone else. "Everyone forgets stuff," she said. "Even important stuff. Like 'oh, hey, I got you your job, no big.'"

He slid her a look. "I should've gone this alone."

She sighed. "Could have, yes. Should have, no. Trust me, you need backup to deal with family."

This had his mouth quirking a little at the corners. "You going to keep me safe, Elle?"

"Hey, I've got a knife."

"Yeah, you do." He paused. "You ever going to tell me why you still have it?"

Well she'd walked right into that one. "Sure. When you tell me why you got me the job."

"We're still on that?"

She sent him her best PMS look.

"I didn't get you the damn job," he said. "I recommended you for it. And I did that because I could. Nothing more, nothing less."

She looked at him, watching as he drove the incredibly busy streets with an ease she never could have managed. "I carry the knife because it's handy."

He shook his head. "It's more than that."

"You're wrong."

"Such a pretty liar." He stopped for a red light and looked at her. "You want me to guess why you're still carrying it after all these years?"

Hell no.

"Maybe you wanted to keep a piece of me," he said.

He was teasing her. Of course since it was also the truth, she got annoyed all over again. "Or," she said, "I want to be able to take a piece out of anyone I need to. Including you, if you get too close. Don't think I won't."

This won her a small smile, like he understood her reasoning perfectly and he'd expected no less. "So you're my body guard for the evening?" he asked.

"Just for the evening, and then we go back to World War III. But yeah, for tonight, I've got your back, whatever you need." She realized her mistake the minute the words left her mouth.

And so did Archer as he sent her a gaze so sizzling she had to look down to make sure her clothes hadn't melted off. Holy. Cow. Where had all that heat come from? "Well," she finally managed. "Within reason, of course."

"Look at you," he murmured. "Always a ready answer for everything."

Is that what he thought? "Have I ever gone back on my word with you?" she asked.

Another considering look. "No. Never. Are you trying to tell me something?"

Was she? She decided to stop talking before she got herself in trouble.

At her silence, he shook his head, a small smile playing on his lips as he continued to drive through the city, still easily navigating the anything but easy to navigate streets of downtown San Francisco.

"Since we're in a momentary truce," he said, breaking their silence. "You're a knockout tonight."

She looked at him but he was concentrating on the road. "Are you trying to soften me up?" she asked.

"Definitely," he said. "But it's also true."

She was wearing one of her favorite dresses, now with his suit jacket around her shoulders. This left him in a button-down that along with his trousers fit him perfectly, emphasizing his broad shoulders and powerful long legs. His sleeves were rolled up. Tie loose. His hair was slightly mussed and he could clearly care less, which of course only made him all the more drop-dead sexy.

He made it hard for a girl to not fall head over heels. "You're not looking too bad yourself," she grudgingly admitted, telling herself not to read into his statement. Not that her body got the memo because it was humming with hyperawareness.

They didn't speak again. The only reason she even knew where they were going was because she'd read the invitation that day in his office. And sure enough, ten minutes later they were in the financial district, parking in the underground parking lot of a beautiful brick and glass building.

"The restaurant that's hosting the party is up on the top floor," he said as he opened his door. He turned back to her, maybe to ask her to stay while he checked to see if they were even welcome, but she slipped out of the truck too quickly for that. "Guarding your body," she reminded him.

"Within reason," he said, mocking her, but then he surprised her by taking her hand.

Which she allowed only because of their truce. They took the elevator up with another couple who were lip locked for the entire ride. And not just lip locked but hand and leg locked too, really going to town, running their hands over each other like they were searching for ticks. They got off on the floor before the restaurant and she let out the laugh she'd been barely holding on to and met Archer's gaze. His mouth was curved into a smile but his eyes were dark and heated. She felt an answering heat in the pit of her belly.

And south.

Just before the door closed, the couple stumbled back into the elevator, looking sheepish.

"Sorry," the woman said. "We missed our floor."

Elle bit her lower lip rather than laugh again. She could appreciate that they'd gotten lost in their lust. Appreciate it and maybe even envy it a little. Because that had never happened to her. She couldn't imagine getting so lost in someone as to lose track of her surroundings. She was just too aware of herself and others.

Still, she was overheated when the elevator doors opened and Archer put his big warm hand low on her back to guide her off. He glanced at her, letting his gaze linger. "You're all flushed." He paused. "Envious?"

"No." She added a scoff. "He probably leaves the lid up and snores."

He looked like maybe he wanted to say something to that but the hostess asked him how she could help him.

"I'm here for the Hunt retirement party," he said.

She thumbed through her iPad. "I'm sorry but that was cancelled."

Archer was hard to rattle but he looked stunned. "Do you know why?"

"Uh . . ." The hostess swiped around on her screen for another moment. "There's only one note here—the retiree decided against a big shindig and cancelled. He had a much smaller dinner party a week ago instead."

Archer, still as stone, didn't answer. Elle slipped her hand in his. "Thank you," she said to the hostess and she tugged Archer aside so the woman could help the next people in line.

"I'm sorry," Elle murmured. "He didn't tell you?"

"No. I think he cancelled because he didn't have any family who RSVP'd." He paused. "Because I'm his only family and I'm an asshole."

She shook her head. "No. Archer—"

He made a rough sound and turned back to the elevator. This time there were no lovebirds and Archer didn't speak. Neither did she. The energy was completely different. In the truck, he took out his phone and made a call. To his dad, she assumed, listening to the phone ringing.

And ringing.

At the beep, Archer pinched the bridge of his nose. "Dad," he said. "I'm sorry. I should have RSVP'd. Hell, I should've called, okay? But I'm calling now." He hesitated and then ended the call and tossed the phone aside.

He drove her back to the Pacific Pier Building in a

heavy wind, a few drops of rain hitting the windshield. He parked on the street and got out to walk her to the pub but she stopped in the courtyard.

"It's not all your fault," she said.

"Yeah, it is."

"Communicating is a two-way street and—"

"We're not talking about this."

"But—"

"Ever, Elle."

The storm broke over them with a boom of thunder, and rain began to fall in earnest as she stared at him. For once she didn't think of her poor shoes. All she thought about was the pain in her chest. "So much for letting me be there for you," she said. "And all that other stuff last night about no debt, no price between us."

He just looked at her, impervious to the rain. To *her*.

"So to be clear, it's only okay if I need you," she said. "But when the shoe's on the other foot, you're not willing to let yourself need help from me, is that it?" She shook her head, all the bottled-up emotions popping free. "God forbid you be vulnerable in any way or show a weakness, right? You probably faked not being able to use those chopsticks with your left hand yesterday, just to throw me off."

"Elle," he said, sounding to-the-bone weary. "Get out of the storm and go get warm—"

"No."

When he sighed, actually *sighed,* she narrowed her eyes. "You know what, Archer? You go get warm, okay? Go straight to hell for all I care."

"I'm already there."

"And that's my fault?" she asked incredulously, having to squint through the rain now.

"Yes. Shit. No." He shoved his hands into his hair, making it stand up on end. "I don't know. You've got me all twisted in knots and all sorts of fucked up." And then on that rare, shockingly revealing statement, he hauled her up against him, spun them into the alley, and kissed the ever loving daylights out of her.

And him too, if his heavy breathing counted for anything.

When they finally came up for air, they were both drenched to the core and she'd completely forgotten the fact that she'd decided to keep her mouth off him. The only thing that helped was that he'd forgotten himself too. He had his hands on her ass, holding her tight to him, nudging her hips up close and personal to what felt like a very impressive erection.

And she wasn't much better. She was climbing him like a tree and making needy little whimpers that she couldn't stop to save her life. They weren't even having sex, their clothes weren't off, they were standing in a damn alley for God's sake, but she'd swear they'd both just nearly come from only a kiss.

"You're killing me," he said, his voice as rough as gravel.

She felt like she was literally going to die if she didn't get him inside her, but she managed to give him a cool look. "So walk away then, Archer. You're good at that."

But he didn't move. Instead, he looked down at

himself. "I couldn't walk to save my own life. Hell, in this condition, I couldn't even get you upstairs to one of our offices."

"This isn't a booty call, remember?"

He tilted his head, clearly taking in her flushed face, her crazy breathing, and then there was the fact that her nipples were poking against the material of her wet clothes like two heat-seeking missiles, which he could clearly see because his jacket was slipping off her shoulders. She tightened it around herself.

He didn't make a smartass comment. Instead he shocked her when he said, "At the moment, Elle, I'd get down on my knees and beg."

This revealing statement knocked her for such a loop that she was still staring at him when Eddie poked his head into the alley. "Hey, dude. Dudette. Listen, far be it for me to interrupt a melding of the minds and all but I'd like to come through here and—" He caught Archer's expression and backtracked. "Actually, you know what? You two take your time."

When he was gone, Elle touched a hand to her mouth and stared at Archer. "That was not on my agenda," she said. "*You're* not on my agenda."

His eyes were dark and unfathomable. "Ditto. Tonight was just an overreaction to an emotional evening."

She stared at him some more and then stepped back, her heart thundering in disappointment now. She shrugged out of his jacket, thrust it at him, and then turned and left the alley, only to hear Eddie murmur "Don't take it personally, son. Women are born crazy."

Hard to be insulted by the truth, she thought as she strode across the courtyard through the driving rain, not even feeling the chill as her blouse and skirt stuck to her like a second skin. She took the elevator, heading to her office simply because she needed a moment alone. An immediate moment alone. She'd gotten her key in the lock when she felt the air pressure change as someone came up behind her.

Didn't take a rocket scientist to figure out who. "Overreaction to an emotional evening?" she repeated in angry astonishment, not turning to face him. "Seriously?"

"I was wrong."

"Maybe I should get that in writing, you admitting you're wrong. It's like seeing a unicorn and I need to capture the moment."

A tanned, sinewy arm encircled her, taking over unlocking the door. Then he nudged her inside, flicked on the lights, kicked the door closed, and pushed her up against it. He was big, hard, and drenched.

"You know what?" she asked, proud of her steady voice in spite of her trembling legs. "I'm going to have to pass on the caveman act—"

His mouth came down on hers, fusing their lips in a hot, searing kiss that she felt from the tips of her frozen toes to the ends of her wet hair and every single inch in between. Huh. Turned out she'd been wrong too, very wrong to think she could resist this with him.

Lightning flashed, followed immediately by a boom of thunder. Her office lights flickered once, twice. An electric surge, she thought dizzily, the scent of rain and sexy Archer making her press into him.

"I want you, Elle," he said, voice low and rough. "It's a goddamn ache, I want you so much. Just like this, dripping wet in every way, blind with need."

"Yes." Mindless at this point, she shoved up his wet shirt. He tore it off over his head and then unbuttoned her blouse and spread it open, a low, muttered oath on his lips as the lights flashed out again.

And stayed out this time.

In the far back recesses of her mind, she told herself to stop, that she was going to get hurt, but the part of her in control didn't care. He needed her. And she sure as hell needed him. His fingers wrapped around hers and he gave a tug. She had to hand it to him, he knew her office as well as she did because in the next beat she was free-falling onto her small, narrow love seat, followed down by a hundred and eighty pounds of highly sexually motivated male.

The love seat, built for show rather than actual use, complained with a splintering *crack* and then collapsed beneath them.

They hit the floor. She saw a brief flash of Archer's white teeth as he smiled his badass smile in the dark and then rolled, pinning her beneath him, her hands caught in his above her head.

"Your arm," she gasped.

"Worth the pain." His kiss was hot and deep and she almost lost herself in him.

Almost.

She fought the dregs of passion because no way was she going to be passive, not when for the first time in far too long she felt . . . *alive,* from the tips of her hair to her toes, which were already curling. Yanking her hands from his grasp, she placed them on his chest, unable to see much of anything but *needing* to touch, slowly sliding them up and around his neck, pulling him down to meet her lips. "More," she demanded and skimmed a hand down his bare, sleek back and into his trousers. When she then slid that hand around to his front and brushed against a very hard erection threatening his zipper, he growled her name low in his throat, sounding gratifyingly breathless. He had his hands up the back of her dress, each palming a cheek, his fingers dipping in between, and when he discovered how wet he'd made her, he groaned.

She clutched at him, already halfway gone. "Archer—"

"I know. Christ, Elle. You feel amazing."

"Now." She didn't even recognize her voice. "Right now."

"My office." His voice was rough gravel, like he could barely speak. "My couch is bigger and not in pieces on the floor."

"No, here. *Please . . .*"

His low laugh was sexy as hell, damn him. He knew exactly what he did to her. "I do like the please," he murmured. "More of that."

"Archer, I swear to God if you don't do me now, I'm going to hurt you."

"Mmmm. Bossy too." His mouth was busy at her breasts, her bra tugged open, his teeth and tongue driving her wild. "You're a fantasy come true, Elle." His voice was thick with erotic promise, his hands following through on that promise, his fingers especially taking her straight to heaven. "And we're going to get there. But not with you on your back on this floor."

"No?"

"No."

She made an unintelligible sound of objection and he soothed her with a hot kiss before pulling back and tugging her up to her knees. Then he turned her away from him and slid his hand down her back, encouraging her to bend over the coffee table.

Before she could suggest that *he* bend over the table and they'd see if *he* liked it, his fingers were back in play between her thighs and she couldn't remember why she'd wanted to object.

He draped himself over her in a protective shell, his chest plastered along her back, his legs encasing hers, one arm around her middle, palming a breast, the other between her legs, those fingers slowly but surely driving her right out of her ever loving mind. His mouth was just as busy, his teeth teasing the side of her throat, her jaw. "Good?" he murmured.

She nodded and then, to make sure he didn't stop, gripped his wrist to hold his hand in place as lightning flashed through the window. She jerked but he wrapped himself around her. "I've got you," he murmured.

And he did. He had her writhing against him as he urged her thighs open as far as they could get with her panties wrapped around them and his long, powerful legs on either side of hers, all while his fingers teased, cajoled, coaxed her into a hot mess, knowingly moving in an oscillating circle that seriously tugged every single thought right out of her head. She felt surrounded by him, completely surrounded in the very best possible way as his hot, wet mouth played over the nape of her neck and shoulders. Her head fell back, her breath coming in short, desperate little whimpers, her entire world shrunk to this, to the pleasure of his body and mouth and fingers . . . God, those fingers. "Archer—"

"You're close," he whispered hotly in her ear. "I can feel it."

She opened her mouth to disagree because she didn't come quickly. Ever. But apparently she did now. She burst, quivering in delicious orgasm and then, before she could process the shock of that, he'd managed to put on a condom and thrust inside her, and she came yet again. Or still . . .

"Fuck, Elle . . ." His fingers tightened on her hips as he filled her to capacity, reducing her to a puddle of goo. "You feel so good."

She bit her tongue hard so she wouldn't make any noise, but it was almost impossible to remain quiet with him so hot and silky hard inside of her. She could feel every single inch of him as he slid in and out, thrusting harder and deeper with each stroke, and it felt so incredible that she came again, oblivious to the storm around them or the fact that she was on her knees, bent over the table, begging for more.

He gave it to her, everything she wanted, and when she cried out his name, he groaned something back, something hot and erotically dirty, and he shuddered and finally let himself go.

From the dim recesses of her mind she remembered how she'd felt watching that couple go at each other in the elevator like the rest of the world didn't exist, remembered thinking wistfully that she'd never experienced such a thing.

She could now check that box off.

For a long moment they stayed still in that instance in the dark, Archer pressed up against her, the two of them panting for air, muscles trembling, before he finally shifted.

And she thought, okay, that's it. He's going to stand, zip, and walk out the door.

But he didn't, and in perhaps the sweetest thing he'd ever done, he lingered there with her in the dark, stormy night, still inside her, his mouth brushing lazily and warmly up and down the nape of her neck, his arms tight around her.

Cuddling.

He was cuddling her.

When his thumb brushed over her nipple, her entire

body jerked, hungry for more, the greedy thing. A little bit unnerved by that, she elbowed him to give her space, and when he did, she staggered to her feet.

A small beam of light came on and she blinked.

Archer had a penlight between his teeth and was buttoning his trousers. From within his pocket, his phone was vibrating, as it had been on and off for a while now.

Not in any apparent hurry, he set the still-lit penlight on the table where he'd just given her the best orgasms—plural!—of her life.

She'd never look at the table the same way again.

Her gaze drifted to the love seat next. Following her gaze, he laughed. "I'll get it out of here for you," he said.

"No, that's okay." It was Friday night, the courtyard would be a hotbed of action in spite of the storm. She didn't need everyone to see him carrying it out, speculating about what had happened. Although in this case, the truth was probably crazier than anything anyone could make up. "Luis will get it for me."

Archer lifted his head and studied her. His eyes softened and a small smile crossed his mouth. He stepped into her, pushed the hair off her hot and sweaty forehead, and brushed his mouth over her temple. "You okay?"

A low laugh huffed out of her. "I think you know that I am. I didn't expect that to be so . . ." She shook her head, at a loss for words.

He let out a slow exhale. "I did."

She met his gaze and at the look on his face something inside her clutched hard. He regretted what they'd just done. The best time of her life and he regretted it. "Are you about to piss me off again, Archer?" she managed to ask.

"We both know I can do that without trying."

Not exactly an answer. She laughed mirthlessly. "Yeah, well if your next few words are anything along the lines of 'I'm sorry' or 'that was a mistake' or 'I shouldn't have taken advantage of you,' then it's a *definitely*."

He just held her gaze and her heart stopped. "Wow." That she was right gave her no satisfaction at all. "You know what?" She gestured to the door. "I want you to go now"—she pointed at his mouth when he opened it—"without saying another word so that I can still stand the sight of you."

"Let me drive you home first—"

"No, I'm good, thanks. Oh and, Archer?" She waited until he looked at her. "Stay the hell away from me." And then, although she wanted to turn away from him as he walked out her door, she forced herself to watch him go.

Chapter 12

#DeadBoyfriendWalking

Archer prowled the length of his office and back. Two minutes ago he'd been kicked out of Elle's office. One minute ago a big case he and his guys had been working on broke wide open and everyone was coming into work.

He had maybe three more minutes to himself and all he could think was that something had just changed in his world and he was pretty sure he knew what.

Or at least who.

He'd known a year ago that by leading Elle here to the Pacific Pier Building as general manager for Spence things would change. But for most of that year he'd managed to keep his distance, both mentally and physically.

It hadn't been until he'd had a taste of her that night they'd been camping that his world had stopped spinning.

And he'd been a little off his axis ever since.

After what had just happened in her office, he'd lost

all balance whatsoever. The funny thing was that a year ago he'd have said his world worked just as it was. That he had everything he needed. He had a home he loved and a business he'd built from the ground floor up that was both successful and also satisfied him.

But something had happened to that satisfaction over time. He'd felt less fulfilled and more . . . restless and unsettled.

Unsatisfied.

But unable to pinpoint why, he'd ignored it.

Then she'd come into his life and for the first time he'd been out of his league. With her, he was never sure of anything.

Maybe it was because her smile lit up his world. So did the way she cared so fiercely for those in her life, even him, which made him one lucky son of a bitch. When he made her laugh, he felt like Superman. And when he made her melt . . . God. He could still see how she'd looked in her office, trembling for his touch.

And when he'd given in to it, his foundation had cracked. He could tell himself that what had happened had been a mutual explosion of pent-up need and frustration and that was it. But that was a lie.

It wasn't over and it wasn't done. Ever since that kiss on the mountain, he'd been telling himself that was it. That he wouldn't give into further temptation, he wouldn't play with her, never her.

But the thing was, he wasn't playing at all. He was dead serious.

And suddenly that no longer scared him or had any

sort of power over him. He didn't want it to be over or done. Truthfully, she was the best thing in his life and he was a complete idiot if he let her walk away from him.

Unfortunately, or maybe fortunately, the guys piled into his office at that moment and they were off and running the job for a high-profile criminal attorney involving a missing witness and a cover-up. It spilled over into the weekend and through much of the week, it was Thursday morning before he had a moment to breathe or think of anything outside of the job.

He'd texted Elle several times and had gotten no response. It was early, too early to catch her in her office because he'd disturb her while she was in class. So he went into his office, trying to make a dent in the ever growing paperwork, his mind playing Friday night in Elle's office on repeat.

Christ, he'd screwed up all year, keeping his distance like he had. But then Elle had upped the ante, offering him emotional support at every turn like . . . like they were something to each other. And he realized she was right. They *were* something to each other. They were everything.

Stay the hell away from me . . .

He'd long ago promised himself he'd never hurt her. He'd die first. But with Friday night flashing through his mind—the crazy storm, the feel of Elle's sweet, curvy body against his, the sound of her soft sighs in his ear, how she'd reached for him as she'd come, his name on her lips . . .

He wasn't going to be able to stay the hell away from her.

He'd given her time this week only because he'd had no choice, but the job was over now and he wanted, needed, to see her. Something had changed for him, in a big way. And he was over watching her from afar. Over worrying about their past and whether she might be with him now because of gratitude or a sense of debt.

He'd take her however he could get her and he wanted her at his side, for keeps.

Aware that it would be a hard sell, he was working on his pitch but he hadn't gotten anywhere when Spence called him up to the roof. Few people knew about the best spot in the building, from which there was the kind of view of San Francisco and the entire bay that postcards were made of.

Spence had brought breakfast burritos and they sat, legs hanging over the edge of the five-story building, watching the world go by.

"What's the occasion?" Archer asked.

"The week sucks. Breakfast burritos make it better."

Archer looked over at him. Because while it was true—breakfast burritos *did* make everything better—there was more to this story, he could tell. He felt like a jerk because he'd been so focused on himself—and Elle—that he'd neglected his best friend. "You still working on that new drone prototype with Caleb?"

"We accidentally blew it up."

Archer grimaced. "Sorry, man. How about your date

this past weekend, the secret one you made me swear on my life not to tell anyone about—"

"Didn't work out," Spence said glumly.

"Why?"

"She'd looked me up."

Shit. This was unfortunately all too common. Once a woman caught a whiff of Spence's net worth, she usually pulled out all the stops to hook him. "I told you to let me vet her," he said. He—or Elle or any of the others—always tried to vet all Spence's dates because, although the guy was a genius, he had zero ability to weed out the ones looking for their MRS degrees.

"She seemed normal," Spence said.

"But?"

"But she thought I'd be interested in getting married ASAP. No prenup."

Archer had to laugh. "On date one, no less. She definitely gets this month's Gold Digger Award."

Spence shoved some more fries into his mouth. Spence often said much more with his silences than his words. He wasn't shy or introverted but he could be quiet, focused on his work, and come off as uninterested.

Elle called him a sexy geek, but Archer knew the guy's love life hadn't been all that exciting.

Neither had Archer's, until Elle. Now he felt both like the luckiest son of a bitch on the planet and the most terrified because she had all the power. And that was a true first for him. "You ever been in love?" he asked.

Spence blinked. "I'm sorry, did you just ask me a relationship question? Because you're allergic to relationships, remember?"

Archer shifted uncomfortably, already sorry he'd brought it up, but it was too late now. "Well, have you?"

"Are we really going to talk about . . . love? The two most emotionally stunted guys I know?"

"Humor me," Archer grated out.

"Okay then . . ." Spence shrugged. "Yeah. Or at least I thought I was. And you know this already."

"But you felt like you'd protect her, no matter what?"

"Of course. Why?" Spence slid a look his way. "Do you, uh, love Elle? Wait. Shit. Don't answer that. I don't want to know." He ran his hands over his face. "This way if Elle ever asks me if we talked about this, I can deny it." He dropped his hands and glared at Archer. "But the next time you're having an emotional meltdown, call a professional like Willa or Pru."

"It's not a meltdown," Archer said, but he was talking to himself because Spence was walking to the stairwell door. "At least not a big one."

He'd just gotten back to his office when Mollie buzzed to tell him that someone was there to see him. He looked at his schedule. "Who?" he asked, not seeing any appointments or meetings until later.

"Morgan Wheaton."

He stilled. It'd been a long time since he'd heard or thought of Elle's sister. "Send her in."

Morgan walked into his office with the same easy,

natural confidence her younger sister, Elle, usually displayed but there was a subtle difference.

Elle's grace came naturally.

Morgan only imitated it.

"Well, look who traded up," she said, eyeballing his office. "Nice digs." She smiled but it didn't quite meet her eyes. "How've you been, Officer Hunt?"

"We both know I'm not a cop anymore."

"No shit." She walked to his window and looked out. It was only February but she wore a flimsy sundress with a thin denim jacket opened to reveal her assets. Her bare legs went on for days, and she wore the kind of sandals that strapped up her calves to her knees, all carefully orchestrated for maximum effect, which wasn't that difficult to achieve with the Wheaton-family genes.

She looked a lot like Elle but with something important missing.

The spark of vulnerability.

Okay, so maybe Elle hid that spark every bit as well as her sister to most of the world, but he'd never had any trouble seeing it.

A fact he knew she hated.

"Nice view," Morgan said from the window, taking in the marina, the bay, and the slice of the Golden Gate Bridge.

While she studied the sights, he leaned back and studied her. There was only two years' difference in age between the sisters, but Morgan had always looked older than her years.

While acting much younger.

There was a quality to her that said life had sucked so far and she didn't expect it to get much better, and it frustrated him. By keeping Elle safe that night, he's ensured that both girls had gotten out without facing the cops, but only one of them had used the opportunity to change her life, turning herself around, and it wasn't the sister standing at his window.

"What's going on?" he asked her. Because something was going on, he was certain of it. She'd never have come here otherwise. She needed something and for whatever reason she thought he could give it to her.

"Not much," she said with a shrug.

With Morgan, this could go easy or hard but he was going to guess hard. "You need something."

She shrugged again.

Hard it is then, he thought. "Does Elle know you're here?"

"I saw her last Thursday. She didn't tell you? She took one look at me and shut the door in my face. Didn't even want to talk."

This didn't surprise him. Elle had been hurt by her family in many, many ways, and that hurt ran deep. Bone deep.

And Elle wasn't exactly the forgiving sort.

"When I realized you both work in the same building," Morgan said, "it came to me that you're still playing the knight in shining armor and protecting Elle."

"You're wrong."

She gave a smile that said she didn't believe him.

"Get to your point, Morgan."

She let out a breath, her eyes surprisingly free of cynicism and guile. "I've been clean for twelve months," she said. "No drugs. No booze." She paused and looked at him.

He looked right back at her.

"You don't believe me?" she asked.

"It doesn't matter what I believe."

She sank into one of his chairs, leaning forward, hands on his desk, eyes earnest for once. "I'm proud of what I've done this year. I got a real job. I rented a room from some old lady. She's got a lot of rules but"—she lifted a shoulder—"she's nice. She doesn't know me from before. She likes me."

Archer sighed. "You're likeable, Morgan. You deserve to have people care about you. That was never the problem."

Her gaze met his. "My point is that I've changed. And I thought Elle might be able to help me but she . . . she hasn't forgotten. Or forgiven."

"You're her family," he said. "She's forgiven. But yeah, probably not forgotten." He paused. "She's been through a lot too."

"You're defending her." She said this with a small smile and a good amount of surprise. "That's cute."

When he grimaced, she laughed. "Didn't mean to threaten your masculinity. Do you need to go lift weights now, or maybe fix your truck?"

He had to laugh. "Still a smartass."

"It's a Wheaton genetic trait," she said. "It's like our shield against our shit parents. We were born with it. Don't tell me Elle's changed her wiseass ways."

He didn't answer that and she laughed again. "I guess you two are good for each other, huh?"

She was fishing, but the truth was he and Elle had been better than good, they'd been . . . combustible.

"Guess that was a pretty personal question, huh?" Morgan asked. "I forgot, you don't do those."

She was trying for light and casual, and he got that. Put up a good front. Fake it until you make it and all that. But something about her worried him. If she'd been all attitude and bravado, he could have blown her off.

But she was afraid, although of what he had no idea. With her, it could be anything. And if she brought the trouble to Elle . . . "Tell me what's going on, Morgan."

Her smile faded. Her mouth trembled, although she put her fingers to her lips quickly as if to hide the weakness. "Oh, you know, just always trying to outrun my stupid past."

"How?"

"You know I didn't stop grifting after that night."

He nodded and she looked away. "It was harder for me to get out than it was for Elle."

Bullshit. But he said nothing.

"I was all on my own," she said.

Elle too, he thought, but again he held his tongue.

"I kept cutting things too close."

"You actually did cut things too close," he said. "Twice."

She met his gaze. "You know?"

"That you went to jail five years ago and again two years later?" he asked. "Yes."

She stared at him. "I know it's hard to believe but I really have gotten my life together. I'm sober. I'm taking some general ed classes, working toward my AA degree. I told you my current living situation and I'm cleaning houses for cash."

"But?" he asked.

"But I want something different, something on the books and legit." She laughed shortly with little amusement. "I know this sounds ridiculous given who I've been, but I want to pay taxes. I want to save money to get my own apartment. But no one's going to hire an ex-felon. I need a fair shot, and I won't blow it. Not ever again." She looked at him, eyes defensive and a little defiant, like she expected him to laugh at her.

"You mean it?" he asked.

"I've never meant anything more."

"So what is it you need?"

"A job reference, for starters," she said. "The coffee shop downstairs has a sign in the window that says they're looking for a part-time barista for the early morning shift. There's also a sign in the pub for a waitress."

No way in hell would he blindly trust her at one of his friends' places of business but he'd figure something out for her. *If* she really meant it. "And that's all you want from me, a job reference?"

She looked away. "And a co-signer on a lease for that apartment, when I find it."

"And . . . ?" he asked. "Lay it all out, Morgan."

She gave a brief smile. "Upfront and brutally honest as ever, I see."

"Always," he said.

She looked at him again, right in the eyes. "I don't want anyone from my past to be able to find me. I know you have ways to make people invisible."

"You want to be invisible?"

"I want to be safe," she said. "I want a fresh start. I want to be able to get those things for myself but apparently I'm unable to do that." She looked very unhappy. "I need help, Archer. I don't want to but I do."

He took a deep breath. "Everyone needs help sometimes. There's no shame in that."

Some hope came into her eyes. "Does that mean you'll do it? You'll help me?"

He'd never been able to turn away from a Wheaton, trouble or not, and he doubted he was going to start now. "I'm not going to keep this from Elle."

She arched a brow. "Interesting."

Yeah. Or terrifying.

Elle sat on the counter of Willa's shop, sipping her morning tea. The pet store was always fun and an adventure. Today there was a huge Siamese cat snoozing near the cash register, a cockatoo perched on a stack of bird feed, and Vinnie the teeny pup sprawled in the sole sunspot near the door, his manly bits on display to the world as he snored away.

Elle, Willa, Pru, and Kylie were eating muffins from Tina's coffee shop. Once upon a time Tina had been Tim. Tim had made good muffins but Tina was happier than Tim had ever been, and that happiness had spread to her muffins. People came from far and wide for her muffins, which as far as Elle was concerned were the best on the planet.

Elle chowed down on a mini blueberry muffin while listening to Pru and Willa argue over the last lemon muffin in the bag.

"I only had two," Pru said.

"I only had two too," Willa said.

"Me too on the two," Kylie said.

"But there were ten in the bag," Pru said and added that up on her fingers. "Where're the other three?"

They all turned and looked at Elle. She unapologetically popped in the last bite of her third muffin. "Hey, there is the quick and then there's the hungry," she said, getting down from the counter. "I've got to get back to work."

Willa held out a hand to stop her. "Not so fast, missy. You've been lying low all week. We haven't seen or heard a peep from you."

"It's been a busy one."

"Uh-huh," Willa said. "We'd sure love hear about your interesting date last weekend."

Elle didn't let her expression change because, much as she loved her friends, she didn't intend to discuss what had happened between her and Archer.

Not when she didn't have a handle on it herself.

Although you had quite a handle on him . . . And at that thought, images flooded her mind. Her on her knees. Archer wrapped around her like a glove, enclosing her in the heat and strength of his body. His hands holding her right where he wanted her, his fingers doing wicked things, his mouth at her ear urging her on.

Just thinking about it had her breath quickening. Other reactions happened too, nothing that should be happening in public under the razor-sharp scrutiny of her friends who could spot a lie or misdirect a mile away. But mostly she remembered the *stay the hell away from me* that she'd uttered. The last words she'd spoken to him. "You heard wrong," she said. "That wasn't a date between Archer and me, it was . . ."

Hell. A booty call. Exactly what she'd promised she wouldn't be to him. But whatever, mistakes had been made and orgasms had happened. It was all just a singular momentary setback from her Archer-embargo.

Pru went brows up. "Archer? I was talking about Caleb. But do tell about Archer."

Well crap. "He and I had a few things to discuss, is all. Business things. So we took it to my office. The end."

Willa grinned. "I once jumped Keane's bones in my office while all of you sat right here, and I too used the excuse of"—she used air quotes—"'things to discuss.'"

Pru went wide-eyed. "Wait," she said to Elle. "So you and Archer *discussed things?* Wow. We all knew it was only a matter of time before the tension between you two exploded but I thought we'd all hear the nuclear reaction, or at least smell the smoke."

"Ha-ha," Elle said, and then she blinked. "Wait. What do you mean you all knew it was only a matter of time?"

Everyone was suddenly very busy stirring her coffee or crumpling her napkin or anything other than answering that question.

"Hello?" Elle asked but then Spence walked in and distracted everyone. Elle hadn't had a chance to confront him about Archer getting him to hire her. She wasn't sure she was ready to have that conversation.

He had a large brown bag that smelled like more of Tina's muffins and the conversation was momentarily put on hold while they practically jumped him.

"Back off," he said, lifting the brown bag above all of their heads. "Mine."

"Gimme," Willa said.

He put a large hand on her head and held her off. "Get a hold of yourself, woman."

"But they smell good!"

"Then go get your own," he said.

"Did you know that Archer and Elle did the deed?" she asked, still eyeing his bag.

Archer was a stone when he wanted to be, giving little of himself away, but Spence . . . Spence was a mile-high, mile-long brick wall. A fortress. But at this question, he did a comical neck twist and stared at Elle.

Be calm, be calm . . . She sipped her tea to give herself a minute. But she clearly didn't pull off the calm because Spence tossed his head back and laughed.

Elle crossed her arms. "You're an ass."

"Yes." He was still grinning. "But come on, it's been a long time coming."

"That's what we said!" Pru exclaimed.

Spence was still smiling at Elle, fully enjoying her discomfort. "So what do we know?" he asked the girls. "Facts only."

They started talking at once and he held up a hand. They all promptly zipped it on command. Then he pointed at Willa.

"They were seen arguing," Willa said. "In the courtyard. And then they moved to the alley."

Elle stared at her. "How did you—"

Spence pointed at Pru, who continued where Willa left off by saying with glee, "They reportedly shoved each other up against the wall and went at each other."

"That's not fact," Spence chided. "That's speculation."

"Okay, true," Pru allowed. "But they definitely moved to the alley."

"Oh!" Willa said. "And they broke her love seat! Luis dragged it to the Dumpster this morning."

Elle felt her face flame.

"Hmm," Spence said, stroking his chin, smiling at her. As their resident genius, nothing much got by him.

Granted, he'd been adrift since selling his start-up last year, not yet having found his thing, but he was still present. As far as she knew, not one of them except herself—and undoubtedly Archer—knew Spence had bought this building. But sometimes he was too smart for his own good and she didn't want to deal with his opinion of her and Archer because it didn't matter. She and Archer weren't a thing. Yes, they'd had a thing, a very momentary thing, but that was over now. Completely. One hundred percent.

At least, she was pretty sure that's what she'd meant by *stay the hell away from me*. And anyway, he had. He'd vanished. And on that depressing thought, she headed to the door. "I'm out."

"See," Willa said excitedly. "It must be true, she's leaving."

"Leaving won't stop us from talking about you!" Pru called after her.

Elle responded with a single finger gesture that had them all cracking up again. She pushed open the door to the courtyard, and as was her habit, which she never admitted to, her gaze automatically slid up to the second-floor walkway to Hunt Investigations.

Someone was coming out of Archer's offices and she stilled because it wasn't Archer.

Nope, it was worse. It was her sister.

Chapter 13

#OneOfTheseThingsIsNotLikeTheOther

Frozen in place by shock, Elle watched Morgan vanish into the elevator. What the hell? She found herself moving across the courtyard and got to the elevator just as it opened.

Morgan stepped out and then did a double take at the sight of Elle standing there.

Elle gave a short laugh. "See, now I know why I'm surprised to see you. But I have no idea why you're surprised to see me since I work here."

Morgan recovered quickly. "Look at that, you *can* string together more words than *no* and *goodbye*. Good to know."

"Just tell me why you're here, Morgan."

Her sister settled her purse strap higher on her shoulder. "Because you're so sure that I'm up to something, right?"

There was actually more than a little hurt in Morgan's tone and it gave Elle pause. Morgan didn't do vulnerabilities. Morgan didn't do weaknesses.

Morgan didn't do family.

So why then was her sister suddenly breathing a little too fast? Why were her eyes so suspiciously shiny, like she was on the very edge of a breakdown? Elle took a deep breath for calm. "Just talk to me."

Morgan arched a brow. "You sure you don't just want to slam your door on my nose again first?"

"I'll decide after you tell me what you were doing in Archer's office."

At this, Morgan smiled. "Jealous?"

"Okay, forget it," Elle said and she spun on her heel to walk off.

"Dammit, Elle, wait. Look, I'm a bitch when I'm up against the wall, and . . . well, I'm sorry, okay?"

Elle turned back. "You're in trouble?"

Morgan blew out a breath. "Not like you're thinking."

Elle walked back to her. "Keep talking."

"I'm sober," Morgan said. "I'm going to school. I'm working on getting and keeping my shit together. I'm looking for a job and my own place, and I need references."

"Been there, done that," Elle said. "When we left Mom, remember? We lied about my age so I could sign the lease. Same with the credit cards we got to keep us going, the ones we put in my name to build and estab-lish credit since you'd already trashed yours. And then you bailed on me. I was sixteen and alone and you up and vanished, leaving me holding the bag for twelve thousand dollars of debt that you'd racked up. And then you showed up two years later and we did a wash and repeat. And okay, that time was on me. Fool me once and all that. I was stupid for trusting you again."

Morgan closed her eyes and when she opened them, there were tears of regret. "What do you want from me, Elle? I'd say I'm sorry for every shitty thing I've done but we'd be here all day, and in the end I'm not sure you'd believe me anyway." She paused and sighed. "But I am, you know. Sorry. I was *such* a shit and I hate that and I wish I could take it all back, I really do."

"Just tell me what you really want."

Morgan made a low sound of frustration. "Is it so hard to believe I might have really changed this time? Have you lived your own life so perfectly that you can really look down your nose on me? You don't have anything you're ashamed of?"

Of course she hadn't lived her life perfectly. She'd made more mistakes than she cared to admit. But as for being ashamed of anything . . . No. She couldn't say she was.

Except for maybe this—she wasn't willing to believe that Morgan had changed her stripes. She couldn't, because if she did, then she also had to admit she gave up on a sibling when she shouldn't have.

"Look," Morgan said quietly. "I can tell you one thing I *didn't* come here to do, and that's fight with you."

"Why were you at Archer's?"

"Because you shut me out and I need help."

Guilt niggled at her. But so did anger. "You shouldn't have gone to him. We've cost him enough."

"Maybe," Morgan said. "But go figure—the big, tough, hard badass has quite the heart beneath that broad, sexy chest of his."

When Morgan had walked out of the courtyard, through the wrought-iron gate, and vanished onto the street, Elle tried to talk herself off the ledge. She was going to go upstairs and bury herself in work until all murderous urges faded. She even passed the elevator, deciding that taking the stairs might expel some of her temper.

But nope. At the top of the stairs, she was breathing heavily and her toes hurt . . . but she was still mad as hell. Enough to forget her Archer embargo and head into his office instead of her own.

Mollie smiled at her from behind the reception counter. "Hey, you. Great dress and pretty little crop sweater to go with. But aren't you cold?"

Elle looked down at her sleeveless baby blue wrap dress and the lacy sweater that wasn't really a sweater so much as something that was too pretty to leave hanging in her closet. "Freezing, actually," she admitted, "but I bought some summer stuff on sale and this one didn't feel like waiting for a season change."

Mollie laughed. "What's a little discomfort to looking good, right?"

Exactly Elle's thinking.

"So what's up?" Morgan asked. "What can I do for you?"

"I just need a moment with your boss to strangle him—er, talk to him."

"Oh, do go for the first," Mollie said. "I could really use the rest of the day off."

Elle smiled grimly and headed back. Archer's office door was closed but she didn't let that stop her. He was in the middle of a meeting with Joe, Max, and Trev, the four of them bent over a set of plans. Carl was sprawled across the middle of the floor, taking up nearly all of it, snoring. The big Doberman lifted his head, eyeballed her, and leapt to his feet, eyes hopeful and on the look-out for a treat.

Elle patted him on the head. Archer had been listening to something Joe had been saying but his eyes cut to hers and held, making her heart kick hard as the previous Friday night came flooding back to her, the sexy erotic memories doing a number on her temper.

The message in Archer's eyes said he might be thinking about that night too, which didn't help.

"Clear the room," he said.

"Aw, man," Max said. "Just when it's going to get good."

Trev smacked him upside the back of his head.

Joe rolled up the plans on the desk, and as he turned to follow Trev out, he smiled at Elle. "Who ate your bowl of sunshine this morning, thundercloud?"

"Bite me, Joe."

He winked at her. "I would but boss man would object."

"Out," Archer repeated in a voice that had Joe hopping to attention.

Max snapped his fingers at Carl, who'd gone back to snoring on the floor. The dog stretched, farted, and then, his work clearly done, trotted happily to the door.

"Sorry," Max said, waving the air. "He ate Mollie's Egg McMuffin and it didn't agree with him."

"No shit." Joe coughed and choked. "Literally."

Elle wrinkled her nose. "Is he a dog or an elephant?"

Max just grinned and walked out.

This left Archer and Elle alone, which wasn't going to be good for his health, a fact he seemed blithely unconcerned with. In fact as she moved toward him, he came around his desk and then leaned back on it, legs casually crossed, body language deceptively relaxed and calm.

The leopard at rest.

He wore faded jeans that fit him in all the right places and a soft-looking black T-shirt that stretched across his chest like it was made for him. He stood close enough now that she felt that intangible thing happening again, the old and undeniable pull of his personal force field. It was a combination of the intensity of his personality, the power of his will, and the focus of his attention. And it all added up, binding her by her own attraction to him. She took a step back to try to break the spell before she threw her arms around his neck and it wouldn't be to strangle him.

"I'm putting a temporary hold on the 'stay away from me' thing," she said, "just for a minute while I yell at you, and then we're definitely going right back to it."

"I don't think so," he said, eyes glittering with an emotion she couldn't place. Determination maybe, which gave her pause because that made no sense.

"You saw Morgan?"

"Yes," he said without hesitation, which took some of the wind out of her sails.

"So you admit it."

"Have I ever lied to you?"

"You've omitted and avoided," she said. "Sure thing."

His expression said they disagreed there. "She came to me for help," he said. "And she went to you first, so you can't be surprised she's here."

"But I am surprised. I'm surprised that you would help the one person who destroyed both of our lives."

He stilled, eyes on her. Then he pushed away from his desk and shifted past her to shut and lock his door before turning to face her. "We need to talk."

She crossed her arms and hugged herself. A revealing stance, she knew, but she couldn't help herself. "I told you, there's nothing to talk about."

"I think there is."

"The thing that happened between us *didn't* happen," she said.

"I beg to differ but we'll circle back to that," he said. "Morgan didn't destroy my life, Elle."

"Fine. Then I did."

"No," he said.

"You were a rookie cop, fast-tracked by your captain dad on an undercover sting that should've defined your career and set it into motion. I was a stupid teenager on my own fast track—to nowhere. I not only jeopardized the whole operation, I got you fired."

He stared at her for a very long beat. "I didn't get fired," he finally said. "I quit."

This was so off the rails from what she'd expected from him that she could only gape. *"What?"*

"You're right, I was a rookie," he said. "That night was my first experience on a joint task force. I shouldn't have even been there in the first place but my dad pulled some strings and cut through all the red tape. He was . . . intent on my career."

This, she knew. His dad was a lifelong cop. He'd lived and breathed the life, and he'd wanted the same for his son.

"Everything was carefully choreographed that night," he said, "with no room for error, no room for the unknown. I had explicit directions, I was to observe and stay the fuck out of the way even though everyone was so certain, from the top to the bottom, that it would go smooth, textbook."

"Except I showed up," Elle said quietly, remembering the terror of it all, knowing she'd been in *so* over her head.

"Yeah, there you were, right in the middle of it, young, scared . . . out of your league. I knew you'd get pulled in along with everyone else on that takedown. What I didn't know was if anyone would care that you were innocent or if they'd consider you collateral damage." He looked right at her, into her, and she knew he was seeing her as she'd been that night—in a ragged tank top and shorts, hands and knees bleeding from a fall she'd taken, a bruise blooming on her face where Lars had hit her.

She still hated that Archer had seen her like that, hated it to her very core. She'd worked so hard to become the person she was right now, the person who had her shit together, who would *always* have her shit together.

But the depressing thing was, no matter how far she ran from her past, no matter how much she changed, grew up, matured . . . Archer would always think of her as *that* girl, a secret humiliation she could hardly bear. "Go back to the part where you weren't fired."

"I disobeyed orders," he said. "I broke protocol and rules. I didn't respect my dad's authority."

"Right," she said. "Because of me."

"No," he said firmly. "I'd have done it for anyone I thought innocent in that situation. And I *should've* been fired. Everyone knew it, but everyone also knew my dad wouldn't do it. Instead, he suspended me."

"You were only suspended?"

"Yes. But I couldn't go back to the job."

She stared at him. "So you quit?"

"*Yes* and you need to know that it was the best thing

I ever did. So if you're harboring some secret guilt, let it go. It's unfounded."

If Elle knew one thing about Archer, it was that he did what he thought was right, not what was easy. He'd saved her life and maybe he hadn't been fired because of it, but regardless of what he said, she was still responsible for the change in course his life had taken.

She'd cost him so much.

She couldn't bear to cost him another thing and yet Morgan was back. Which meant it was only a matter of time now before they ruined his life again. "You can't trust her, Archer," she said. "I don't understand why you would."

"I don't trust her," he said. "But that doesn't mean I don't want to know what she's up to."

"Fine. It's your life, but—"

"But you're still going to tell me what to do?" he asked, a small smile on his lips.

She went into defense mode at his amused tone. "Well, I'm sure as hell not going to be quiet about it."

"Duly noted," he said dryly. "And for the record? I *never* want you to be quiet, Elle."

She felt her face get warm. They both knew he'd inspired all sorts of noises from her that night, both while clothed *and* unclothed. "I told you, we're not discussing that. Because it didn't happen."

"You know what I think?"

"That I'm right?" she asked with false sweetness.

He snorted. "Elle, you're always right. It's your world and we all just live in it."

At that, it was her turn to snort.

His tone was amused. "I think you get off on yelling at me."

True story. And although she'd come in here to do just that, they were now somehow smiling at each other, cynically or not, and they were also standing close.

Very close.

She stared at his mouth, remembering how it had brushed against the sensitive skin beneath her ear, whispering dirty promises as he'd driven her to heaven and back.

Twice. Okay, three times, but who was counting?

That mouth smiled. "You want to yell at me some more, don't you?" he murmured.

Yes. But that wasn't what troubled her. It was the other urge she had—to take off her clothes and climb him like a tree. "I don't always give in to what I want," she said stiffly. "For instance, I wouldn't mind wrapping my fingers around your neck right now and yet I'm not. Admire my restraint, won't you?"

His smile widened, the sexy ass, and then he shifted so they were actually touching, chest to chest, toes to toes. "Go for it," he murmured.

Chapter 14

#CantHaveJustOne

Archer watched, fascinated and mesmerized as always by the energy that shimmered off Elle in waves. Her cheeks were flushed and her eyes flashing as she slapped a hand to his chest and opened her mouth, undoubtedly to let him have it, and he couldn't help himself.

He kissed her.

Maybe it'd been to keep her from letting him have it, but mostly it was to get his tongue in her mouth again because he needed the taste of her more than he needed anything on the planet.

Elle held herself still for all of a single heartbeat and then in typical fashion she dove right in, flinging her arms around him with that soft, sexy little moan that came from deep in her throat.

She undid him, every time. Desperate for her, he held on tight. Her breath fanned his face, her lips just grazing his as she pulled back to look at him, her mouth wet.

He stared right back, unable to move, hell, unable to so much as fucking breathe until he had her again. To that end, he slid his hands over her body, knowing now how to make her gasp and writhe against him with that sexy little needy whimper. He had his hands gliding up the back of her thighs when she stopped him with one word.

"Wait," she gasped.

He froze. "Wait? Or no?"

She hesitated at that and then dropped her forehead to his shoulder. "Okay, here's the thing."

Oh good. There was a thing . . .

"I'm still really mad at you."

"Understood," he said, wanting to be agreeable.

"I mean really, *really* mad," she said. "But now it's all sort of mixed up with something else."

"And that is . . . ?"

"I want you," she said, stirring him up with nothing more than the words. "But," she said when he started to talk. "I want you on my terms."

"I'm listening." In truth, he didn't care what the terms were, he'd give her whatever she wanted.

"We do this," she said, "but only with the understanding that it's within our temporary hold."

"The temporary hold of me, and let me quote you here, 'staying the hell away from you'?"

"Yes," she said. "You good with that?"

No. Hell, no. But he'd worry about it on the other side. He wrapped his hand in her hair and gave a gentle tug so that she was looking at him.

"Archer? You hear me, right? This is happening in another time continuum only?"

"I hear you." He just happened to disagree. Lowering his head, he leaned in to kiss her but once again she stopped him.

"Another rule?" he asked.

"The light's on," she said.

"Yes."

"But it's already full daylight and these are fluorescent lights. No one looks good under fluorescent lights, Archer."

"You do. You look good under anything." He flashed a grin. "You're going to look amazing under me." He leaned in to get started on showing her but she put a hand to his chest.

"I'm serious."

"I know," he murmured soothingly while dragging his mouth along the slope of her collarbone, thinking the sooner he got her naked, the sooner she could start to fall for him the way he was falling for her . . .

"Look, I know I carefully cultivate this whole ice queen thing"—she broke off with a moan when he nibbled at her throat—"and that you might think I'm perfect and all, but—"

He snorted against her skin and she smacked him in the chest. He caught her hand and she played tug-of-war with him, giving up when he placed her hand flat on his chest.

"Elle," he said. "You always look perfect to me."

"But this is what I'm trying to tell you! It's all an illusion. It's the magic of good clothing." She peered into his face, sweetly earnest. "Do you understand what I'm trying to tell you?"

"No."

She sighed. "I just don't want you to . . ."

Cupping her face, he lifted it to his. "What?"

"Be reminded of that girl I used to be," she whispered.

He frowned at that, completely lost. He'd thought they were playing but clearly they were not. "What are you talking about?"

"The girl who came from nowhere and had nothing and didn't have any direction or even know who she was," she said. "That girl! I don't want you to see her when you look at me."

He stilled in shock. "Elle, *that* girl was braver than anyone else I'd ever met. She was willing to do anything to protect her sister, to save her sister, in spite of having zero odds in her favor."

Her breath caught as if she desperately wanted to believe him but was afraid to. "I'm not her anymore," she said quietly.

"Yes, you are. Beneath the veneer, beneath the makeup and pretty clothes and badass sexy shoes, you're exactly who you've always been. You just need someone to remind you." He tugged her cute little sweater off her shoulders and tossed it to his desk. "Show me," he said softly.

"Show you *what?*"

"Show me who you are beneath it all."

She laughed a little breathlessly. "What, I'm just supposed to put on a striptease for you?"

"Reveal," he corrected. "Reveal the real you."

She crossed her arms. "Why would I do that?"

"Because I'm going to do the same." He checked the lock on his door and hit the intercom button on the phone on his desk.

"Yes?" Mollie asked sweetly, knowing damn well that she'd sent Elle back here without warning him.

"I'm unavailable until further notice," he said.

"What if any of the guys need you?"

"If they like their jobs, they won't."

"But you have a meeting in fifteen minutes—"

"Unavailable, Mollie."

Elle stared at him as he disconnected, her arms falling back to her side.

Archer did his best to look like something she couldn't live without. He must have succeeded because she said, "You seem like a man with plans."

"I have you all to myself." Finally. "I do have plans. Big plans." Plans to make you want to keep me . . .

"You're . . . flirting with me," she said, sounding surprised.

"I've been in denial about that but yes. I'm flirting with you."

She continued to stare at him for a minute and then seemed to come to a decision. She stepped back and untied her wrap dress at her waist.

It fell open.

So did his mouth because she was gorgeous in nude-colored, sheer lace and a pair of black fuck-me pumps.

Going up on tiptoe, she kissed him, soft. Slow.

He wanted to crush his mouth to hers and kiss and nibble and suck on every inch of her body, but she was still giving him those teasing little tastes, her breath warm against his face every time she sighed in pleasure. She rocked her hips against his and when she found him hard—which he'd been since she strode into his office to call him out—she hummed in approval.

A groan shuddered through him as she went on like that, torturing the both of them, her breathing becoming more and more labored. His would have done the same, but he wasn't breathing at all, not even a little bit.

Her hands slid up his back, bringing his shirt with them. "Off," she said.

Whatever the lady wanted. He yanked it off and had barely tossed it aside when she bent forward to kiss his knife scar, making his heart melt. Then she curled one of her hands around the back of his neck, wrapping the strands of his hair around her fingers as she slowly deepened the kiss, giving him her mouth, giving him everything.

He wrapped his arms around her, keeping his hands pressed against her back, doing his best to let her dictate the pace. Not easy with her tongue in his mouth and her body rocking against his. When they finally broke apart for air, she gestured for him to lose more clothing.

While she waited, he kicked off his shoes and socks and straightened, meeting her gaze. "Your turn."

She took in his chest and abs, and he was pretty sure her pulse took a good, hard leap as she bent to take off her heels.

"Leave the shoes."

She straightened with an arched brow. "Really?"

"Oh yeah."

"You have some catching up to do," she noted.

Obliging, he unsnapped, unzipped, and stripped out of his pants, leaving him in black knit boxers that did little to hide how hot he found her.

She was staring at that very evidence when she licked her lower lip, prompting him to groan and move toward her, stroking his hands up her torso. When he assisted her bra to the floor, she sucked in a breath.

"Gorgeous," he whispered, his mouth at her jaw, his hands gliding over her trembling body. "So gorgeous you take my breath away."

"Finish," she said, a quiet demand that had him smiling because even when she was down, she was never out. She wanted him naked first and he didn't have a single problem with that. He shucked the black cotton.

This time her inhale was audible, a low feminine murmur of appreciation.

"Now *you're* overdressed," he said, his mouth at her ear and he hooked his fingers into the scrap of lace masquerading as panties at her hips and slowly drew them down, crouching before her to ease them all the way down her legs. Leaning in, he brushed a kiss across one of her thighs, and then the other. And then a hip. Her belly button.

And then just south of it.

"Archer," she gasped, her hands going to his hair.

"Right here," he said, and he kissed her again, this time letting his tongue snake out and stroke. He worked her over, following the clues of her body as her fingers tightened in his hair and writhed against him.

He made her come that way, loving the breathy way she moaned his name. And when her knees gave out he caught her, lifting her to his desk. Sliding his palms up the insides of her thighs, he pushed them open and stepped into the vee of her legs. "One of these days we'll actually make it to a bed."

"That will be hard to do since after this we're going back to staying the hell away from each other." She sank her teeth into his bottom lip and then slowly let it slide free and kissed him softly, which he felt all the way down to his toes and back.

"Condom?" she whispered.

He froze, eyes locked on hers, wondering how she felt about seeing a grown man cry. "I don't—Christ." Had he seriously forgotten about a condom for the first time in his entire life? "We used my emergency stash from my wallet the other night."

"I see." She hesitated, eyes on his. "Before that, I hadn't been with anyone in over two years. I'm on the pill."

His heart was in his throat. "Two years?" He cupped her face. "Why?"

Her eyes shuttered. "You want to talk about that or do this?"

Good point. "I've not done this without a condom . . . ever," he said.

She rocked against him again, taking him into her hands, giving a playful tug to bring him right where she wanted. Leaning into her, his hands on the desk on either side of her hips, his breath decidedly uneven, he teased them both until she moaned and wrapped her legs around him.

"So what's the holdup?" she asked, impatient to the end.

Gripping her sweet ass in his palms, he jerked her forward and slid into her.

Their twin gasps comingled in the air and he was pretty sure he blacked out for a minute. "Oh fuck, Elle," he whispered, only vaguely aware of her nails digging into his shoulders where she was holding on for all she was worth, her head back, her hair brushing his forearms, her throat bared for his mouth. Her lips were parted, her breath came in little whimpery gasps and he felt her clenching tighter and tighter around him.

God. He already couldn't remember what it'd been like before her. He'd thought everything was great in his life but then he'd been thrown a curveball in the

form of this gorgeous, passionate woman who he suddenly couldn't get enough of.

Which made it official. He was hers, completely.
"You're beautiful, Elle," he said, pressing tight against
her. "The most beautiful thing I've ever seen."

She shuddered, whimpering against his mouth as
she came, and while she was still clenching and puls-
ing around him, he lost himself in her. When he was
with her like this, he found himself. It was as simple
and terrifying as that.

Chapter 15

#DidIShaveMyLegsForThis?

After, when they were still entwined, hearts pounding against each other as they attempted to recuperate, Elle tried to memorize everything about the moment. The way his arms wrapped around her tight, protective, one hand cupping the back of her head, the other settled possessively on her ass.

It'd been such a bad idea, she knew this, but somehow she always lost focus of that when he touched her the way he did. Things were unbearably complicated between them. Always had been. But not this. This was easy.

And she didn't know what to do with that.

Hopping off the desk, she gathered up her clothes and escaped into the bathroom connected to his office and stared at herself in the mirror.

She had Hair Gone Wild and her mascara was

smudged. Her lips were bare but curved, like she was a woman who'd been well and truly taken care of. Business handled.

That it was true didn't help. And how was it that he seemed to know her body better than she knew her own? She didn't know whether to be horrified or amazed.

A little bit of both, she decided as she pulled on her clothes. She smoothed down her dress and stared at herself some more. Wow. Sex was good for her skin— she was glowing.

But it didn't change the fact that she'd decided to take control of her life. She'd also decided against Archer and yet she'd fallen right back into his bed. *What was wrong with her?*

One glance in the mirror at the after-sex glow told her what was wrong with her. She was in denial.

Dammit. She hated when that happened.

It didn't matter. She'd been in worse spots before, far worse, and she'd managed to pick herself up. This time would be no different. Yes, maybe a mistake had been made, a big one, but she'd learn from it if it killed her.

The way she saw it, she had only one choice here, if she wanted to save any face at all. She would gather her dignity the best she could, give him a kickass smile and walk right out the door, playing it as cool as he always did.

Her heart started pounding again at the thought,

but she fixed her hair and slid a finger beneath each eye, sweeping away the smudged mascara. Without her purse, she couldn't do anything about the bare lips and suddenly she felt more naked than she had without a single stitch of anything on her except Archer's body.

Since that thought made her inner thighs quiver in memory, she turned away from the mirror, took a deep breath, and walked out of the bathroom and back into Archer's office, heading straight for the door.

Archer was dressed and back to his inscrutable self. "Hey," he said with a smile. He had his cell phone out. "I'm going to order us some food. What do you feel like?"

A mess. She felt like a mess. "Can't," she said.

His smile faded. "Don't run off, Elle. Give this a shot. Give us a shot."

Her heart just about stopped. "Us?" she asked in shock. "There is no us. There's a you. And there's a me. And okay, so sometimes we get crazy and become a very momentary us but it's not real."

"It could be," he said.

She gaped at him, completely gobsmacked. "You pushed me away for a year."

"I was wrong."

She shook her head, unable to process this. "So now what, we live happily ever after?"

"Depends on you. What do you want?"

What did she want? Had he lost his marbles? "Okay,"

she said slowly. "I thought you were kidding but now you're scaring me because I don't think you are."

"I'm not."

Who was he and what had he done with Archer? "Is this so we can keep having time-outs that involve naked time?"

"God, I hope so." He barely caught her when she whirled for the door. "Elle, wait. I'm serious."

She searched his gaze. "You expect me to believe your feelings changed just like that?"

"Well not just like that." He flashed a smile. "You wore me down over time."

"This isn't funny, Archer."

"You're right, it's not. You need time and we have that. Take all you need. You free tonight?"

"Yes."

"I'll pick you up," he said. "We'll try the date thing."

Her phone rang and she looked down at it. It was maintenance, reminding her she had a meeting with them. "I have to take this."

"It's okay." Archer leaned in and kissed her gently. "After work, Elle," he murmured, and then he walked out of his office, giving her some space.

Elle locked herself in her office, brain going a hundred miles an hour. She paced the small space, unable to decide on a feeling. Shock and panic worked, she decided. She purposely changed gears to problem number two by pulling out her phone and sending a text to Morgan.

Meet me at O'Riley's in fifteen minutes.

Forget Archer and the fact that he knew her better than anyone else. Forget the amazing orgasms or how he always had her back. She needed to forget all of it for a few minutes and give herself some breathing room.

Instead she'd concentrate on her sister. If anyone was going to help Morgan, dammit, it'd be her. She headed downstairs.

"Hungry?" Finn asked when he saw her.

"Starving."

"What do you want?"

"Everything you've got," she said as she slid onto a stool next to an already seated Morgan.

"Worked up an appetite today, huh?" Finn asked.

If he only knew . . .

Morgan laughed. "Used to be, she was always hungry. It was like she was hollow."

True story. Living as they had, three squares hadn't always been part of the program. There'd been long stretches of time when they'd lived off apples, peanut butter, and Top Ramen.

And just like that, she suddenly wasn't hungry anymore. "Maybe just some tea to start." She turned to Morgan. "Okay, let's have it. What is it you really want?"

"I already told you. I wanted to see you."

"And?"

"And . . . I was hoping you'd give me references, and maybe help me get on my own feet with a place,"

Morgan admitted quietly. "But when you weren't interested, Archer became my Plan B."

"Archer isn't your Plan B," Elle said. "You need to leave him out of this."

Morgan reached for the drink in front of her and took a leisurely sip. "You know, it's amazing how potatoes give us chips, fries, *and* vodka. It's like get your shit together, every other vegetable, you know?"

Elle narrowed her eyes, wrapped her hand around Morgan's wrist, and brought the glass under her nose for a sniff.

"It's 7UP on the rocks," Morgan said.

Feeling like a jerk, Elle let go and nodded. "I'm sorry. That was rude."

"No, that was on point." Morgan met Elle's gaze. "You've got every reason to err on the side of caution with me. I get it, Elle. I really do. But people change. Look at you, for instance—family used to mean everything to you. There was a time you'd have done whatever you could to keep us together."

"We weren't ever a real family."

"Yeah," Morgan said as she stood up. "I know. I'm just saying, people change, including you. In fact, you've changed a whole hell of a lot." She tossed some money onto the bar and walked out.

"Morgan," Elle said. "Wait."

But she didn't. Watching her go, Elle drew a deep breath and before she could let it out, Spence slid onto the stool Morgan had just vacated.

"Am I crazy, or did I just see you and your doppelganger sitting together?"

"That was my sister."

Spence lifted a brow. "The elusive Morgan Wheaton?"

"The one and only. Long story."

"I love long stories," he said.

So Elle told him what Morgan wanted, leaving out most of their wretched past. She loved Spence, she loved *all* her friends as if they were family, but no one knew the whole story.

Well, except Archer.

Spence was quiet a moment. "You don't think she's good for it this time? You think nothing's changed?"

Elle hesitated and then shook her head. "I don't know."

Spence nodded slowly. "And I'm guessing you've been burned by her in the past."

Elle lifted a shoulder.

"Yeah, you have, and I'm guessing you're worried you're wrong about her this time."

"Yes," she said softly.

Spence slung an arm around her and kissed her on the top of her head. "What does your gut say?"

"That I'm a bitch." Elle resisted the urge to burrow in and pretend her life wasn't in complete uproar. She wanted her calm quiet back. But she managed a smile. "I like to stick with what I'm good at."

Spence smiled back but his eyes said he was onto

her. "I don't know, Elle. If you were such a bitch, you wouldn't be giving this the time of day; instead you're sitting here hoping she proves herself."

"Is that what you think I'm doing?"

"Isn't it?"

Yeah, she supposed that's exactly what she was doing. She wasn't big on trust and Morgan would be the first to tell her that was wise. Hell, it'd taken her an entire year to trust Archer.

And look how that had turned out . . .

"I know you hired me because Archer asked you to," she said, and then she grimaced. She'd meant to finesse that statement but it was too late now.

Spence looked confused. "What are you talking about? Archer didn't ask me to hire you."

"Then how did you end up with me in the pool for the position?"

"I started out with a headhunter," he said. "Your resume came to me in a stack of a hundred others. Getting them down to the top ten nearly killed me. Archer helped." He paused and gave her a quiet look of speculation. "And yeah, he recommended you personally but I made the final decision on my own. The truth is, once I met you, I knew you were the only one for the job."

Okay, that didn't seem nearly as intrusive as she'd imagined.

Finn brought them a tray of sliders and fries. They dug in for a few long minutes before Spence got a text. He snorted, responded, and put his phone away.

"What?" she asked.

He slid her a look and said nothing.

Annoying alphas. *"What?"*

"Caleb wants to know if he should bother trying again."

"And you said?" she inquired, brow raised, not sure she knew what she wanted the answer to be.

"I said that we're not in high school and he could figure it out for himself. Although I should've told him not to bother because you're all sorts of screwed up."

"Gee, thanks."

"You are."

"Don't start," she said.

"Then you don't start," he said seriously, putting down a French fry—which meant he was very serious indeed. He blew out a sigh, muttered something about hating being forced to discuss feelings, and then looked at her. "Okay, so you're you, which means you're going to bury your heart deep and you're going to continue to wear that ice shield you're so fond of. Poor Archer probably doesn't know what hit him."

"Poor Archer?" she asked in disbelief. *"Poor Archer* is a big boy." A *very* big boy . . . "He plays by his own rules and anyway neither of us even has a copy of the rules. So trust me, Spence, he's not the one who's going to get hurt here. He probably has them lined up."

"Are you talking about other women?"

"No, I'm talking about kittens and rainbows!" she said, exasperated. "Yes, I'm talking about women!"

Spence blinked at her unusual vehemence. "Elle there's been no other women for him, not in a long time. A year, in fact."

She narrowed her gaze. "Did he tell you to tell me that?"

Spence laughed. "Yes, right after we talked about what to wear to the prom. Jesus. No, we don't talk about this shit, thankfully."

Elle sighed. "He said he wants to have something with me."

"Something . . . like dinner?"

She had to laugh. "I think he meant more than dinner. I think he meant a relationship. Not that it matters."

"Let me guess," Spence said. "Because you don't trust him."

"He didn't want me until I started going out with other men."

It was Spence's turn to laugh. "If you believe that then I've got some swampland to sell you. The truth is, you don't trust him. Hell, you don't trust *anyone* with your heart. And shit . . ." He pushed away the food in disgust. "Not only did you just trick me into a relationship conversation, but you just made me say *heart*. I hate you right now, but I've got one more thing to say and then I'm cutting out my tongue. I think you're just looking for reasons to hold back. There." He tossed up his hands and stood up. "I've done my Dr. Phil for the day. Hopefully for the year." He pointed at her. "And if you tell anyone we had this conversation, I'll deny it."

When he was gone, she sat there thinking too hard. *You're just looking for reasons to hold back.*

Was that true? No. No, it couldn't be. This was all about Archer and how screwed up *he* was. Not her. And that's what she continued to tell herself the rest of that night as Archer didn't come to take her out as promised. And she'd continue to tell herself as long as she needed to hear it.

Chapter 16

#YouWantFriesWithThat?

Later that night Archer paced the ER waiting room restlessly until Mollie took his hand.

"Archer, sit," she said softly. "Please."

So he sat. For her. Joe had been jumped on what should've been a routine surveillance job. He'd been hit over the head with a baseball bat and hadn't regained consciousness at the scene. Archer, the guys, and a teary Mollie had been huddled in the waiting room for well over an hour when Elle came in and sat at Archer's side.

"Any word?" she asked quietly.

He no longer questioned how she seemed to know everything. Maybe Mollie had texted her. Or Spence, who'd called him a few minutes ago. Archer hadn't been able to do anything but concentrate on Joe. He remained still, leaning back, eyes on the ceiling, exhausted to the bone, very aware of her gaze on him. "No word."

Her hand settled on his arm, stroked up and down a few times and then her fingers entwined with his and she gently squeezed.

No empty platitudes, no promises of "it'll be okay" or "don't worry" because she knew more than anyone else just how not okay the world could be.

She just held on.

He appreciated that more than anything she could have done. He closed his eyes and after a few minutes she set her head on his shoulder. Her breast pressed against his arm and a fast tactile memory rose in his body—the feel of her smooth skin, her nipple pushing against the palm of his hand.

A strand of her silky blonde hair stuck to the stubble on his jaw. The scent, some complicated mix of feminine magic, made him want to inhale her. Maybe it was his sheer exhaustion that did him in but he turned his face and buried it in her hair. "I'm sorry about tonight."

"Don't be."

He knew she said that so easily because she honestly didn't believe in them. He'd do better, but for now he'd believe in them enough for the both of them. And so they sat there like that, quiet, taking comfort in the moment—or at least he did—when the doctor appeared.

Everyone stood. Elle did too but she hung back a little bit as Archer and Mollie spoke with him.

The news was grim but not nearly as bad as it could've

been. Concussion, brain swelling, but it was coming down on its own and he'd regained consciousness several times but was sleeping now. Mollie sagged in relief against him and Archer hugged her tight.

"I'm going to go see him," Mollie said, and she followed the nurse back.

The tension in the waiting room drained considerably. Archer took in some deep breaths himself and watched Elle vanish into the little gift shop. Five minutes later she was back with a big bag of jelly beans.

"His favorite," she said and Archer didn't bother to ask how she knew that either.

She was magic.

They kept Joe company while he dozed. Archer sat on a chair at one side of Joe's bed, Elle on the other side reading a *Cosmo* magazine whose cover claimed "Guys Think about Sex Every Five Seconds."

"Is that true?" he asked.

"I don't know," she said flipping pages without looking up. "You tell me."

He thought about it. "I mean I think about it a lot, but I also think of other things."

This had her lowering the magazine to eyeball him. "Like . . . ?"

"You," he answered truthfully.

She cocked her head. "In what way?"

"Naked."

This had her arching a brow. "Always?"

"Depends," he said.

"On . . . ?"

"On if I'm hungry or not."

She snorted and went back to her magazine. But she was smiling now and he felt like he'd won the lotto.

Archer stayed all night with Joe and Mollie, and so did Elle. He figured that had to mean something. At dawn, Joe woke up and said he wasn't going to die and that they all needed to get some rest because they looked like zombies.

Archer gave Elle a ride home.

"You're not coming in," she said when he parked in front of her place. "Don't follow me up." She started to get out, sighed, and then turned back. "But thanks for the ride home."

He smiled because it was hard to be polite and murderous at the same time but she managed it like no one else, looking sexy and adorable at the same time. "I'm going to follow you up, Elle."

"No, you're not. I've been preoccupied, but I had time to think all night and I realized something. In order to get me this job when I needed it, you must have been keeping track of me for longer than this past year. You've been keeping track of me for eleven years and I had no idea. And now I want to be alone with that and stew in my mad." She pointed at him. "And you're going to let me."

Yeah, he was. He had to. She deserved the time. "Get some sleep," he said quietly.

"I only have time to shower, I've got homework."

She'd be exhausted by the end of the day. "At least let me in and I'll make you breakfast while you shower."

She held his gaze. "No cracks about wanting to help me soap up?"

"Well, I don't like to brag," he said, letting a teasing tone come into his voice, hoping to lighten the mood, "but I'm really good in the shower."

She snorted.

"Admit it," he said with a smile. "You're a little tempted."

"Maybe," she said, her gaze dropping to his mouth. "And maybe more than a little. But I'm also angry and confused. I need to get unangry and unconfused, Archer."

"I could help you with that too."

"I'll let you know," she said.

That had been two days ago.

Joe was out of the hospital and laid up at home, pissed off because Archer wouldn't let him work until the doctor cleared him for light duty. This meant Mollie was also off because she was taking care of Joe, leaving him without a receptionist, forcing them all to pick up the slack—which, for the record, they hated.

Archer had had no idea just how much Mollie did until she wasn't around. All of them universally hated answering the phones, so they were taking turns and fighting about it.

Yesterday Morgan had showed up out of the blue and offered to answer phones. He'd been desperate enough to let her, but there was a steep learning curve and he wasn't sure he'd ever heard a bunch of big-ass grown men whine or bitch so much.

Morgan appeared in his office doorway. "The latest searches are in your email," she said.

In his line of work there was a lot of computer foot-work, something else they all hated. It was quiet, boring work that none of them wanted to do, and he figured it was safe enough to put her on it. Also it would keep her occupied and out of trouble while he figured out if *she* was still trouble herself.

His own investigation on her had assured him that she'd been in things deep as late as six months ago but that she'd kept herself clean ever since. Still, the dif-ference in her claimed timeline and the truth troubled him. "Thanks," he said.

She nodded and shifted her weight around, giving herself away. Elle would never have done that but Morgan was far more transparent.

"What's up?" he asked.

"I know it's only been two days and I haven't done all that much yet," she said. "But I wanted to thank you for the opportunity to prove myself to you."

"You don't have to prove yourself to me."

"To my sister then."

He leaned back and met her gaze. "I'm not sure that your working here is going to do that."

"I'm hoping that seeing me work a real job is going to help change her mind about me."

"I don't have that much power," he said. *God* didn't have that much power.

"You underestimate yourself. You could talk her into being my sister again if you put your mind to it."

He let out a low laugh because he doubted his ability to talk Elle into *anything*.

"I know I've asked a lot of you but will you at least think about it?" she asked. "About helping me get back on Elle's good side?"

He looked into her baby blue eyes that were so like Elle's and sighed because he knew he'd try. Not for Morgan.

But for Elle.

Because she deserved that. She deserved family. Hell, she deserved the damn moon. He didn't know if it was because he was so fucking proud of who she was and what she'd made of herself, or if it was because he'd had a taste of her now and was afraid he might never get a chance at another, but he wanted, needed, to make things good for her.

The next night Archer managed to catch Elle as she was coming out of her office.

"Still stalking me?" she asked politely.

"Maybe I just missed you," he said as they stepped into the elevator together.

"That would require emotion, Archer."

"You think I don't have emotions?"

She sighed. "I know you do. I just think you don't like them."

"Are we talking about me or you?" he asked.

She rolled her eyes as they crossed the courtyard and headed to the street, where she began to walk at a pace that amazed him given the height of her heels.

"You're walking all the way home?" he asked.

"The girls and I ate pizza and brownies for lunch. I've got about two thousand calories to work off."

He kept pace and she glanced up at him. "You my bodyguard?"

"You're the one with a knife."

She snorted. "You probably had more adventures today than I'll have in a lifetime. Walking must seem tame to you."

"Elle, you're more of an adventure than anything that's ever happened to me."

She ignored this and made a few stops, one for some flowers, another for a loaf of fresh bread from a bakery, and then again for a bottle of wine, making him wonder if she was prepping for a date. He hoped not because he'd have to kill the guy.

"Having fun?" she asked dryly.

"Yes."

She laughed. "Liar. You're not into fun."

"I have my moments."

She blushed, which he found both charming and adorable, although she recovered quickly.

"Hmm," she said. "Because after breaking up two dates in a row, I'd have said you were actually a fun-sucker."

"Elle, I didn't want to mess up your fun either time. You think I don't know how long it's been since you let yourself have a life?"

She flushed and looked away.

He turned her face back to his. "But seeing you go out with other guys when we're . . ."

She arched a brow. "Do tell."

Shit. He'd walked right into that land mine. "I'm not going to apologize for a single thing I've done," he said.

She wasn't impressed. *"Shock."*

"I'm not going apologize for the things I've done," he repeated, "because I'd do all of it again if I had to in order to keep you safe."

"You're not paying attention, Archer. I'm not in danger these days. I don't need you to keep me safe. I can take care of myself."

"I know. And I get it," he said. "You're smart and strong. You've got it all handled. And okay, maybe I should've told you about the job—"

"You think?"

"Look, I have faults, okay? A helluva lot of them actually, but . . ."

"Don't let me stop you," she said. "But *what?*"

But . . . she was the most important person in his life. Without his family, she was basically his best friend, even when they went long stretches without communicating. But he'd never told her that because doing so would've made him feel . . . vulnerable.

And he didn't do vulnerable.

Elle strode past him, nose in the air.

He followed her up the stairs. At her front door she turned and faced him. "I don't need a boogeyman check."

"Humor me," he said.

"Actually, I think I've humored you long enough." She turned to unlock her door and stilled.

He looked around her to see what had stopped her and saw that her door was ajar.

Someone had broken in.

Chapter 17

#ShadyBusiness

Elle stood there in front of her opened door, barely registering, when Archer put a hand on her hip, firm and protective, pushing her behind him so that she couldn't see past his broad shoulders. But she had no problem seeing the gun he'd pulled out of nowhere.

He nudged her to the side of the opened door, her back to the wall. "Stay here," he said and then he vanished inside.

She stood there, torn between following him or doing as he'd asked, but in the end she decided that following him would make her the dumb chick in every horror movie ever filmed.

Someone had broken into her place.

It'd been a damn long time since fear had ruled her body, but it took over now like an old friend, as if no time had gone by, making her feel as if she was a kid in perpetual panic all over again.

Archer reappeared as silently and efficiently as he'd vanished, tucking his gun away behind him. "I don't see anything out of place but I need you to come look to make sure."

She nodded numbly and he took a second look at her, frowning as he slid his hand in hers. "Hey," he said, pulling her into him. "You're shaking."

"No I'm not."

"Okay," he said gently, squeezing her. "Maybe it's me."

She let out a small mirthless laugh and followed him inside, still holding tightly to him. Her laptop was still on the table. Her TV hadn't been disturbed. Nor anything else that she could tell. "I didn't leave my front door unlocked," she said.

"I know."

"You do?"

He squeezed her waist, making her realize he was still holding her to his side. "You'd never have left it unlocked," he said. "You're too smart that. Not to mention anal."

She choked out a laugh at the compliment and insult sandwiched together and knew by the way he smiled that he'd meant to get that reaction from her. "Should I call the police?" she asked.

"Already did."

An hour later the police had come and gone. Archer walked around checking the windows and then he grabbed her purse. "Okay, let's go."

"Go where?" Elle asked.

"To bed. You're done in."

"I don't need my purse to walk down the hall and get into bed," she said.

"That's not the bed you're going to."

It took her a minute to respond, as her body and brain had two very different reactions to the thought of sleeping with him again. Her body wanted to jump up and down and pump a fist in anticipation. Her brain wanted to scream that she was in far more danger from Archer than anyone or anything else.

At least her heart was anyway . . . . "This is a really bad idea," she said.

"Why?"

"Because you'll flash me your panty-melting smile and my clothes will fall off."

This got her the wolf grin. "And?"

"And," she said, "we're no longer mutual orgasm givers."

He just looked at her, purse held out, the thing looking small and feminine in his big hand.

"Fine." She snatched it. Someone had broken into her home. Touched her things. And she had no idea why or what they'd been looking for. The truth was that her knees were still knocking and she didn't want to sleep here alone anyway. "I'll sleep on your couch."

"Wherever you want," he said, and then he drove them through the night, in his zone, quiet. Watchful.

Elle didn't have a zone, but she could pretend with the best of them. "It was probably Morgan," she said.

He gave a slow shake of his head. "I called her. It wasn't."

She stared at his profile in the dark, slashes of ambient light slanting over his face at every streetlight they passed. "Excuse me," she said. "You called her? You and my sister are on calling-each-other terms?"

He parked in front of his building and turned to face her. "While you're still good and pissed off at me, there's something you should know."

"Great. What now? No, wait," she said. "Let me guess. You've kept track of my period as well as everything else, and you know I'm a day late."

He stilled. Blinked once. Not another muscle moved on that big body, not a single one. After a very long beat went by—during which she cursed herself for opening her big, fat mouth—he said with deceptive calm, "You're late?"

What the hell was wrong with her? She hadn't meant to say that. Hadn't meant to say a damn word. She'd only just realized this morning. She was one hundred percent certain it was stress. Or ninety-five percent anyway . . . "Guess you don't know everything, do you?"

There was a muscle ticking in his jaw now, and he took a moment to visibly compose himself. It was pretty fascinating really, the control he had over his emotions. She considered herself quite the emotion controller but Archer was the master.

He got her inside his place and then, in a move that shouldn't have charmed her as thoroughly as it did, put on some hot water, presumably for her nightly tea.

Dammit. He knew exactly what she needed, always.

Well, almost always. Because right this minute stand-ing in his kitchen, she could've used a hug.

He came to her and for a minute she thought he'd read her mind. He pulled off her jacket and set it over the back of a chair. He took her purse and tossed it on top of her jacket. Then he put his hands on her arms, gently stroking up and down as he bent at the knees to look her in the eyes. "Can I ask you to sit without start-ing a fight?"

She lifted a shoulder. "Asking would be nice."

She thought, but wasn't sure, that she saw a very small smile curve his mouth. "Will you please sit?"

With another shoulder lift, she headed back into the living room to the couch and sank into the cushions. It was the most comfy couch she'd ever sat on. It seemed to embrace her and she lay her head back and closed her eyes, suddenly and completely exhausted.

For whatever reason, Archer let her be. She heard him tinkering around in the kitchen and the thought made her smile. Archer tinkering in the kitchen . . . The image that conjured up felt incongruous, the big badass Archer in an apron bent over the stove.

"What are you smiling about?"

Shit, the man moved like smoke. She jerked and opened her eyes to find him crouched in front of her. He set a steaming mug of tea on the coffee table.

"You're not wearing an apron," she murmured.

With a frown, he palmed her forehead.

"I'm not sick," she managed with a low laugh and

pushed his hand—the one that felt far too good on her skin—away from her.

He didn't budge. "Talk to me, Elle."

She blew out a breath. "I'm not ready to talk to you." She picked up the remote on the coffee table and aimed it at the biggest TV she'd ever seen.

It came on, the volume up high, the screen flashing through channels so fast it made her dizzy. "I think I just launched a lunar module, but I'm not sure."

He reached over and turned it off. "You're exhausted. You need sleep but there's no sense in trying to go to bed when you're this pissed off. Let it all out, Elle. You're . . . late?"

"Only a single day. It's nothing."

He didn't take his eyes off her. "So you've been late before?"

"No," she admitted. Normally she was so regular she could be a calendar. "It's probably stress."

His gaze held hers. "But maybe not."

"I'm on the pill," she reminded him.

"Not foolproof."

"It's too early to worry," she said, "it's highly unlikely I'm . . ." She couldn't even say the word.

He put his hand over one of hers and linked their fingers. "Whatever happens, we'll deal with it."

We. At that one single word, her throat went tight. Not a *you.* Or an *I.* They were a *we.* They couldn't get along to save their lives, he was bossy and manipulating and controlling and alpha, and he drove her crazy.

But that *we* . . . That *we* definitely staggered her.

"You hear me past that stubborn, beautiful brain of yours, right?" He squeezed her fingers. "You're not alone in this, Elle."

She couldn't speak. She was completely undone.

He gave her a minute. Or hell, maybe he needed a minute too. Finally she found her voice. "I'm not pregnant."

"You mean you don't *want* to be pregnant."

Right. *That.*

Chapter 18

#ThereIsntAnEmojiForThis

Archer watched Elle rise to her feet and pace his living room a few times, muttering to herself, something with a lot of pronouns like *you* and *me* and *we*. She was making no sense at all but he was smart enough to keep his mouth shut. Which was easy enough to do because he was completely thrown for a loop.

She could be pregnant with his baby. He needed to sit down more than a little but instead he locked his legs into place and waited her out.

Finally she turned to him. "What did you mean, we'll deal with it? You don't want children any more than I do."

"Things change."

She stared at him and then turned to continue her pacing. Then suddenly she stopped, standing in the middle of his living room, body language tense, blonde hair pulled back from her face, twisted in some fancy do that made her look like a goddess.

One pissed-off goddess who he absolutely wouldn't mind having his baby.

"Are you actually telling me you'd want kids?" she asked in disbelief. "And be careful here, Archer, because you've very purposely perpetuated the image of impenetrable badass. You're an island and you don't need anyone, you never have. In fact, it's taken you by my calculations eleven years to want . . ."

"A relationship," he supplied helpfully.

"Yes," she said. "That. Eleven years, Archer. So I'm not sure how I'm supposed to believe that you see yourself with a white picket fence, the same woman every night, and . . ." She appeared to struggle for what might be worse than a white picket fence and the same woman every night. "And a tricycle in the front yard!" she came up with triumphantly. "Because honestly, you just don't fit the profile."

He realized he was going to have to give her something to get anything in return. "I agree," he said. "I've led the life I've wanted and it's been a selfish lifestyle, not leaving much room for a relationship."

"Convenient."

"Yes," he agreed. "It has been. When I left the force, I did so with the knowledge that I'd be walking the line between right and legal. I also knew I'd be cutting myself off from a family who wouldn't understand what I was doing, or why. I did it knowing I'd be alone because I couldn't ask anyone else to get on board with it all, and I was good with that."

She stared at him. "But . . . ? Because I sense a big one."

"But," he said, "although I would've sworn that everything in my life was just as I wanted it . . . something's been missing."

She hadn't blinked. Hell, he wasn't sure she was breathing. "I'm not ready for this conversation. I'm still mad at you. If you want to discuss *that,* I'm totally game."

"Let's do it," he said.

"You've been meddling in my life this whole time, keeping tabs on me like I was your responsibility."

"The college thing doesn't count," he said.

She stilled and the room temperature dropped twenty degrees. "What?" she asked very quietly.

Oh shit. "What?" he repeated, taking a step back, both mentally and physically. "You know what? It's late. You're tired. So am I. We'll just circle back to this another time—"

She picked up a pillow from the couch and chucked it at his head with deadly accuracy.

His own fault. He'd been teaching her all year how to play darts in the pub and she was a quick learner.

"You got me my job *and* into college?" she asked in an outside voice.

Note to self: *never* speak first. "I wrote a letter of recommendation," he said. "That's all. I knew someone on the admission committee."

She stared at him for a full minute and then backed

to the couch and sat. She blindly reached out for another pillow and he stepped toward her, intending to grab it and ward off another attack but she pressed it to her stomach and huddled into herself a little.

Blowing out a breath, he sank next to her. "You weren't given any breaks growing up. I hated that for you. Everything I did, I only wanted to help."

"Helping would have been calling me and asking if I wanted the assist," she said. "Instead you've been acting like a puppet master, directing my life. I hate that, Archer."

He took the pillow from her and put his hands on her arms, turning her to face him. "I'm not a puppet master. I didn't direct you in any way. I just . . ." He shook his head. "Gave you a helping hand when you needed one."

"But it wasn't help I wanted from you. I wanted—"

"What?" he asked when she broke off. "You wanted what from me?" Say it . . .

But she only shook her head.

He sighed. "Look, you didn't need my help. But you had no one else. I just wanted to make sure you were safe. And protected."

"Because that's what you do, right?" she asked. "You keep people safe and protected."

"Well, yeah," he said, not sure they were having the same conversation.

She shook her head. "See, that makes me a job to you. And that's the one thing I never wanted to be, Archer."

He stepped into her path, pulling her in until they were toe-to-toe. "I need you to listen to me," he said. "Can you do that?"

"Depends on the level of bullshit you're going to try and feed me."

A rough laugh escaped him and he dropped his forehead to hers, taking it as a very good sign when she didn't try to knee him in the 'nads or gouge his eyes out. "No bullshit," he said quietly, willing her to really hear him. Risking his life, he stepped even closer because the only thing he had going for him was their sheer physical chemistry. And yeah, he was enough of a dick to use that if he had to. Anything to make sure she heard what he had to say. He waited until she met his gaze, and even then he nearly drowned in the blue depths.

"That night," he told her, "there was just something about you. You came onto my radar and"—he shook his head—"you stayed there. I was worried about you staying safe." And alive . . . "I don't have a lot of nesting instincts, Elle, but you brought out the ones I had. I wanted to put you in a hot shower, wrap you up in a blanket, and feed you." His smile was wry. "And then I wanted to make you sleep and watch over you while you did."

"You did all that," she reminded him. "You took me to the urgent care and then brought me home with you like I was a half-drowned puppy. You fed me and put me to bed. Alone," she added. "Even though I asked if you expected to be paid with sex." She shook her head. "You laughed. I was serious and you laughed at me."

"Elle, you were bleeding, drenched from the rain, and

wearing only shorts and a tank top and no shoes. Trust me, I wasn't laughing. I was pissed off at the life you'd been forced to lead. You'd seen shit you should never have seen. You'd done shit you never should have had to do. I wanted to kick someone's ass for that. Still do."

She stared at him and maybe it was his imagination but she looked a little less mad. "In the morning you fed me again," she said. "Scrambled eggs, sausage, and toast."

"The only thing I knew how to cook," he said with a small smile, remembering every minute of that night, how he'd watched over her through the long hours, unable to understand his need to make sure she was safe given that his entire world had imploded.

"After breakfast . . ." She closed her eyes, clearly embarrassed by the memory. "I tried to kiss you and got turned down again." She shook her head. "You gave me a sweatshirt. There was money in the pocket."

"I didn't want you out there with nothing."

"I thought it was a test at first," she admitted. "But it wasn't."

"No," he said, remembering how she'd tried to give him back the money.

"You told me to follow my instincts and not let anyone distract me from them," she said. "You told me that there was right and there was wrong and that there was also a gray area, and that was okay as long as I stayed as close to the right as I could get. And then I left and I never saw you again."

He nudged the mug of tea to her mouth and watched her sip.

She took her time, taking a few more long swallows before she set the mug aside. "But you were around. Watching over me," she said. "Weren't you?"

"Yes."

"Tell me why I didn't realize that. Why you didn't just let me know you were there at my back, watching my every move."

"I wasn't watching your every move," he said. "I never did that."

"Are you suggesting you've never invaded my privacy?"

That question wasn't nearly so easy to answer honestly. Neither was the question she was really getting at—why hadn't he wanted her?

She looked at him for a long moment. "Okay, let's see if I've got all of this straight. You didn't want to be with me, not even as friends, and yet you kept tabs on me, even going as far as to direct me into school and a job—"

"The school of your choice," he pointed out. "And a job you love."

She narrowed her eyes. "You didn't want to be with me," she repeated. "So instead you basically stalked me—"

"Not stalked," he said. "Kept safe and protected."

"But I didn't need that from you. I needed—" She broke off and turned away. "Look," she said, clearly striving for patience. "I get that you've been there for me, more than anyone else . . . ever. But the way you went about it . . ."

"You were underage."

She turned back. "What?"

Fuck it. "You were sixteen, Elle. I was twenty-two. We couldn't. I couldn't." He drew a deep breath. "And then after you left, you worked hard and got your life together. Seeing me would've been a reminder of shit you didn't want to remember. So I stayed away."

She stared at him, not looking particularly flattered that he'd tried to do the right thing. "I make my own decisions," she finally said. "I don't need anyone making them for me."

"I'm getting that, but as long as you're still mad, I need to add one thing to your list of my infractions."

"Oh boy."

"I hired your sister as a temp," he said. "Morgan's doing some background checks and online searches until Mollie comes back to work."

Her mouth fell open. "So on top of ruining the only two dates I've had in ages and being a part of my life for the past decade without my knowledge, you've hired a known grifter who happens to be the sister I asked to leave me alone?"

"Well technically you and I are on a date this very minute, and in spite of the break-in thing, it's not going so bad, right?"

She stared at him and then laughed.

"And Morgan is . . . well, Morgan," he said. "But she's also your sister. Family. And family trumps everything else."

"Then why haven't you reconciled with your dad?" she asked.

"I'm working on that one."

She blew out a breath. "I'd like to say the same," she admitted. "But I'm not sure Morgan and I can get there. I don't have many good experiences with family. Or relationships, for that matter. The most important people in my life are my friends. And in spite of everything idiotic you've done, and there has been a *lot* of idiocy"—she hesitated—"you're one of them."

Something new slid through him. It was warming and it felt . . . amazing. What didn't feel as amazing was the fact that she'd just put him in the friend zone.

Because that part sucked.

Elle took a long time in Archer's shower. At first she'd just stood there letting the hot water beat down on her shoulders, attempting to steam away her troubles, of which there were so many she couldn't keep them straight.

But then the scent of his soap, a visceral reminder of the man and how he made her feel, just about did her in. Rubbing the suds over her skin awakened every desire for him that she'd worked hard at tamping down. By the time she turned off the water, her body was on high alert, practically quivering with need and hunger.

Stay strong, she ordered herself as she wrapped herself up in one of Archer's towels.

"You smell like me," he murmured when she strode out of the bathroom.

She ignored the way her body quivered at that.

He handed her a folded T-shirt. "PJ's," he said.

"Thanks." She turned from him and drew the shirt over her head, letting it cover her body before carefully reaching under it to pull out the towel.

From the careful way he sucked in a breath, she took it that she hadn't been entirely successful but when she turned to glare at him, his expression was calm.

She had no idea how he did it, how he kept that illusion up in the face of . . . well, anything. But she intended to pretend to do the same.

Fake it until you make it, that was her motto.

"Share my bed, Elle. It's big and warm."

Said the Big Bad Wolf to Riding Hood. She shook her head. "I'll take the couch," she said.

"Come on, just take half the bed. I can control myself if you can. Friends, right?"

She stared at the huge bed with the invitingly thick bedding and swallowed hard because she knew firsthand that he could indeed control himself. What she didn't know was if she could say the same.

He laughed knowingly, the bastard, and she stomped off to the couch. He brought her a pillow and a blanket and then walked around the place turning off lights and checking the windows and doors while she lay still like a statue and pretended not to be straining there in the dark, strung tight and filled with tension.

"You going to be okay?" he asked quietly.

"Always."

He paused for a long beat like he had something else to say, but in the end he didn't, he simply turned and disappeared into his bedroom.

She fell asleep with shocking ease, but she didn't stay that way. She was worried about who'd broken into her apartment. And still pissy about Archer directing her life for the past eleven years. And she was wondering about her sister . . . And then there was the elephant in the room. What if she was really pregnant, what then? Would she do better than her mom? God, she hoped so, but shuddered at the thought that she might not.

Shaking her head, she forced herself to relax, but talking about her past had dug up stuff best forgotten. Dreams haunted her, stupid memories long buried. Like the time when she'd been somewhere around five years old and her mom had vanished. She and Morgan had been alone for three days before child services found them and took them to foster care. They'd remained there until their mom bailed herself out and claimed them. That had happened twice more before she and Morgan had learned to evade social services entirely, but, at turns hot and sweaty and then freezing cold, she still tossed and turned at the barrage of unwelcome memories.

"Elle. Scoot over."

She jerked in surprise to find the outline of Archer's tall, built body standing over her.

"Shh," he said gently and crouched down to her level. "Just me. Scoot."

"Why?"

"Because you're having bad dreams. I'll beat them off for you."

"How?"

"I'll hold you tight and not let anything get you."

That sounded alarmingly perfect. "You're not allowed to protect me anymore," she said. "I already said so."

"How about just until dawn then, just this one last time," he said quietly, stroking the damp hair from her forehead. "For me."

She huffed out a breath. "Well, if it's for you . . ."

"Come here, Elle."

Oh how she wanted to do just that. "Archer?" she whispered, heart in her throat.

"Yeah?"

"Do friends sometimes sleep together?"

He nudged her over so they were spooning, her back to his front. "When it's you and me they do. Whatever you need, Elle. Always."

Her throat tightened because in spite of the fact that he drove her crazy, she knew he meant it.

He pulled her in even tighter, warm and strong, and as those arms closed around her, she finally let go and slept like the dead.

Chapter 19

#GotMilk?

Elle woke up still on the couch and wrapped around Archer like a pretzel. He was flat on his back, breathing slow and even and very deeply, assuring her he was still asleep.

So she very slowly opened her eyes and stared at him. Or at the part of him she could see, which was his stubbly jaw since she'd pressed her face into his throat at some point in the night. She was in the crook of one of his arms, pressed up against his side, a leg thrown over his like she owned him, an arm across his chest, her hand in his armpit.

That's when she realized one of his arms was thrown out to the side of his body, the other had wrapped around her like Saran Wrap, his hand on her butt.

At the thought, her body gave a slight hopeful quiver. She told it to shut up. Not that there was anything wrong with having her merry way with a man, but she'd already been there done that with him more than she should have, and now she knew it was a one-way street to Hurtsville, guaranteed.

She pulled back very slightly to get a better look. He was no longer wearing a bandage over his knife wound, which was healing up nicely, but it still shocked her to see the red, puckered scar.

Nothing about him was safe.

Not that her life was all that much better, she had to admit.

The warm palm cupping her butt felt . . . sexy and just slightly possessive. And Team Stay Strong took a slight hit because she liked it, way too much. She looked into his face. It was rare to be able to study him so up close and personal without him blinding her with the sheer force field of his personality, and she soaked up the opportunity. He looked so relaxed, even carefree. Not to mention sexy as all hell without an ounce of effort. Men really sucked in that regard. They had no idea how good they had it, while she on the other hand, required at least an hour of prep time before she could be seen in public. And with that in mind, she began to slowly inch away from the hot man who'd kept her dreams at bay for her, slaying her dragons all night long.

But the second she moved, she felt the subtle change in his breathing that told her he was now awake.

And sure enough, he opened his eyes. "You okay?"

If she'd thought his middle-of-the-night voice had

been dead sexy, it had nothing on his morning growl. "Yes, thanks to you."

Their gazes met for a beat and, as if they were connected by some unseen force, they leaned toward each other and—

His cell phone buzzed from somewhere over her head.

"Duty calls," she whispered.

He didn't take his eyes off her as he reached past her for the phone. Saved by the bell . . . But then she took in his frown as he accessed a text.

"What is it?" she asked.

"Your sister needs to see us."

Archer drove himself and Elle to his office and watched the two sisters interact with each other.

Or rather, *not* react.

They sat in the two chairs in his office right next to each other, but emotionally they might as well have been miles apart. He couldn't read much in Morgan's pouty silence but he read volumes in Elle.

She was holding it together, but it was an effort. He met her gaze and maybe he was crazy but the emotion he read in hers warmed him, filled his soul, dismissing all the secret, buried-deep doubts he'd ever had about being enough for her.

"I've got a couple problems," Morgan said. "Two men have been going around to the places I've stayed over the years, asking where I am now. And there's no good reason for that. I just wanted to ask you both, if you're approached, to play dumb."

"Someone who?" Archer asked. "How and where?"

"I don't know." She paused. "But it escalated last night. Someone must've followed me back to the house where I'm renting a room. Because after I went out this morning, apparently they questioned my landlady and scared her to death. They told her I was trouble and that it would spread to her if she wasn't careful."

"Was she hurt?" Elle asked.

"No." A note of amusement came into Morgan's voice. "She has her husband's beloved golf clubs in the foyer. She pulled out the nine iron and waved it around like a baseball bat. When they didn't take her seriously, she swung at one of them. Connected too, sending him flying into her shoe rack." She pulled out a cell phone and placed it on Archer's desk. "The guy lost this. Ran out without it."

Archer pulled out an evidence bag, nudged the phone into it with a pen, and called someone. Two seconds later, Trev strode into the office.

Archer handed him the bag with the phone. "Need everything you can get off this."

Trev saluted him, winked at Elle, and walked out.

"You can't stay there anymore," Elle said to Morgan. "You can't risk letting your past get your landlady hurt."

"You think I don't know that?" Morgan asked, eyes flashing. She nodded to the suitcase on the floor. "I already left."

"*Neither* of you can stay in your own apartments,"

Archer said. "Elle's place was broken into as well," he informed Morgan.

Morgan blinked, the flash of temper in her gaze gone now as she turned to Elle. "Were you hurt?" she whispered.

"I wasn't home." Elle blew out a breath and softened her voice. "We both got lucky. But Morgan, that luck won't last forever, not as long as you're still standing with one foot in that door."

"I'm not."

Elle just looked at her.

"I'm not," she repeated and then sighed. "But for what it's worth, I'm sorry. I didn't come here to bring you trouble. I thought it was all behind me."

"It's never all behind you," Elle said with a grim finality that had Archer taking a longer look at her. He could see volumes of regret and tempered pain in the depths of her eyes. He'd had no idea how much of the past she still held deep, how much she held herself accountable for.

"New plan," Archer said. "Until we've got this handled, you both stay with me."

"Demanding much?" Morgan asked.

Elle's mouth twitched. "He actually thinks he just asked nicely instead of telling us."

"Huh," Morgan said. "Cute."

Elle actually smiled.

"Glad to see you two bonding," Archer said. "But let's get this handled once and for all."

Elle turned to look at Morgan and he watched some silent sister communication going on. Then Morgan stood up. "I'll give you two a moment," she said and got to the door before turning back. "And really, I never meant to do this to you again. Either of you," she said right to Elle, and then she was gone.

Elle stood up to follow her but Archer beat her to the door and put a hand on it, holding it closed.

She dropped her forehead to the wood.

Letting out a breath, he pressed up against her back, stroked the hair away from the nape of her neck, and brushed his mouth across her sweet skin. "Don't blame yourself," he whispered. "This isn't on you."

"Maybe not," she murmured. "But I turned her away when she needed me. That makes me someone I don't like very much right now."

Pulling her around to face him, he slid an arm around her waist, his other hand along her jaw and into her hair to hold her head for a soft kiss. "That's okay, Elle. I like you enough for the both of us."

She rolled her eyes. "You like me because I tried to get naked with you."

"I do like that, a lot." He let a smile free. "And maybe you've got your pic in the dictionary under *obstinate, stubborn,* and *mule-headed,* but you're also there under *resilient, resourceful,* and *pretty fucking amazing.*"

She stared up at him, looking surprised and . . . a lot less wary. Too bad what he was going to say next would probably ruin that. "So here's how we're going to play this," he said. "You're going to let me help you. In return, I'll let you help me when I need it. And I will need it, Elle. That's how this thing between us works, give and take. So let's skip the freak-out from you that you're doing all the taking because you're not. You never would. You hear me?"

She just stared at him.

"Going to need you to say it, Elle."

"You're crazy."

"I know," he said. "Now say it. Say that you're going to let me help you."

She blew out a sigh. "I'm going to let you help me. Dammit."

He smiled. "Are you angry? Because we do some of our best naked work when you're angry."

She pointed at him.

He smiled.

She rolled her eyes and slid out from between him and the door. "And don't think I didn't notice how you managed to get me and Morgan to both stay with you," she said. "Which puts her and me under the same roof for the first time in a very long time. You're going to owe me for that."

"Sex or chocolate?" he asked, and to his surprise, she appeared to give it serious thought.

"What kind of chocolate?" she asked.

He smiled. "Shouldn't you ask what kind of sex?"

She grabbed the front of his shirt. "Maybe I want both." Then she shocked the hell out of him by kissing him hard and quick, and then she was gone.

Trev came back into the room. "You bribe your woman with chocolate?"

"And sex," Archer said seriously. "Don't forget the sex."

Chapter 20

#HaveItYourWay

Back at Archer's that night, Elle tossed Morgan a blanket and watched as she settled herself onto one long length of Archer's huge L-shaped couch.

"He's really quite a catch, you know," Morgan said. "You two could probably make it work if you wanted."

"How do you know either of us wants to?"

Morgan gave her a get-real look. "I have eyes in my head, don't I? That man wants you, bad."

"There's more to a relationship than sex," Elle said.

"I suppose," Morgan said, not overly impressed. "But if a guy looked at me like he looks at you, I'd go for it. You're lucky, you know that?"

Elle didn't know how to respond to this.

Morgan rolled her eyes. "Oh come on. If you were able to believe in Santa Claus for like, what, eight years, you can believe in yourself for like five seconds. You got this, Elle."

"Hey," Elle said. "I'd have believed in Santa a lot longer if you hadn't made me stay up that year to watch Mom con our poor clueless neighbor out of his presents to his daughters, which she then put beneath our tree—and, by the way, our tree was a marijuana plant."

Morgan laughed. "See? I protected you from some stuff."

"I'm going to make tea," Elle said. *Instead of fight with you . . .*

"You and your tea."

"Do you want some or not?"

Morgan smiled. She'd always been amused by the little habits of comfort Elle had treasured. Tea. The same blanket she'd dragged to every place they'd ever stayed. The book of poems that had supposedly belonged to her father. Elle had no idea if that was actually true or not but her mom had always sworn to it and Elle had decided she had to believe in something.

"Fine," Morgan said. "I'd love some tea. Really," she added at Elle's disbelieving look. "And, Elle?"

"Yeah?"

Morgan's smile faded. "Thanks for not hating me."

Elle sighed. "I don't hate you, Morgan. And I don't want anything to happen to you." She paused. "Well, maybe something little and annoying, like every time you make toast it burns."

Morgan laughed but sobered quickly enough. "I'm sorry I keep messing up your life."

A stab of guilt settled in Elle's gut. "You haven't."

"Oh don't be nice now. We both know I've done

exactly that. And I keep messing up my own life too. I'm having trouble with my Plan A."

"Hey, at least there's a lot more letters after A."

"Yeah," Morgan said and then hesitated.

"What?"

"It's kinda nice not to be alone in this anymore."

Elle had been doing her damnedest to hold on to her distance, but it was getting harder and harder because she was starting to understand just how alone her sister had really been. Elle had always thought of herself as being alone too, but that wasn't really true. She had Spence and Willa and Pru and the others at her back.

And despite his deceptions, she was beginning to realize she also had Archer. And although she knew he was trying to back off and let her be her own strong capable self, the truth was that no one was better at watching her back than him.

"Think we'll ever get this sister gig down?" Morgan asked.

When Elle didn't say anything, Morgan's smile faded. "Oh. Right. We're not really sisters anymore."

"Maybe that's something we can change," Elle said softly, surprised to find that she actually meant it.

Morgan stared at her, clearly shocked. "Yeah?"

Elle nodded. "Yeah."

Morgan's smile was tentative but utterly genuine, and it made Elle's stomach hurt. Turning away to give herself a minute, she moved into the kitchen to get the tea.

Archer was in his shower. She could hear the water

running. She could also feel the low-level hum of awareness skittering through her veins at the thought, which left her nipples hard and achy against the silk of her bra. They hadn't gotten the message that nothing was happening tonight.

She'd gone through her adult life appreciating great sex when it came her way, but always being able to walk away and move on without too much trouble. Except she was having trouble walking away from Archer. Her problem was that she'd let him in her bed. Or more accurately, in her body and, she feared, her heart. And that was the problem. Because everything she thought she wanted was now sideways and she couldn't figure out which way was up.

She filled three mugs with tea. She left one on Archer's nightstand for him, glancing at the big bed tempting her to climb in. Instead she moved back to the living room, turning off lights as she went, before taking the other side of the couch from Morgan, who was already snoring softly. Apparently nothing disturbed *her* sleep.

A few minutes later Elle's nipples did their happy dance again and she opened her eyes to find Archer looking down at her in the dark.

She hadn't heard him coming.

He crouched at her side and set a hand low on her belly. "Why are you warming my couch and not my bed?" he murmured, his mouth at her ear, his warm breath giving her an all-over body shiver, the very best kind.

And there in the dark she felt him smile.

He knew exactly how he affected her.

"I'm not getting into your bed with my sister here," she whispered.

"But you can't sleep out here, remember? You end up needing my body. Bad."

He thought this was funny. "I'll manage," she informed him stiffly.

But then he brushed his mouth across hers and her bones melted. Bad, *bad* bones.

"I'll be waiting for you, Elle."

"I'm not coming!"

His soft, sexy laugh ghosted against her lips. "I can promise you otherwise," he murmured.

Incorrigible.

Impossible.

She flipped over, giving him her back with a huff that only made him laugh again as he left.

"Oh for God's sake," came Morgan's sleepy voice, disembodied in the dark. "Go after the hot guy, would you?"

"The peanut gallery needs to shut up," Elle muttered into the cushion.

"Just sayin'," Morgan said. "I'd leave you alone out here in a hot minute to go have sex if I had the chance."

"I'm not going to go have sex while you're out here knowing I'm having sex!"

"Your loss," Morgan said.

"Oh my God," Elle said. "Stop talking!"

The couch was comfortable but she couldn't find her

zone. The room was a good temperature but she was at turns hot and then cold. Her pillow wasn't working.

Morgan had started snoring again in less than two minutes and Elle forced herself to relax. She wasn't sure exactly when her fantasies became dreams, dreams of how Archer's hands had felt skimming over her body, the touch of his mouth on her skin. The way he'd murmured hot, sexy things while he'd stroked and kissed her . . .

She woke up and blinked blearily at the low light of dawn peeking in the bedroom windows. Wait—What? She sat straight up and stared down at Archer. His eyes were closed and he looked quite relaxed and comfortable.

And shirtless.

She peeked under the covers and found him in knit boxers.

"If you wanted to look at me, all you had to do was say so," came his sleep roughened voice.

"Why am I in your bed? *How* am I in your bed?" she demanded.

"You were tossing and turning and muttering and getting no real sleep. Which means I was getting no sleep either, so I brought you in here."

Where clearly she'd proceeded to sleep like the living dead.

"And that wasn't me rescuing you," he was quick to point out. "Or butting in on your life either. It was me doing Morgan a favor because you were keeping her up too."

She met his gaze, which wasn't amused. Wasn't

sardonic. Wasn't anything but dark, warm, and concerned. For her. Because she was probably having a mental breakdown and also maybe pregnant . . .

"You okay?" he asked softly.

"Yes." It was her ready-made answer but she paused and drew a deep breath. "Maybe." She paused again. "Archer?"

"Yeah?"

"If I admit I'm not okay, just this once, you've got me, right?"

"Yeah, babe. I've got you." He tugged her into him and she snuggled close, closing her eyes as his arms closed around her.

"What is it with us?" she murmured.

He laughed softly.

"How is that a funny question?"

"Because I try very hard to always know what I'm doing," he said. "But I'm winging it here, Elle. I have no idea what we're doing but one thing I'm sure as hell not doing is walking away from you. Not ever again."

She waited for her heart to hit her toes but it didn't happen. There was no panic. No anxiety. In fact, she felt . . . warm. Safe.

Secure. "This is just another of those temporary breaks from you staying the hell away from me," she said. "Don't forget."

"I wouldn't think of it."

Archer loved waking up with Elle in his arms. It was the second night that he'd held her close with an intimacy born of something far deeper than physical wanting and he thought he wouldn't mind sharing his space with her every single day of his life.

All he had to do was convince her of that, but he was working on it, one brick of the wall around her heart at a time.

The morning was a serious eye opener in other ways too. Turned out that sharing a bathroom with two females was an experience.

Or rather, *not* sharing.

They spent forty-five minutes in there. Each. By the time they finally cleared it for him, he was late to his own office meeting for the first time in his life.

When he walked in, the only one who dared say anything was Joe, who had refused to stay home any longer and was on light office duty. "Got the time, boss?" he asked with a smirk.

"You got something to say?" Archer asked him.

"Nothing you'd *want* me to say."

"How about 'I'd love to stay on light duty for another few weeks'?" Archer asked mildly. "Would you like to say that?"

Joe swore beneath his breath. They all hated light duty.

Max snickered.

Joe reached out and shoved Max into the wall.

Carl jumped up and started barking, excited that there was going to be roughhousing. Carl loved roughhousing.

Max put Joe into a headlock.

Carl completely lost his shit and jumped on both of them, trying to get in on the action.

"Hey," Mollie yelled from down the hall. "We just replaced that wall from the last time you two got playful. Knock it off!"

Archer turned to Trev. "What did you get off the phone?"

"It was a burner, but we're still working on it."

"Work faster."

"Yes, sir."

The rest of the meeting was finished without further damage to any property.

Even though Mollie was back, Morgan stuck around to help her catch up, which was probably an impossible feat. At the end of the day, she offered to stay late with Mollie, and since Max and Carl were staying late as well, Archer let it happen, assigning Max to bring Morgan to Archer's place when she was done for the night.

This left just the other troublesome female in his life. He went down the hallway and gathered Elle to go home.

"I need to stop by my apartment," she said.

"For what?"

"Stuff."

He thought of the huge duffle bag she already had at his place but decided that pressing further would be a hazard to his health. At her apartment, he walked her in.

"Most likely, the only thing I'm in danger from is

you," she noted, but she humored him, letting him prowl through the rooms, flicking on lights and taking a look around while she stood at the front door, waiting.

When they got to his place, he did a wash and repeat of the safety check.

"You chase away all the scary things that go bump in the night then?" she asked from the foyer when he was finished.

"All but one." He stepped into her, gratified to notice the hitch in her breath.

"What are you doing?" she asked.

He figured it was self-explanatory when he backed her to the wall.

She allowed it, that small wry smile still in place. "You think you're scary, Archer?"

Christ, he loved when she said his name. She could convey an entire volume of things in the one word. Irritation, amusement, temper, frustration . . . and then there was his favorite—arousal. Right now it was good humor as she allowed him to press up against her and kiss her, and then keep on kissing her until they were definitely no longer amused but something else entirely, something that called to the very heart of him. "Elle?"

"Yeah?"

"Are we in one of those time-outs from you being mad at me?"

Slowly Elle lifted her head and met his gaze. "No." She paused, killing him. "But as you've mentioned before, we do some of our best work when I'm mad at you."

With heat and need and something much stronger barreling through his veins, he lifted her up against him and then turned to head to his bedroom.

Her arms came around his neck, her fingers sliding into his hair to fist it, and she nibbled on his lower lip.

Still walking, palming her sweet ass, he let his fingers dip and play, making her gasp. He swallowed the sound with his mouth and then pulled back a fraction to meet her hot gaze. "Elle—"

The knock at the front door was loud and important. "Hey," Morgan said through the door. "Max is here with me and he's in a hurry to get home to his girlfriend, Rory. You two doing it or are you going to let me in?"

"I blame you for her," Elle said to Archer, who reluctantly let her go. Elle vanished into his bathroom and into his shower, leaving him to let Morgan in.

"So?" Morgan asked Elle when she came out of the shower. "Were you two going hog wild?"

"No!" Elle said.

And to Archer's eternal frustration, they didn't go hog wild at all because Elle stubbornly took the couch for the night.

Elle spent the next afternoon with a set of new tenants who were moving into the empty space on the ground floor between the coffee shop and Reclaimed Wood. They were going to put in a bakery, and Elle, fond of any baking that she didn't have to do on her own, thought it would be a great addition to the building.

By the time she was finished with them, she needed a caffeine hit so she made her way up to Spence's penthouse apartment, where he kept some of the good stuff for her. She found him in his huge, sprawling living room working on . . . something. There were parts and pieces everywhere, of what she had no idea. Spence could take anything apart and put it back together. He could also build whatever he could imagine.

"What are you working on?" she asked.

The only word she understood of his answer was *prototype*.

"Trudy's going to be pissed at the mess," she said.

He was head deep in whatever that thing was on his coffee table, which looked like it could fly to Mars and back. "I asked her not to come clean this week," he said distractedly.

"You trying to break her heart? She loves to clean for you."

"Yeah, but yesterday she came in without knocking and—"

"Caught you getting laid?" Elle asked hopefully.

Spence snorted. "I wish, but no. I was flying a drone and it nearly hit her in the face. She left here screaming about the zombie apocalypse arriving early."

Elle went into his kitchen and pulled out the tin of tea he'd ordered for her from England. "I think I'm all screwed up over Archer," she said, bringing him a cup. "Emotionally."

He sniffed at the tea suspiciously, like she was trying

to poison him. "Why am I always the one to get roped into conversations about people's feelings?"

"Because you're so sweet and sensitive?" she asked dryly.

"Exactly, I'm none of those things so why do you all enjoy making me discuss your love lives?" He downed the cup she'd brought him and made a face because it was unsweetened. Shaking his head again, he went back to work.

"Well excuse me," she said. "Next time I'll come up here to discuss more important stuff, like how big our dicks are."

He was laughing when she left him. She'd been back at her desk for an hour when two men let themselves into her office. Big. Mean-looking. Mouth-breathing knuckle draggers.

"We're looking for your sister," Thing One said, expression blank, mouth grim, beefy body tensed for trouble.

"I don't have a sister," she said.

The two men looked at each other and some silent communication happened. Thing One went to her window and looked out. Thing Two, just as nasty-looking as his buddy, stood between her and the door.

Okay, so they weren't here about the vacancies in the building . . . She started to rise out of her chair but Thing One at the window turned and shook his head at her, like *don't even think about it*.

Fine. She had her laptop open and within reach. She

could get an SOS email out, possibly even a text message if she had that screen up. But before she could get her fingers on the keyboard, Thing One lunged close and slammed her laptop shut.

She dove for her cell phone but Thing Two was faster, shoving her hard as he wrapped his fingers around the phone.

Off balance, she spun, but not fast enough to avoid crashing into the credenza behind her desk and stumbling on her heels. Unfortunately for her, she'd left a drawer open and she hit it going down.

With her face.

It didn't take a genius to figure out she was in trouble. But her phone was on the floor and she stretched for it, just barely grabbing it with the very tips of her fingers, hitting Archer on speed dial.

Two legs came into view as she scrambled up to her knees, hopefully leaving the phone connecting to Archer. She put a hand to her throbbing temple and cheek, hoping, praying she'd diverted his attention from the phone.

"Let's start over," Thing One said, hauling her up to her feet. "We're looking for your sister."

"I already told you, I don't have a sister."

He put his hands in his front pockets, the casual gesture revealing the big gun at his hip. "Try again."

Oh boy.

"Look, our beef isn't with you," he said, clearly the talker of the group since Thing Two had done nothing but grunt. "Just tell us where Morgan's at and we'll leave you alone."

If they knew things like Morgan's name and where Elle worked, the gig really was up and she was in bigger trouble than she'd thought. "What do you want her for?" she asked, hoping like hell Archer was listening to this and on his way.

"She cut us out of a deal and our boss isn't happy," Thing One said. "He wants to talk to her."

"Who's 'he'?"

"Lars Maddox."

Only half feigning dizziness now, Elle leaned on her desk and let one of her hands fall onto her heavy-duty stapler. Lars had been Morgan's boyfriend a lifetime ago and he wasn't a nice guy. He was the *opposite* of a nice guy. Back when she and Morgan had been teens, he'd had Morgan doing some grifter work for him. In fact, he'd been the one Elle had been attempting to return the stolen Russian brooch to the night their lives had all imploded. The night Archer had saved her. If Lars was still in Morgan's life, Morgan had been lying about getting her life together.

Which sucked.

"I'm losing patience," Thing One said. "Where the fuck is she?"

"Under my desk," she said, and Thing One laughed.

When Elle didn't, he sighed. "Shit. You're just crazy enough to be telling the truth." He peered around her desk and when he dropped his gaze from hers for a second to take a peek, she hit him over the head with the stapler as hard as she could, connecting with a gratifying thunk.

He went down like a stone.

Thing Two narrowed his eyes. "Hey! You can't do that."

She readjusted her now sweaty grip on the stapler, preparing for a round with this guy as he started toward her all good and pissed off. That made two of them, she thought, just as her office door flew open with enough force to bang against the wall and embed the handle in the drywall. Damn. That was going to be costly to fix.

There was a blur of movement and Thing Two took a roundhouse kick from Archer and flew back eight feet, hitting the far wall of the office with a satisfying splat before sliding down to the floor.

"Stay down," Archer told him, and he turned to Thing One, his eyes flat and hard and scary as hell as he gave the guy a "come here" gesture with his hands.

Thing One rushed him but Archer did a quick, sharp movement with a bent arm and an elbow. Thing One expelled a breath of air and hit the floor.

He didn't get up.

Archer turned back to Thing Two, kicking him over so that he was facedown, putting a knee in his back to cuff him with some plexicuffs he pulled from one of the pockets in his cargos.

Thing One got the same treatment, and then Archer rose to his feet and leveled that sharp, intense gaze on her. "You okay?"

Here was the thing. She'd been born okay, and she'd

had things under control. Mostly. Her point being that she'd made it through relatively unscathed, but at Archer's three words uttered with calm steel, *are you okay,* she felt her throat close up.

With the same swiftness he'd used to take in her office with one sweeping glance when he'd first crashed into it during her fight, he grasped her impending melt-down. Reaching out, he snagged her by the front of her dress and hauled her into his very capable arms.

And although she was her own woman who stood on her own two feet, who fought her battles for herself and usually won them too, sometimes being alone wasn't all it was cracked up to be. So she fisted her hands in his shirt, buried her face in his throat, and held on tight.

Chapter 21

#BigGirlsDontCry

The police came quickly and arrested the two men, taking statements from everyone involved. The story they got from the suspects was questionable at best, leaving Elle with more questions than answers.

In the middle of the chaos, Archer tugged her to a quiet corner and met her gaze. "Do you need a doctor?"

"The cops already asked me but I'm fine."

"Elle." He slid a big palm to her stomach. "I'm going to ask you again. Do you need a doctor?"

"No. *No*," she repeated when he just looked at her. "I'm really okay." Maybe pregnant, but okay. At least physically. In truth, she hadn't really let herself think about the implications of being a few days late. Not yet.

Managing to slip away a few minutes later, she walked down the stairs to the courtyard, her goal being a moment alone before she hunted down Morgan for some answers.

The fountain water was shimmering beneath the bright sun as she passed by. Several people were milling around, including a young couple holding hands and laughing as the guy teasingly held up a quarter to toss in.

"You sure you're ready for true love?" the girl asked him.

He gave her a goofy smile.

Elle tried to picture Archer giving her that same goofy smile and couldn't.

And then Archer himself was suddenly right there, pulling her around to face him. The dark mirrored lenses of his sunglasses glinting in the bright daylight. "Where are you going?" he asked, his gaze roaming over her face, which was stinging like a son of a bitch. "I wanted to treat your cut and ice your face."

"I was going to do that." And she would. Right after she fortified herself, shored up the brick walls around her trembling foundation. She was thinking some of Tina's muffins would be a really great start.

Archer stroked the hair from her face, looking over her features, his own tight. "Are you dizzy?" he asked. "Do you feel sick? How many of me do you see?"

"No, no, and the one of you is more than I need at the moment," she said, pushing his hand away. "And stop looking at me like you're itching to toss me over your shoulder and drag me back to your cave."

"I'm more likely to toss you over my knee," he said, his voice sounding amused now.

An older woman standing near them gasped and glared at him.

Elle realized that given what her face looked like, she probably thought Archer had already beaten her, and she found a smile on this shitty day.

Archer didn't look amused in the slightest. "We're just messing around," he said to the woman.

"Males your age have no manners," she said. "In my day, women were wooed with flowers and handwritten love letters. Now it's all chains and whips and hand-cuffs." She pointed a bony finger in Archer's face. "You men wouldn't be so amused by the whole BDSM trend if we were the ones holding the floggers!"

And with that, she huffed off.

"She actually thought I was going to beat your ass," he said, sounding shocked. "She took one look at me and laid judgment."

She laughed. "Oh, put on your big-boy panties and deal with it."

He shook his head and looked into her eyes. "And you. You've got a black eye coming on and you're laughing. Why aren't you upset?"

"I am. But I held my own and that felt good." She flashed a smile. "Thanks for the stapler-to-the-head tip."

He let out a reluctant smile. "You're pretty amazing, you know that?"

"Amazing enough to buy me muffins?"

"Tell me you want more from me than that," he said.

They'd just been joking but suddenly she could tell he wasn't and her smile faded. "Can we just start with the muffins?"

He stared at her for a long beat and then nodded, surprising her by sliding his hand down her arm to link their fingers, holding her hand as they crossed the courtyard to Tina's coffee shop.

Tina's welcoming smile faded at the sight of Elle. "Sit," she said, pointing to a free table. "You sit right there and don't move."

Less than a minute later Tina was back at their small table with an ice pack, a basket of muffins, and a steaming tea.

"I love you," Elle said fervently.

"Right back at you," Tina said, and then she turned to Archer. "Whatever you want, on the house, both of you."

"Coffee will do it for me," he said. "Thanks."

Tina didn't budge. Instead she put her hands on her hips and stared at him. "You got this, right?"

Archer's gaze slid to Elle's for a beat and then back to Tina. "I do."

"You need any help kicking ass and taking names?"

"If I do, I'll let you know," Archer said, taking Tina's request as seriously as she'd uttered it.

Tina nodded curtly, squeezed Elle's shoulder, and went back to get Archer his coffee, which she brought right away.

Archer thanked her and then reached across the table and peeled the ice pack from Elle's eye, looking it over before gently pushing it back to her skin.

"Am I going to live?" she asked, trying to lighten the moment.

"Yes, but I might not." He shook his head, a very small smile curving his grim mouth. "Christ, you actually swung a fucking stapler at a guy twice your size . . . when you told me that, my heart nearly stopped."

"*Heavy-duty* stapler," she said. "Just like you taught me."

He let out a low laugh.

"I got him pretty good," she said proudly.

His eyes were just as proud. "That you did, slugger. You didn't need me, you had it under control on your own."

"Maybe," she said. "But boy, was I ever happy to see you. You got my call."

"I got your call. And now we have more questions than we do answers."

There was that *we* again but she nodded. "I know. And Morgan's not answering her phone."

"Because I thought this should be done in person." Morgan had appeared at their table looking pale and shaky. "I need to tell you both something."

And just like that, Elle knew the men really had been telling the truth. Morgan had been pulling a Morgan—she'd been holding back.

On everyone.

Archer nudged out a chair for Morgan. "I'm thinking you've got more than one thing to tell us," he said evenly.

"Yeah." Morgan sat like her legs were too weak to hold her and then dropped her face into her hands.

"Stop with the dramatics and just tell us," Elle said with what she thought was remarkable calm. "Tell us what you've neglected to mention. You're still in Lars's life. Or he's in yours."

"How did you know?" Morgan asked, voice muffled.

"I know everything," Elle said, wishing that was really true. For instance, she'd like to know if she'd get straight A's this semester. Or if she had a big enough tax refund coming that she could buy a new pair of boots.

Or if she was really doing as she feared and starting to trust Archer with the one thing she'd always promised to withhold—her heart.

He met her gaze and she tried like hell to hold it, to be cool, but he was scruffy and delicious sitting there all badass and pissed off that she'd gotten hurt, and she wanted to jump his damn bones, so she broke eye contract first. "Talk," she said to Morgan.

Archer watched as Morgan lifted her pale face and snatched a muffin from Elle, who gathered the basket close to her like it was a pot of gold.

Even he wasn't dumb enough to take food from Elle. And the most ridiculous thought came to him. If she was pregnant, say with a silky haired, blue-eyed little girl, he was a dead man.

Morgan sighed, took a huge bite, and swallowed. "I told you I'd gone to rehab a couple of times and that was true. What I didn't tell you was that in between I had a few rough patches where I . . . well, continued on in the family business of grifting to keep myself afloat."

"Hey," Elle said. "Not everyone in the family is a grifter."

"Fine," Morgan said. "I'm the only screw-up. But I'm serious about that all being so last year. I've been working hard at the jobs I could get, but nothing's paid enough to support myself. I can't do it on my own. I need a village. I need *my* village . . ." She looked at Elle.

But Elle shook her head. "You know," she said. "Yesterday I might've believed you. Why are you here, Morgan? What do you really need from me, because clearly it's not just a job referral."

Morgan sagged like her lungs were balloons that had just popped. "Lars contacted me and asked for my help, one last time."

"To which you said, 'when hell freezes over,' right?" Elle asked.

Morgan bit her lower lip.

"Right?" Elle repeated.

Morgan blew out a sigh.

"Oh my God, Morgan." Elle tossed up her hands. *"Seriously?"*

"Listen, I wasn't thinking straight, okay? I was

having trouble making rent. I don't have any friends I can trust and you . . ."

"I what?" Elle asked, eyes narrowed.

"You deserted me."

It wasn't easy to catch Elle off guard, Archer knew, and given that she probably still had adrenaline overloading her system from what had happened upstairs, he set a hand on her arm. Not that he would stop her from jumping over the table to go for Morgan's throat—hell, he'd help her hide the body if that's what she needed from him—but he just wanted her to think it through first.

"I didn't desert you," Elle said to Morgan, possibly through her teeth. "*You* deserted *me,* remember?"

"I was trying to protect you." Morgan eyed the muffin basket that Elle was still hugging.

"No muffins until you tell me the rest," Elle said. "Tell me what you did and I'll buy you your own damn basket."

Morgan hesitated.

"I just beat a man over the head with my stapler," Elle warned. "Start talking or I'll do the same to you."

Archer lifted a brow.

"What?" she said defensively. "She's my sister. I can talk to her like that."

Morgan stilled, her eyes going suspiciously watery.

Elle narrowed her gaze. "What now?"

"You just called me your sister," Morgan whispered and put a hand over her own trembling mouth.

Archer watched Elle struggle to hold on to her anger and fail. She could be as cold as ice when she needed to be, but she also had a heart of gold. He'd always thought that a weakness, but now he was starting to see it was really the opposite. It was a strength. And it made her a far better person than he could ever be.

Elle reached out and slid her hand into Morgan's. "You *are* my sister," she said gruffly. "You'll always be my sister. And if you meant any of what you said when you first came into town—"

"I did," Morgan said fiercely.

"Then tell me everything," Elle said. "Everything, Morgan, or so help me—"

"I know, I know. Stapler upside the head." Morgan nodded. "Okay, so you know Mom and Lars worked together back in the day. He had her doing cons for him, for a bigger payout than she could get by herself. She often pretended to be a Russian gypsy who could read fortunes. She went around finding 'family curses' and promising to remove said curses, which of course she always located in their priceless, heirloom jewelry. Sometimes she had me play the part of the curse expert on the phone—"

Elle frowned. "How did you let him sucker you into that?"

"It was Lars. But all I had to do was make a few calls to the mark. And again, this was years and years ago. But as we both know, one of the cons went bad. The police got involved and Mom rolled over evidence to stay out of jail. Lars wasn't so lucky. He was out on bail and then the case got delayed but eventually he went away for a few years. When he got out, he immediately messed up and violated parole and then went back for a few more years. He just recently got out again, and he somehow has it in his head that I still have the pot of gold—or in this case, a suitcase full of jewelry from that job."

"Which you don't," Elle said. "Because all you had was the brooch, and I returned that the night we all got caught."

The now infamous night, a night Archer had always looked at as a tragedy but that wasn't true at all. It was the night that had brought Elle into his life.

"You don't still have the loot," Elle repeated tightly to Morgan. "Right?"

Morgan sucked her lower lip into her mouth. "Not a whole suitcase." She grimaced. "But I do have a nineteenth-century pocket watch that supposedly belonged to Russian royalty."

Shit, Archer thought. Here it came.

Elle stared at her sister. *"Why?"*

"You're not going to understand."

"Try me," Elle said tightly.

"You don't let emotions rule over logic," Morgan told her. "You have a healthy mistrust of feeling deeply for anyone, and honestly, I wish I was more like you."

For the briefest flash, Elle looked like she'd been slapped, but she recovered quickly. "Tell me about the watch, Morgan."

Morgan rolled a shoulder. "He cheated on me. Once way back during the time of the first con, and then again when he was out on parole. I was angry and betrayed. I wanted him to feel some of that. So yeah, I took the watch. I'm not exactly proud of it and I didn't do it to sell the thing out from beneath him or anything like that—although I thought about it. But it was more of a . . . victory prize. He didn't want me, he threw me away. Mom told me to think of it as my tip."

Elle just stared at her. "If Mom taught us anything from day one, it was to never hold on to anything, not for sentiment, not for love, not for profit, not for *anything* because it would take you down, every single time."

"It wasn't for profit," Morgan said as she closed her eyes. "But it was for sentiment."

"What does that mean?" Elle asked.

Morgan opened her eyes and looked at Elle. "I kept the watch because it reminded me of you."

"Me?"

"Because it was from that night," Archer said quietly, understanding Morgan more than he expected.

"The watch goes with the brooch you returned," Morgan said to Elle. "And now I've set Lars on your trail because he thinks that I have more than that. I've broken your trust and screwed everything up."

Elle sighed. "This isn't all on you. It's also on Mom."

"And me. I did this," Morgan said. "But I can fix it."

"No," Archer said. "But I can."

They both turned on him at that, two sisters unexpectedly unified. "This is our problem," Morgan said. "*My* problem."

"She's right." Elle met his gaze. "I can't let you get involved, Archer. Not again. God knows what we'll ruin for you this time."

He took her hand in his, needing her with him on this. "This is right in my wheelhouse, Elle. I need you to let me and the guys handle this."

"Only if you let me in," she said. "I'm not letting you do this without me."

"Or me," Morgan said, equally stubborn.

Well, hell. This had all the makings of a complete clusterfuck but he had these two women looking at him, trusting him, and all they wanted was for him to do the same. "We do this my way," he warned. "Which means you're both still staying with me." He looked at Morgan. "No more vanishing. If you leave this building, you go together or you take one of my men with you."

"Can I have the cute one with the tats?" Morgan asked.

"Reyes?" he asked. "Definitely not."

"Why?"

"Because you'll eat him alive," Archer said.

"Well of course I will," Morgan said on a laugh. "But I promise you he'll like it."

Elle rolled her eyes.

Morgan cocked her head in her sister's direction, still looking at Archer. "You must be doing something wrong if that annoys her. Need some pointers?"

Archer was rethinking his stance on strangling her when she laughed again and stood up. "Okay, I'm going upstairs to earn my keep." She paused. "But I just want to say again . . . I'm sorry. I know that's not good enough, that I should've trusted you sooner. But I really am sorry."

And then she was gone.

"You do too much for me. I hate that you're doing this too," Elle said.

"You do plenty for me in return."

"Such as?" she asked.

"Keep me human."

She looked a little stunned at the admission and he couldn't say he didn't feel the same. He stood up, dropped some money into Tina's tip jar, and then pulled Elle out of the shop. He tugged her past the fountain and into Old Man Eddie's alley, thankful to find it empty.

Gently he pressed Elle up against the brick wall and kissed her. It was a relentless need, driven by worry for her safety, by the strange sensations in his chest that flooded him at her nearness, and by a driving need to wrap her up in his arms and never let go.

Elle surprised him by seeming to have the same need because she wrapped her arms around him just as tight and deepened the kiss. When her tongue touched his, her taste invaded his senses and he lost his mind a little bit. He wanted to eat her up. Every inch of her.

She pulled away breathless, shaking her head as if to clear it, laughter glinting in her blue eyes. "Trying to kiss some sense into me?" she asked, her fingers still tangled in his hair.

"Trying to kiss some sense into *me*." God's truth. "You're killing me here. You need me safe, right?"

"Of course," she said.

"So can you try to understand that I have the same need for you?"

She studied him intently and then slowly nodded. "Yes."

He trailed a finger down the curve of her cheek, across her lips, and down her throat, absorbing her shiver with his body. "Is that a yes, you'll let me keep you safe?"

"Yes, I'll try not to kill you while you do."

She was playing, but he wasn't. Couldn't. He cupped her face. "Tell me you understand."

Still not breathing all that steadily, she nodded. "I do. Just as you should understand that if there's any dirt on my backside from this alley wall, you owe me a new dress."

That night Elle stared at the L-shaped couch in Archer's living room. It was comfy but if she was being honest with herself, she didn't want to even bother with the pretense of getting ready to sleep on it.

Once again, Archer was in the shower. Morgan was on the couch, watching her with a knowing smirk.

"Shut up," Elle said, and she stalked into Archer's bedroom, shutting the door harder than strictly necessary.

She climbed up on the great big mattress and got under the warm bedding, hugging Archer's pillow to her face, inhaling his scent deeply. God, he smelled amazing. If she could bottle it, she'd make a million bucks . . . She didn't know how long she'd lain there drifting on that thought when she realized she wasn't alone in the room. And given the way her nipples got happy, she knew exactly who'd joined her.

Chapter 22

#HashtagGettingLucky

Archer stopped short at the sight of Elle facedown on his bed, apparently trying to inhale his pillow. She froze as if sensing him, and rolled onto her back.

"Your bed is comfortable," she said.

"Thanks, Goldilocks." Smiling, he moved to the edge of the bed, admiring the sight of her in it. "Were you just sniffing my pillow?"

"No." She sighed. "Maybe a little. You always smell so good." She sat up and let the covers fall to her hips. She was in one of his T-shirts and—he was hoping—nothing else.

"Tired?" she asked.

"Not even a little," he said as he sat on the bed, planting a hand on either side of her hips, caging her in.

She pulled him in and he let her roll him to his back

and pin him to the mattress. She was looking quite determined as she bent over him, holding his hands down on either side of his head.

"I wanted to surprise you," she said, shaking her head like she was surprised herself. "I don't even like surprises."

He flashed a grin. "But you like me."

She shook her head again. "In spite of myself."

He flexed his hands beneath hers but let her hold him down. "You seem like a woman with a plan."

"I always have a plan. But this one involves us being"—she wriggled on him and he bit back a groan—"very quiet." Then she oscillated her hips and the T-shirt rose up high enough on her thighs to flash him a tantalizing view of heaven on earth. "Can you be very quiet, Archer?" she murmured, bending over him to nip at his jaw.

"I was born quiet." He slid his hands from hers and up her shirt to cup her bare ass, wrenching a very satisfying moan from her throat. "I think the real question is—can *you* be quiet?"

She bit her lower lip, clearly remembering just how *not* quiet she was whenever he got his hands or mouth on her. It made him grin. "Lose the shirt, Elle."

"*My* plan, remember?" And then she grasped his hands, pressing them to her breasts. "All you have to do is lie there and look pretty."

He choked out a laugh that turned into another groan when she slowly lifted the shirt over her head, leaving her in nothing but smooth, soft skin and seriously mouth-watering curves.

"You're gorgeous," he said reverently. "The best thing that's ever happened to me." He met her gaze. "I've never wanted anything or anyone the way I want you."

She faltered for a beat as if stunned by this statement. "Morgan said I don't let emotions rule me," she said. "And she's right—"

"No, she's not—"

"She is," she insisted. "But I feel when I'm with you, Archer. I feel . . . hungry. As in my mouth actually waters for you." Then she leaned down and whispered in his ear. "And I plan on tasting every . . . single . . . inch . . ."

He pulled in a ragged breath as she traced the shell of his ear with the tip of her tongue. She then spent the next several moments touching every inch of his body with her mouth, leaving the sole part that ached most for her until very last.

By the time she placed her mouth on him he was no longer coherent. And moments later, as the world spiraled out of control, it was apparent that she not only owned his body, she was also the keeper of his soul.

The next morning Elle sat straight up in bed and found Archer standing by his dresser buck naked, searching through a drawer. He pulled on black knit boxers, cargo pants, and a black T-shirt. Then he walked to a wall safe and began to strap on weapons. Glock on his right hip. Knife clipped to the inside of one of his pockets.

Cell in another pocket. Black baseball cap on backward, boots on and laced up, flak vest strapped across his chest and back.

Why this turned her on so much, she had no idea but she could scarcely breathe for wanting him.

When he was loaded for bear, he turned and caught her staring at him, probably drooling, and his eyes darkened.

"Say the word," he said, "and it all comes back off. You'll be late for class, very late, but I'll make it worth your while."

She felt herself go damp and was so tempted she had to bite her tongue to keep the "oh yes, please" in.

Apparently reading her mind, Archer started toward her with sexy, wickedly dirty intent blazing in his hot eyes. He got to the bed just as a knock came on the bedroom door.

"Hurry up, bitches," Morgan yelled through the door. "I need the shower."

Archer groaned and dropped his forehead to Elle's shoulder.

"You should've let me kill her," she said.

At the end of the day, Elle was still at her desk when her phone went off with a text.

Morgan: I'm staying in the building instead of heading to Archer's with you. Got plans.
Elle: What plans?
Morgan: Poker game in the basement at seven.
Elle: No. Hell, no. I refuse to let you grift my friends out of their money.

Morgan: I won't cheat! The sexy geek said he'll bring me
to Archer's afterward. Okay with you, MOM?
Elle: Don't even think about sleeping with Spence.
Morgan: Aw. Worried about me?
Elle: Worried about HIM.

Morgan's response was the middle finger emoji. Elle rolled her eyes and stood up to get ready to leave when her phone buzzed again, a call this time.

"You hanging in there?" Archer asked.

She could hear the exhaustion in his voice. "Better than you, it sounds like. How about dinner?"

"You cooking?" he asked with such wistful hope that she was caught off guard.

"Yes," she said, then she stilled in shock. *Yes?* Was she insane? "I'm leaving now."

"With Morgan?"

"No, she's staying for tonight's poker game."

"Take Joe," Archer said. "Give him five minutes to get to you."

"Not necessary."

"There's a missing dickwad out there sending his goons after you and your sister," Archer said. "Humor me."

Three minutes later, Joe was at her door. "I've gotta stop at the grocery store," Elle warned. They got under way and after a while she eyeballed him. "I don't suppose you know how to cook?"

"Hell yeah I know how to cook," he said. "It attracts the ladies."

She rolled her eyes and dragged him into the store with her. "Help me pick out something that an idiot could cook and still impress someone."

He grinned. "You going to seduce boss man tonight?"

"None of your business. Can you help me or what?"

He set her up with a pack of steaks, potatoes, and a ready-made salad. "Doesn't get better than barbequed steak and potato, and a little green to make you feel healthy," he said.

"I don't know how to barbeque," she said.

"You turn a knob, toss these babies on the grill, wait a few minutes and then flip them over. Trust me, you'll have that man eating out of the palm of your hand." He flashed a grin. "Or wherever you want him eating . . ."

She gave him a long look.

This didn't faze him in the slightest. "Call me if you have any problems." He walked her into Archer's place, checked for monsters in all the corners, declared her good to go, and left her alone.

Elle walked out the living room sliding-glass door and stared at the biggest barbeque she'd ever seen. There was indeed a knob on it. As well as instructions engraved on the steel side. Turn on gas. Point knob to desired flame height. Grill.

"Easy enough," she said out loud. She turned on the gas. She heard it hiss out. Then she cranked the knob and—

Whooomph.

The flame ripped out from beneath the grill and just

about took her eyelashes and eyebrows along with it. "Holy shit!" she gasped, leaping back, tripping over a lounge chair, and falling to her ass on the deck. Sitting there, she reached up to touch her face.

Still there.

Relieved, she got to her feet and studied the flame before turning it down a little. Note to self: men are stupid. Five minutes later she had the steaks and the potatoes on the grill.

"Take that, *Iron Chef,*" she murmured as she poured herself a very big glass of wine. She went back onto the deck and stared down at the busy streets below, at the marina past that, and the gorgeous bay. The view made her sigh with pleasure. If she had this view, she'd never leave. She'd take off her heels and curl up on the chair and watch the world go by.

Which, in the end, is exactly what she did. She kicked off her heels, hiked up her dress enough to get comfy, and took in the view as she sipped her wine, feeling damn content and righteous as hell that she'd made dinner with her own hands for the man she . . . well. Wasn't that a little complicated? She liked him. A lot. She also admired his strength, both inside and out. He was smart, self-made, and when he chose to be, funny as hell.

And yeah, she possibly, maybe, probably loved him.

She leaned back and closed her eyes at that terrifying thought while images flashed through her mind. Archer giving her that just-for-her smile that very morning, the smile that said he got her . . . and damn but he did always seem to get her, in a way no one else ever had. Archer, ticked after that distraction job and yet he'd still taken her into his arms on the dance floor, rocking her to that slow song. Rocking her world while he was at it because there was no one who could make her as crazy as he did, and no one else on the planet who could make her feel as much as he did either. Archer, busting into her office, willing to put his life and limb on the line to save hers, always, without question . . .

The only thing more shocking than that was that she knew she'd do the same for him . . .

She had no idea how many minutes later she jerked awake. The smell came to her first, charbroiled meat. The smoke came next. And then when she whipped her head around, she saw the flames shooting out of the barbeque.

She flew to her feet, stubbing her toe on the leg of the barbeque as she slammed the lid of it down and cranked the knobs to off before crouching low to turn off the gas below as well.

By the time she straightened, the flames had died.

And so had the black lumps that had been the steak and potatoes.

Dead. She'd killed them dead. Reaching out, she picked up one charred lump, burned her finger, and dropped it. With a sigh, she shoved her hair back from her sweaty face—the heat coming off the barbeque was surely giving her a sunburn—and whipped out her phone. "You suck," she said to Joe.

"Only if you ask real nice," he said.

Ungh! "I burned everything!"

"Did you trim the fat?" he asked. "Keep the flame on medium? Turn the steaks after three to four minutes? Immediately remove from the flames?"

No, no, no, and a solid no. She disconnected on him and went hands on hips, staring down at the mess. Then she whipped her phone back up and called her favorite Italian restaurant, which delivered. She placed an order, offering to double the tip if they rushed it.

By the time she'd cleaned up the barbeque mess and discarded the evidence, the food had arrived. The delivery guy had a ready smile that faltered at the sight of her. Not having time to give that a single thought, she paid him and went into the kitchen to dish everything out onto plates and set the table.

She'd just finished when Archer strode in. He tossed his keys to the counter and headed straight toward her, his nostrils flaring. "What's that smell?"

She panicked. She'd lit the two candles she'd been able to find and she'd shut the patio door, but not before standing there like an idiot in the living room waving a magazine around, trying to get the burnt smell outside. "Um . . ."

"Italian," he said with a smile, staring down at the table. "I thought so. Chicken Parmesan? Looks amazing."

She took a breath and smiled with relief.

"I had no idea you could cook," he said.

"Oh well, I—" She gasped when he curled an arm around her waist and tugged her into him.

He gave her a smacking kiss on the lips and then pulled back, cocking his head as he studied her.

"What?" she asked.

"Like the look."

Pulling free, she turned to eyeball her reflection in his stainless-steel refrigerator and barely repressed a shocked shriek. Her hair had rioted and there were streaks of what looked suspiciously like charcoal across her jaw and cheek and forehead.

Archer came up behind her, leaving not even air between them, his hands on her hips, his jaw pressed to hers. He had to bend to do it too because she'd left her shoes on the patio.

Along with her brain, apparently.

"Barefoot in my kitchen," he murmured, his hot mouth against her ear.

And maybe pregnant . . . She thought of the test kit she had in her purse. One of these days she was going to take it. Soon. "Don't get used to it," she managed.

"What, you being barefoot?"

"Me being a mess."

He turned her to him and cupped her face, suddenly serious. "I've wanted in under your armor for a long time, Elle. Don't deny me now."

This just about undid her. It certainly left her speechless.

He smiled again, looking pleased with himself. "Can we eat now? I'm starving and your food looks amazing."

She watched as he moved away from her to sprawl into a chair and dig in. Guilt consumed her. "So about the food—"

"Hang on a second," he said around a huge bite, leaning back, his eyes closed. "I'm having a moment."

"But—"

"I skipped lunch," he said. "And this is almost as good as an orgasm. Only almost because let's face it, nothing's as good as an orgasm."

"I didn't cook it," she blurted out.

He flashed her a smile. "I know."

She stared at him. "You knew the whole time?"

"Well yeah." He was slathering a thick hunk of Italian bread with enough butter for a heart attack with one hand, spooning more chicken Parm onto his plate with his other. She had no idea how he ate the way he did and stayed so leanly muscled.

Bastard. "How?" she demanded. "How did you know?"

He slid her an amused glance. "My barbeque's still smoking and smells like you torched it in a bonfire. You've got soot on your face and on your feet. The trash isn't shut all the way and even from here I can see a take-out container near the top."

"Do you have to be so observant?" she demanded.

"How else would I be able to keep up with you?" An arm snaked out and he yanked her onto his lap, where he buried his face in her hair. "You cared enough to want me fed. That turns me on about as much as you barefoot in my kitchen. Barefoot and—"

She put a finger over his lips. "Don't say it." She didn't want to hear the word *pregnant* on his lips. Behind her hand, he was smiling. "You're a very odd man," she said.

"Have you taken a pregnancy test?" he asked around her finger.

"Not yet."

"Take the test, Elle. We need to know."

But it would change his actions, she thought with a catch in her gut. He'd stay with her out of even *more* obligation to her and—

"Stop." He lifted her face to his as he read her thoughts, making sure she knew his. "Whatever we find out," he said, "I'm here for you. Whether it's just you, or you and our baby. Always. But it's a fact that you're getting the raw end of the deal."

She shook her head. "Not true."

He nipped the finger she still held to his mouth.

"Very odd man," she repeated softly.

Not insulted in the least, he smiled and pulled her hand away from his mouth and then took that mouth on a leisurely tour up her throat, letting it make its way along her jaw to her ear.

"Here, Archer?" she asked breathlessly, tilting her head to give him better access as she eyeballed the table.

"Not the table. I've been dreaming about all the things I want to do to you and I don't want to be interrupted."

"There's more . . . things?" she asked a little breathlessly.

"Oh yeah."

While she quivered at the thought of that, he rose and carried her to his bedroom, where he kicked the door closed, hit the lock, and dumped her onto his bed.

Elle expected Archer to quickly strip her out of her clothes but instead he made himself at home between her thighs and nudged her face to his. "I want in your life, Elle. All the way in."

"Well if I'm not mistaken . . ." She rocked against an impressive erection. "You're about to get as far in me as you can."

But he wasn't playing. "You know what I mean. I'm trying to give you the time you need but I need a hint on how this is going."

"The fact that I'm halfway to orgasmic bliss in your bed should be a pretty big hint," she said.

He smiled. "So you're halfway to orgasmic bliss already, huh? Damn, I'm good."

She kissed his jaw and nuzzled his throat. "You are." She pulled back and cupped his face. "You're going to be able to stop manipulating me?"

He sighed. "I manipulate everyone."

"Yes, but I'm not everyone."

Their gazes locked and held. The silence stretched and finally he spoke. "Stay with me." It was worded like a command but he said it softly. Probably as close to asking as he would come, she thought, her heart pounding hard. God. Was she really going to do this, give him the power she'd never really given anyone by falling for him? "How about if we go one night at a time?"

"Works for me," Archer murmured. And closing the distance between their mouths, he kissed her.

Chapter 23

#GoingGoingGone

The next morning Elle walked into the kitchen followed by a dressed for general badassery Archer. He headed straight to the oven, turned it on, and set a bagel on the rack. He looked at Elle questioningly but she shook her head.

Carbs were the devil.

Instead she hit the coffeepot and poured two cups, handing one to the big, silent alpha leaning against the counter while he waited for the bagel to heat up. He gave her one of those smiles that made her knees wobble.

Morgan came in and eyed them both. "Cozy," she noted.

Ignoring that, Elle found an orange in the fridge and commandeered it.

"Seriously," Morgan said. "The big guy's even smiling." She turned to Elle. "Nicely done."

Elle rolled her eyes. "Gotta get to class," she said as she grabbed her purse.

"I'll take you." Archer looked at Morgan. "And you."

"I can call a cab."

Archer shook his head. "I got a call from Trev. They managed to triangulate the last calls from the burner phone, which were all placed from the Tenderloin District. We have a job we can't get out of this morning but this afternoon we're going to try to root Lars out. Until then, I need you two to stay in the Pacific Pier Building."

They drove in silence, everyone apparently locked in their own thoughts. As for Elle, hers bounced all over the place, from the danger Morgan had brought to their door to giving Archer another shot at her heart—which was possibly the most terrifying.

When they'd parked and were walking through the courtyard, Morgan turned to Elle and said quietly under her breath, "I'm really not okay with you all putting yourselves in danger to keep me safe."

"I get that," Elle said. "But I don't see another choice right now. The guys will get to the bottom of this soon."

"How?"

"They'll find Lars."

Morgan looked worried. "He'll hurt them." She reached for Elle's hand. "Can we talk?" She glanced at Archer, who'd gone on ahead of them. "Alone?"

A bad feeling went through Elle. "Yes, but I have a class and then two meetings. Can it wait until after?"

"I'll come to you at lunch."

Elle nodded and caught Morgan's hand, in which she held her phone. "You trust me, right?"

Morgan blinked. "Um . . . yes?"

Uh-huh. "If that's really true, you won't mind loading the Find My Friends app on your phone so we can keep track of each other."

To her credit, Morgan barely hesitated before relinquishing her phone to Elle so she could load the app. Elle decided to accept that gesture as a giant step in the Trusting Each Other Program . . .

Until Morgan didn't show for lunch.

At twelve thirty, Elle called Mollie, looking to see if her sister was maybe caught working through lunch. She'd gotten a text from Archer several hours earlier reminding her that he and the guys were leaving the building and he didn't want her going anywhere alone.

Mollie told Elle that Morgan had vanished about thirty minutes ago without a word.

Since it took two minutes tops to walk from Archer's office to Elle's, this wasn't good news. What was Morgan thinking? That she could really take down a dangerous man on her own?

Oh shit. That's exactly what Morgan was thinking. Elle brought up the Find My Friends app on her phone and sat there, heart pounding while it loaded Morgan's approximate whereabouts.

The Tenderloin.

She called Archer but she went straight to voice

mail. She tried Spence next. "I've got a problem," she said.

"Your problems are my problems," Spence said.

She'd been hoping he'd say that. "It's about Morgan."

"Okay."

"I need you to come with me to stop her from being stupid."

"Meet me out front in five," he said.

When she got out to the street, Spence was there in an old beat-up Ford truck. He leaned over and pushed open the passenger door.

It took her a minute to figure out how to climb up into the truck without flashing the world her goodies and when she did, she found Old Man Eddie squished into the backseat.

"It's his truck," Spence said. "He's not allowed to drive it anymore, hasn't been since the seventies when he got his license taken away."

"And it still runs?" she marveled aloud.

Spence flashed a smile. "Let's just say I've done a lot of work on it here and there when I've had time."

Eddie snorted. "Don't be modest, boy. You took the entire thing apart and put it back together again. Baby's better than brand-spanking-new. She's bionic." He looked at Spence. "Bionic's still a thing, right, boy genius?"

"Sure," Spence said. "But she's only bionic on the inside." He looked at Elle. "He didn't want anything on the outside to change."

"Of course not," Eddie said, stroking the truck. "Baby likes flying under the radar."

"And as for your next question," Spence said to Elle. "She's *almost* legal."

"I never question a favor." Elle searched for a seatbelt, finding only a lap one. It'd have to do. "But we're in a hurry. Does baby hurry?"

Spence laughed and revved an engine that sounded Formula One race ready.

Elle pulled out her phone. "I'm calling Archer to leave a message and let him know what we're up to."

"Good idea," Spence said. "Since I already did."

She slid him a look that usually had a man's testicles going north for the winter. "You didn't trust me to know that was the right call?"

"Bros before hoes," Eddie said from the backseat.

"He tried calling you back," Spence said. "You didn't pick up."

She stared down at her phone. Yep. A missed call.

"Text him where we're headed," Spence said. "He's going to meet us there. Do it now before he kills us both."

"I've got Morgan's dot on the map but I want to try calling her again for her exact location." Elle nearly collapsed in relief when her sister answered.

"Yo."

"Yo yourself," Elle said. "Where the hell are you?"

"Well, you're not going to like it."

"Try me."

"I'm on my way to Lars's place—"

"No—"

"I didn't want you or Archer to get hurt. I need to do this, Elle. I want to clean my slate. I want to start over without anything hanging over my head. That way I can get myself a life like you, with a great job, a great guy—"

"Morgan—"

"And I'm going to turn myself in," Morgan said firmly. "With the Russian pocket watch. It'll go back to its rightful owner and when it's all over and done, I'll be free and clear and finally in the right place to start anew."

Elle's stomach dropped. "Morgan, I don't know the statute of limitations on stolen antiques. You could go to jail."

"I stole it, Elle," Morgan said softly. "I did this. I'm coming to terms with paying the consequences for that, but first I want to make some things right. I hate all the crap and danger I've brought to your life and I'm furious at Lars. I need to see him."

"No," Elle said firmly. "No way—"

"I'm going to tell him I have the watch hidden safely away and that I'll give it to him if he promises he'll leave me and you alone."

Panic and fear were unhappy twins inside Elle. "He'll never do it. And you're not naïve enough to believe otherwise."

"Of course not," Morgan said. "But you know how

arrogant he is, how much he likes to talk about himself. I'm going to record our conversation and hopefully get him to implicate himself. I'm going down but he's coming with me. And the beauty is, he won't see this coming. He'll never believe a grifter like me would actually go to the police. But that's exactly what I'm going to do."

"You don't even know if he's going to be home."

"If he's not, I'm going to search it for the brooch and turn that in too. Lars inherited his grandma's house in the Tenderloin while he was in jail. It's a pit, but it's a free-and-clear pit, and he's living there."

The age-old need to protect her sister reached up and choked Elle. "This is sheer insanity. You know that, right?"

"He's probably not even home, in which case I'll get to B&E one last time." Morgan laughed a little but it didn't ring true. "You're not going to be a spoilsport and ruin the last bit of fun I'm going to have for a while, are you?"

"Fine, but wait for me," Elle said. "Okay? Just wait a few more minutes. I'm on my way. I'm bringing the cavalry."

But Morgan had disconnected.

"You hear that?" Eddie asked Spence excitedly from the backseat. "We're the cavalry!"

Before Elle could correct that notion, her phone buzzed.

Archer.

"Morgan's making a move without us," she said immediately. "I'm on my way to stop her."

"Address." His voice was his usual calm, although she detected enough heated tension coming through to pop corn as she gave him the best address she could.

"I'll meet you there," he said. "Wait for me."

"Absolutely."

"I mean it, Elle. This guy's a nutcase."

"I know," she said but he'd already disconnected. What was it with the people she loved and their terrible phone manners? Irritated, she shoved her phone away. "You know what's more infuriating than knowing he's right all the time? Having *him* know he's right all the time."

From the backseat, Eddie patted her on the shoulder in sympathy. "I've been told it's a male genetic disorder."

Much of what Archer did was hurry up and wait. Ninety percent of that hurry up and wait was routine, and if he and his guys did their job right the odds got even better.

But there was always a possibility of things going fubar and completely out of their control. Archer was trained and prepared for that, so he rarely felt a leap of sheer adrenaline and genuine fear going into a job.

But he felt it now.

He, Lucas, and Reyes pulled up to the address Elle had given him and parked behind Eddie's ancient, old Ford. He was relieved to see Elle in the passenger seat, which allowed him to take his first breath since Spence had called him and filled him in.

He'd felt a whole lot better when Elle had called him as well, but it wasn't until right this minute, seeing her sitting there tense and worried about her sister but still waiting for him, that he recognized what he was feeling.

Relief, absolutely, but also something much, *much* more. He went straight to the passenger door and yanked her out of the truck and into his arms.

"What?" she asked. "What's wrong?"

He tightened his grip and for a rare moment let his vulnerability show as he took comfort from her embrace. "You waited."

"You asked me to," she said a little ungraciously.

He was undone. He made it a habit to never be vulnerable and he was good at it, but with this woman, all bets were off. "Fill me in."

"I think Morgan's already inside. Her plan was to taunt Lars with the Russian pocket watch, telling him that she had it hidden, that she'd give it to him if he promised to leave her and me alone—"

Archer made a derisive noise.

"She's not stupid—she knows he's an arrogant asshole," she said. "But he's an arrogant asshole who will happily run his mouth to show off. She wants to implicate him. And then turn the both of them in."

He met her gaze. "And your plan was to go in after her."

"No, because you told me to wait. Oh and side note—you still suck at asking."

Eddie bobbled his head on his thin neck. "Girls like to be asked. It's a feminist thing."

"It's a *human being* thing," Elle corrected. "You wanted me to wait for you and I did. I don't see a car out front so probably Lars isn't even home. We can just get Morgan out of there and—"

"There's no 'we' on this," Archer said.

"No?"

"Hell no." He looked at Spence. "Watch her." Then he turned to Reyes and Lucas. "You've got the front, I'll go in the back."

The guys moved like smoke, mobilizing at Archer's orders. Archer started to vanish around the back of the house.

Elle followed him, hearing Spence swear from behind her. She didn't care.

Archer flashed her a quick look of irritation but she took it as a good sign when he nodded at Spence. "Watch the street."

The alley was narrow, lined with fencing and the occasional trash can. They counted buildings and Archer stopped Elle at the right gate. "I can get in and out faster alone," he said.

"But I can keep her from doing something stupid," she said.

He didn't like this, she could tell, but again he didn't try to hold her back. The back door was unlocked, the handle turning easily in her hand. She looked at Archer, surprised.

With a grim expression, he reached out to stop her

from going in, stepping in front of her. "Go back," he ordered.

Before she could follow his direction, shots rang out. Elle stood frozen in shocked horror as Archer spun toward her, tackling her down off the steps and onto the grass, hauling her behind a tree and pressing her down low there.

She reached out and grabbed his shoulders. Morgan. *Morgan was in there!* "Archer, we have to get to her—"

"I know. Stay here," he demanded in her ear and then he was gone.

She was wholly on board with that. She stared down at her shaking hands and gasped in horror.

One of them was covered in bright red blood. Blood that wasn't hers.

"Elle." It was Spence, kneeling beside her.

She looked up at him. "Archer was hit."

Chapter 24

#Crickets

Elle tried to control her crazy breathing but couldn't. Spence had her by the hand, probably to keep her from running into the house more than for comfort. They couldn't see much. There'd been no more gunfire and the odd silence scared her more than the shots had. She pulled out the knife Archer had given her all those years ago, the one she tucked into her pocket every morning out of habit, and slowly peeked around the tree.

"Holy shit, Elle," Spence said, looking impressed at the sight of the knife.

Reyes and Lucas burst out the back door from inside, guns drawn. Morgan was between them, looking unharmed. They located Elle with unerring ease, so either she wasn't all that well hidden or Archer had told them to come find her.

"Thank God," Elle whispered as she hugged Morgan

fiercely. Then she turned to Reyes. "Archer," she demanded, fisting her hand in his shirt. "Where's Archer?"

He looked down at the knife in her other hand and arched a brow like Spence had. "He's right behind us."

"He's been hit," she said, heart in her throat.

"Shit," Reyes said, turning back to the house just as Archer pushed through the doorway, shoving Lars in front of him.

Reyes and Lucas rushed up to detain Lars as sirens wailed in the background.

When Archer was relieved of his burden, he hesitated, weaved, and then dropped to his knees.

Elle rushed to his side, gathering him against her as he started to slump over. "I've got you," she said, clutching him to her. She had him and she wasn't letting go no matter what his stubborn ass said. She tore at his shirt to see how bad it was.

"You're carrying my knife again."

"Still," she corrected.

He let out a tight smile. "Better than diamonds any day."

Her vision got hazy when she realized he'd been hit in the groove between his chest and shoulder and that he was losing way too much blood way too quickly. His face was pale and he was cool to the touch as she lowered him down and carefully placed his head in her lap so she could apply pressure and try to slow the bleeding.

"Elle," he gritted out, peering up at her intensely as the paramedics began to cut away his shirt. "Are you—"

"Fine," she promised, letting out a sob as he closed his eyes. She could scarcely breathe. *"Archer—"*

He got his eyes halfway open again. "You're so pretty, Elle. Both of you."

One of the paramedics was working at staunching the free flowing blood, the other checking vitals and speaking into a cell phone. Spence was at Elle's side. "Don't worry. They'll put a Band-Aid on it and he'll be fine."

Archer weakly flipped him off and then grabbed Elle's hand. "You really okay?"

"Yes." She ducked around the paramedics working over him and clutched his hand to her chest. It was utter chaos around them and yet it somehow felt like they were all alone. "And so are you, dammit," she said fiercely.

A tight smile twitched at his lips. "Yelling at me even when I'm flat on my back." His eyes drifted shut and he muttered something that sounded a whole lot like, "Christ, woman, I love you . . ."

The words reverberated through her, rocking her to the very foundation. "What?" she whispered. "What did you just say?"

He didn't respond. Or move. She whirled to Spence. "What did he just say?"

Spence, who'd been watching the paramedics, gave her his worried look. "I didn't hear him say anything."

"But he did. He said—" She whirled back to Archer, leaning over him. "Say it again!"

"I'm sorry," the paramedic said. "He's unconscious."

Elle put her face close to Archer's. "If that was some kind of goodbye, Archer Hunt, I swear I'll follow you and bring you back myself. Do you hear me?"

"Lady, the people in China can hear you," the paramedic said. "Aliens can hear you. *Everyone* can hear you except him. Now I'm going to have to ask you to step back."

Spence pulled Elle back. "Easy, tiger. There's a bunch of cops here. No sense in getting arrested with the actual bad guy, right? I mean I'd bail you out of course, but you might have to spend a few hours in lockup in an orange jumpsuit first, and I know how you feel about orange."

"He was shot." God. Shot. Because of her. "He has to make it, Spence."

"He will out of sheer orneriness, trust me."

All around them was wild pandemonium. First responders were everywhere. Reyes and Lucas had been separated and were answering questions. As was Morgan. Elle gasped in horror when they clicked handcuffs on her sister, and she ran over there.

"I'll bail you out," she promised thickly.

Morgan gave her a tight smile. "Get Archer taken care of first. Don't leave his side for me."

"Morgan—"

"I can wait," she said, voice steady, her eyes not quite as much.

Elle hugged her fiercely. "I'm so proud of you."

Morgan's eyes filled with tears and a low sob escaped. "Right back at you, sis. But seriously, I've survived every single screw-up I've ever made and we both know there've been some spectacular ones. I'll be okay."

Elle gave her another hard hug before they took Morgan away. She turned to Spence. "I want to call a lawyer for her—"

"We'll call mine on the way to the hospital."

The medics were still working on Archer, starting an IV, controlling his bleeding. When they had him where they wanted him, they clicked the stretcher upright and prepared to wheel him out to the waiting ambulance.

"We're following them," Elle said to Spence.

He already had the keys out. "Yep."

This time there were no smartass comments from the peanut gallery in back. Nothing from Eddie but a tense silence. Spence gave Elle his phone, and while he drove, she called his attorney for Morgan.

When they arrived at the hospital, they were told Archer was in surgery and were directed to a waiting room. Elle called Willa, who was better than any calling tree. She called all the others, and within the hour they'd piled into the waiting room with her. Pru and Finn, Willa and her boyfriend, Keane. Haley in her optometrist's lab coat. Kylie, still wearing sawdust and sporting a suspicious Vinnie-sized lump in her sweatshirt pocket.

All of Archer's guys were there too as well as Mollie.

"Didn't expect to be back at a hospital so soon," Joe said.

Spence's attorney called back to let her know that Morgan's bail hearing was set for first thing in the morning. Beyond that, he couldn't say for sure, but he felt that it was possible she'd get off with restitution only, no additional jail time.

Elle knew and believed that Morgan wanted a clean slate more than anything, so this got her more than a little choked up and hopeful for her sister's future. She thanked him and disconnected. "I've got to call Archer's dad," she said.

Spence sucked air in through his teeth. "Not sure if Archer would want that."

Elle looked at everyone else.

Joe shook his head. "He'll be pissed."

"Super pissed," Finn agreed.

"But it has to be done anyway, right?" Elle asked.

No one answered.

That meant the call was hers to make. Fine, she'd made tough and uncomfortable decisions all her damn life, what was one more, right? She didn't have his number but she knew what station he'd retired from. She could at least get a message to him.

Spence did her one better and once again handed over his phone. He had Archer's dad's direct cell number. Elle left a message and then realized how full the waiting room was.

For a man who lived like he was an island, Archer sure as hell had a lot of people who cared deeply about him. She hoped he knew it.

"Sit, honey," Willa said, patting a chair between her and Pru.

Christ, woman, I love you . . . Archer's words echoed in her head. At least she hoped that's what he'd said.

"How do you do it?" Elle asked Pru, the one of them who'd been in love the longest. "How do you handle the sheer, overwhelming emotions of it all? And then there's the biggee—*why?*"

Pru smiled. "When you find someone who knows you're not perfect but treats you as if you are anyway, someone whose biggest fear is losing you, it's worth whatever you have to go through." She glanced over at Finn. "And if that person is someone you can wake up in the morning with and let see you without makeup and whatever other armor you use to hide from the world . . . well, you'd best hold on tight because if you let that go, then there's no hope for you."

Finn pulled Pru into his arms. "Never letting go," he murmured.

Elle's heart took a direct hit. She didn't want Archer to let go . . .

Two hours later, a man wearing scrubs and holding a clipboard appeared in the doorway and looked around the very full room. "Archer Hunt's family?"

She jumped to her feet. Everyone else stood up as well and they all began to speak at once.

The doctor blinked.

Spence and Elle stepped forward, and the doctor look relieved.

"He's out of surgery and in recovery," he told them. "We'll be moving him to a private room shortly and then you'll be able to visit him a few at a time. Shattered collarbone and some soft tissue damage. He lost a lot of blood and required a transfusion, but he's going to be okay."

Several hours later Elle was in Archer's darkened room with Joe. Spence had gone to get them some caffeine. They'd sent everyone else home until morning.

Through the light filtering in from the hallway, Elle could see Archer on the bed, heavily bandaged and heavily sedated. He was breathing oxygen through a tube and a saline IV drip ran into his left hand. The nurse had told her he was very busy sleeping and healing, and that the longer he stayed out the better because he wasn't going to be feeling great when he woke up.

She sat at his side and pushed the hair from his forehead. "That was enough excitement for the rest of my life," she murmured. "But the important thing is that you're going to be okay."

"Don't feel okay. Feel like shit." His eyes were still shut and if she hadn't been staring right at him, she'd probably not have heard him at all. Both she and Joe leapt to their feet.

"You're awake?" Her eyes immediately filled with tears and her throat clogged up. She'd never felt so emotional in her life as she bent over his bed and pressed her lips to his scruffy jaw.

Archer tried to raise an arm toward her but given his grimace and agonized grunt, he was caught off guard by the pain. "What. The. Fuck."

"Stay still." She put her hands on him. "You've got to stay still. You're in the hospital. Do you remember what happened?"

Archer blinked a couple of times, probably trying to shake the cobwebs. "You almost got yourself shot."

"Not even close because you put yourself in front of me and took the bullet yourself."

"Because I'm not the one of us maybe carrying our baby."

Joe stood up. "Maybe I should go . . . anywhere but here." He gestured to the door and then practically ran through it.

Elle sank back to the chair, worn out. Clearly Archer was a little more lucid than she'd imagined possible. And since she'd gotten the proof of not being pregnant an hour ago, she could at least take that off his mind. "I'm not," she said just as a nurse bustled into the room, beaming wide, Spence right behind her.

"Good evening!" the nurse said, all chipper. "Or shouldn't I say good almost-morning?" She moved to the IV pump that was attached to the pole and began hitting buttons. "Nice to see you're awake, Mr. Hunt. You've had a whole waiting room filled with people wondering about you all night. How are you feeling?"

"Fine," he said, eyes still on Elle. "I want to sign myself out now."

The nurse smiled and patted his arm. "Soon," she said and then flashed both Spence and Elle a look that said she'd majored in handling tough patients. She placed a small clicker into Archer's good hand. A cord ran from the clicker to the pump on the IV pole. "Press this if you feel the need for more pain medication," she said. "Don't worry, no matter how many times you hit it, you won't overdose."

"Good to know," Archer replied, stabbing the button with his thumb repeatedly, his gaze still locked on Elle.

"I'm not pregnant," she told him.

Spence blinked. "What?"

Archer just stared at Elle, his face all but impossible to read. "You sure?"

"Yes," she said.

"*Sure* sure?"

"*Yes.*"

He stared at her some more, and she'd have sworn disappointment flashed in his eyes. Good God. Maybe *she* needed some meds. Then he began to struggle to sit up, muttering something about options and how he'd been stupid enough not to narrow them down for her.

"What are you doing?" she cried. "*Stop.*" She rushed to him and held him down. "You need to stay still. What do you need?"

"For you to not sleep with Caleb or Mike. Or anyone with a penis."

"Well that definitely narrows it down," Spence said.

Elle eyed Archer's finger on the pain med button. "That must be some seriously good stuff."

"It's not the damn meds," he said.

"Let me make sure I have this right, okay? Only people with penises are out? So people who don't have penises are okay? Is that what you're saying?"

Archer blinked once, slow as an owl. "Maybe we make a onetime exception," he said. "If I can watch . . ." He was slurring his words. Closing his eyes, he put a hand to his head. "Fucking pain meds."

She turned to Spence.

"Yeah, it's the drugs," he said, looking amused. "He's a cheap-ass lightweight on drugs. He hates them, usually refuses all pain meds. I don't think they gave him a choice this time though, considering he was unconscious and all. He's gonna be seriously pissed when he sobers up."

"I mean it," Archer said, lifting his good arm to try to point at Elle, missing by a good yard. "Not gonna share you, not with anyone, not even Spence."

"Understood," Spence said, lifting his hands. "She's all yours, man."

"Excuse me," Elle said. "I'm not anyone's! I'm my own person! And are you listening to me? I'm *not* pregnant!"

Spence, looking pained, and also like he wished *he'd* been shot, sank to a chair.

"Still mine," Archer said from the bed, eyes still closed.

Elle choked out a laugh. It was that or scream. "First

of all, you're the only man I've ever known who could make me want to hurt him in his own hospital bed. And second of all, if I'm yours, then you're mine, pal. And I don't share either so you'd better tell that to all those women always tripping over their own feet whenever you so much as smile at them."

Archer opened his eyes and stared at her very intently, as if he couldn't quite focus. "We could just bite the bullet and make it official so there's no question."

"Official?" she asked. Maybe squeaked.

"Yeah," he said. "We'll get married. Spence?"

"Yeah?" Spence asked warily.

"Book two seats to Vegas."

Spence pulled out his phone.

Elle just gaped at them both.

Archer actually smiled then. "You're so pretty, Elle. I want to eat you up."

She turned to Spence, who was now on his phone. "He's not going to remember any of this, right?" she asked.

"Hard to say. Morphine's a bitch."

"Apparently." She stared down at Archer some more. His eyes had closed again but he was still smiling. God knew at what. She was torn between enjoying this and taking advantage of the opportunity to get him to talk. She decided to do both. "Spence, we need a minute."

"Gladly." And with what looked like huge relief, he made himself scarce.

Elle sat at Archer's side and reached for his hand.

"Did you mean it?" she whispered, desperately needing to know if he remembered the "I love you."

His eyes were still closed and he was breathing deeply, the kind of breathing one did when one was deeply asleep.

Which answered the question, she figured with more than a little disappointment, but then she nearly jumped out of her skin when he spoke.

"I've meant everything I've ever said to you," he said, just quietly without moving a single muscle, like maybe everything hurt. "I'm passing out now," he announced.

She stared at him as he drifted away from her, her heart pounding.

A few minutes later, Spence came back in and found her still sitting there. "You okay?"

"He lost a lot of blood," she murmured.

"He's been worse off."

"I think he's in shock."

Spence snorted. "Probably he's afraid you'll actually want to use those tickets I just booked for you. I know that'd send me into shock."

Stunned, she stared at him. "Wait—you actually bought us tickets to Vegas?"

"Hey, he sounded pretty serious. And God knows, you drive him freaking nuts. I thought maybe he'd finally snapped."

Elle had no choice but to laugh because she was the one who felt like she'd snapped. She wondered if they gave out morphine for that.

Chapter 25

#TeamArcher

The first thing Archer became aware of was soft, muted beeping. The antiseptic smell came next. Which meant it hadn't all been a nightmare. Fact was, he remembered clear as day stepping inside Lars's back door and hearing a gun being cocked. Push had come to shove and he'd had only a single second to make a choice. And that choice had been Elle. It'd always been her and it always would be. "Fuck. I was hit."

"That's what happens when you play the hero" came a voice he hadn't expected.

Archer forced his eyes open to find his dad standing at the foot of the hospital bed.

"Thought you left the hero game," his dad said.

Archer didn't roll his eyes only because it would hurt. *Everything* hurt. "What are you doing here?"

"My son got shot. What do you think I'm doing here? And why the hell weren't you wearing a flak vest? You forget everything I ever taught you?"

"Hey, I'm feeling fantastic," Archer said. "Really. Thanks for asking. And nice job on calling me back after, oh I don't know, *any* of my phone calls."

His father stared at him for a long beat and Archer did his best to stare back but he had problems. One, he felt like someone had skewered him right through with a hot poker. Two, he was high as a kite. And three—he couldn't see Elle.

Why couldn't he see Elle? "Look, I don't know who called you, but—"

"*I* called him," Elle said. And then there she suddenly was, standing up from a chair across the room.

He stared at her. "What the hell for?"

Anyone else would have backed down. But not Elle. Never Elle. God forbid she back down on anything. Instead she lifted her chin, eyes flashing her temper, although her voice was quiet. Quiet steel. "You lost a lot of blood. You took a long time to wake up." She paused a moment and he realized she was struggling to keep it together.

And suddenly he felt like the biggest sort of asshole. "Elle—"

"So yeah, I called him," she said. "Get mad at me, not him."

The thing was, she knew how he felt, how shitty the relationship was between him and his dad, and the *last* thing he wanted was to deal with it here. "You shouldn't have made the call."

Spence came up to Elle's side and looked down at him. "Hey, man. I'm the one who helped her track his number down so if you need someone to take into the ring, you're looking at him. But gotta warn you, you're down more than a quart so I think I could take you."

"Oh for God's sake," his dad said. "Is all this melodrama really necessary?"

"Take her out of here," Archer said to Spence, eyes on his dad, his every breath sending pain spearing right through him.

"I'm standing right here." Elle glared down at him. "You want me to go so bad, tell me yourself."

No way in hell did he want her to witness the showdown between his dad and himself. He was already flat on his back, as vulnerable as a man could get. He looked her in the eyes. "I want you to go."

She drew in a breath and turned away. Spence slipped his hand in hers and then they were gone, leaving Archer alone with the man staring down at him like he was the biggest disappointment of his entire life.

"Nice going, son," his dad said, "alienating the people who care so deeply for you. You're real good at that."

"Well I did learn from the master."

His dad snorted and then took the chair at Archer's side. He leaned in, elbows on his knees. "They say you're going to be okay. Your shoulder's going to be a bitch to rehab but you're young and in lean, mean, fighting shape so it's doable."

Good to know.

"I'm going to say some things now," his dad went on, "and I want you to hear them."

"I don't know, Dad, I'm pretty busy at the moment, so . . ."

"Smartass. You got that from your mother." His dad paused and when he spoke again, his voice was softer. Warmer. "She was a good woman. She got me, Archer. I mean she really got me. And she would've gotten you too."

He had Archer's full attention now. They didn't talk about his mom much but he wished they would because, Christ, he missed her. He missed her so very much.

"She knew how to handle us both. And she would've known how to keep you a part of the family"—he inhaled and then let it out slowly—"when I failed to do so."

This was more from the man who'd raised him than he'd ever heard in all the years put together. "Are you actually taking some of the blame here?" Archer asked. "Has hell frozen over?"

His dad shook his head. "You can't stop yourself, can you? Not even when someone's trying to hand you an olive branch. I'm trying to fucking apologize here."

Shit. Feeling like an asshole, Archer struggled to sit up, hating to have this conversation from flat on his back but damn, the pain—

"Here." His dad leaned in and fumbled with a remote attached to the bed. He hit a button that had the mattress jerking as the lower half of the bed raised, wrenching a string of oaths from Archer.

"Shit!" his dad said. "Hang on—" He pounded another button that had the mattress jerking again, this time lowering Archer's head.

"Shit on a stick," his dad muttered, randomly stabbing buttons now. All of them.

Dizzy, swearing, Archer wrangled the remote from his dad's hands, but he was trembling and now sweating to boot and it slipped through his fingers.

"I've got it!" his dad said, and he dropped to the floor. On his knees he hit a few more buttons until he managed to get the bed straightened out.

"Holy fuck," his dad said, swiping his forehead as he sank back to the chair. "That was harder than getting through the police academy."

Archer laughed and then groaned as that caused another wrenching pain. "Are you sure you're not trying to kill me?"

His dad's smile vanished and he blew out a long breath. "Son."

It'd been a damn long time since his dad had said that word in that voice. Not his cop voice. Not his in-charge-of-everything voice. But a *dad* voice.

Archer's chest went tight and they stared at each other.

"Elle's call took ten years off my life," his dad finally said. "So the question is who's trying to kill who?"

Archer managed a small smile. "Admit it, we're both surprised we haven't killed each other before now."

His dad snorted and looked down at his tightly entwined fingers for a minute before meeting Archer's gaze. "I know why you left. I even know why you stayed gone. What I don't know is why we're still doing this, pushing each other away. I don't want to do it anymore. I'm an old man, Archer. I don't want to die alone."

"Dad, you're fifty-two. That's only halfway old, and anyway you're far too ornery to die."

His dad laughed. "Yeah, that's probably true. And something else that's also true—I miss your stubborn ass."

Archer's chest tightened again. "You don't. No way do you miss that asshole kid who questioned your every word, the one who not only crossed every line you ever drew but butted heads with *all* authority figures. Cuz I'd think it'd be a relief to be free of that."

"Don't be a chip off the old block, dammit. Not right now. Say you miss me too." His dad leaned forward and put his hand on Archer's. "I fucked up, more than once. And eventually I'm going to meet up with your mom again and hell if I want her first words to me to be 'you messed up with our only son.' When she was dying—"

"Dad—"

"No, I'm going to say this, goddammit. When she was dying, she made me promise to . . . well, not be me. She made me promise to be gentle and kind and . . ."

His mouth shut and his eyes went suspiciously shiny. He cleared his throat. "My point is that I thought she was wrong. I thought the way to deal with my son was the way my father dealt with me. Like a hard-ass. Tough. Unbending. To build character." He shook his head. "But I promised her, even knowing I wasn't going to do it. And I failed her. I failed *you*."

"No, you didn't," Archer said. He squeezed his dad's hand. "I wouldn't have responded to gentle and kind and you know it. I was a serious punk-ass, Dad."

"Yeah." A small smile. "You were. You were also smart, sharp, and intensely serious. You had to be. I never let you be a kid. I didn't listen." He leaned in, his eyes serious. Intent. "But I'm listening now, Archer. I want more than this, just seeing each other at holidays or when we're shot."

"Yeah, let's *definitely* stop meeting when we're shot." Archer closed his eyes.

"So you'll consider it?"

"What?"

"Being my son again."

Again that tight sensation in his chest made it hard to breathe. He opened his eyes and met his dad's gaze. "I never stopped."

His dad reached out and hugged him then, slapping him, thankfully on his good shoulder, as he did.

"Don't squeeze," Archer gasped.

"Shit. Right. Sorry." His dad pulled back, swiped an arm over his wet eyes. "Goddamn, there's something in my eye."

"Or you're crying."

"Shut up."

Archer managed a smile but it faded at the look on his dad's face. "What now?"

"That woman you kicked out of here. Elle. She hasn't left your side once since you were brought in here, until now. She hasn't slept, and from what I understand your friends had to pressure her to even eat and she barely did that. She clearly loves you very much. You're going to owe her an apology. Loving you ain't gonna be easy, trust me."

"Tell me something I don't know. Dad?"

"Yeah?"

"Maybe you could get her to come back in here. But you have to ask, with a *please*. She likes the *please*."

"I'll send her back in if you want."

A few minutes later, Spence came back into the room. Alone.

"Where's Elle?"

"Gone," Spence said.

"Gone where?"

Spence didn't answer and Archer took his first good look at his best friend. His shirt was wrinkled, his hair standing up like he'd used his fingers as a comb, and he had black circles of exhaustion beneath his eyes. "You look like you should be lying in one of these beds."

"You sure you want to insult me?" Spence asked. "Because I'm the only thing protecting you from the girls, who want to know what the hell you've done to Elle. And on that subject, you're an idiot, by the way."

"What are you talking about?"

"You told her you loved her at the scene, you know that? The bullet nicked an artery and you went downhill fast. We thought you were going to bleed out and you told her you loved her. Like you were saying goodbye. And then you wake up and tell her you don't want her here."

"That's not what I meant."

"Actually," Spence said, "now that I think about it, you're not just an idiot, you're an asshole. An idiot asshole."

Archer tried like hell to remember telling Elle he loved her but he couldn't. Still, he knew one thing. "I meant it."

"So did I." Spence pointed at him. "Idiot asshole."

"No, I meant I love her. Shit—give me a phone."

He must have looked even worse than he felt because Spence actually hit Elle's number before handing Archer his phone.

He went straight to her voice mail. Fuck. He struggled to sit up and gasped at the pain, vision going all cobwebby. "You need to get me out of here."

"Yeah, I don't think you're ready," Spence said. Captain Obvious.

He definitely wasn't ready but Elle was out there somewhere, doubting him. Again. And it was all his own fault. "I'll sign out AMA."

"Against medical advice is a dumbass move," Spence said.

"Okay, Plan B. You go get her for me. Bring her back here."

"Not against her will," Spence said. "I value my life more than that. Did I mention that you're an idiot asshole?"

"Yeah. And thanks, that's super helpful." Archer's eyes drifted closed again. The lids were just too heavy. He felt like shit. He could handle the pain and the drug hangover. What he couldn't handle was Elle out there thinking . . . he didn't even know. He was stupid in love with her and that scared him but what scared him even more was living without her. "Go get her."

Spence just looked at him and Archer narrowed his gaze the best he could while high as a damn kite. "Where is she, Spence?"

"Hard to say. And we both know that if she wants to lie low, she's got the skills."

"Did she ask you for time off?"

Again Spence just looked at him.

"Christ. She did."

"Look," Spence said on a grimace. "I'm between a rock and a hard spot here, okay? You're both my best friends and—"

"Yes or no—she asked you for time off, Spence."

Spence blew out a sigh. "Yes."

Shit. He was definitely too late.

Chapter 26

#GivingMeLife

It was the next day before Archer was finally released from the hospital. He'd spent every second of that time sending his friends to hell and back searching for Elle.

But she was good at hiding.

He found out that Morgan was out on bail, thanks to Elle getting her a solid attorney. She'd be pleading for a reduced sentence and restitution. Lars hadn't made bail, and thanks to his priors, he probably wouldn't be seeing daylight anytime soon.

Archer had torn out nearly all of his hair and aged ten years by the time the nurse handed him a stack of prescriptions.

"Take the first on an empty stomach three times a day," she said.

From one of the chairs near his bed, Pru snorted. "I haven't had an empty stomach since 2001."

Archer's dad smiled. Yeah, his dad was still there. Even in her absence, Elle had managed to put father and son back together. Which meant in the end, *she'd* saved *him* and not the other way around.

And if that wasn't a big, fat pill to swallow. He'd always done the saving, but not this time.

He wanted to thank her. He wanted to grab her and haul her in close and never let go. But since he was in no shape to do that—he wasn't supposed to use his shoulder or arm until further notice—it would be tricky. Hell, at this point, he'd settle for just getting his eyes on her.

But she still wasn't answering her phone and if anyone knew where she was, they had a good poker face.

Joe tossed a small duffle bag on the bed. "Clothes, boss. Figured you might like some undies and shoes to go with that pretty hospital gown and sling."

Archer flipped him off, snatched up the bag, and staggered into the bathroom. When he came back out after changing, he was trembling like a baby. Sweating, he sat heavily on the bed. "I feel like I've been hit by a fucking truck."

"Or a fucking bullet," Joe said.

"Still nothing from Elle?" he asked casually.

But he didn't fool anyone. They all looked at each other awkwardly. According to all of them, no one had seen or heard from her, but he wasn't buying it. They were basically family, close-knit, and they were all connected daily by at the very least an ongoing group text or Snapchat. He suspected that the girls knew where Elle was, which meant that the guys likely knew as well, but at least in the case of Finn and Keane, no one wanted to risk being cut off by the women.

"Look," he said. "I messed up. We all know that. I messed up big too, on more than one occasion. But I'm trying to fix it. I need to convince her I'm the right man for the job of making her happy, so one of you has got to help me out here." He paused and sighed. "Please."

The *please* boggled everyone in the room. They weren't used to the *please* from him. But he wasn't messing around. "Well?"

Willa came and sat next to him, carefully nudging her shoulder to his good one. "Do you know the most beautiful part about loving a guarded woman? It's that when she finally decides to trust you and lets you in it's not because she needs you. We all know Elle stopped needing people a long time ago. Elle let you in because she wants you. She wants to be with you, Archer, just as you are, faults and all. She just needs to know that she can trust you to do the same, to love her as she is, faults and all."

"I do. Get me out of here so I can go fix this."

Spence was out front in Archer's truck as planned. There were three additional faces pressed against the back passenger window. *Not* planned.

"No," Archer said.

The back window rolled down and all three faces started talking at once.

"We can help," Pru said.

"You might need us to plead your case," Willa said.

"Because you're alpha," Kylie explained. "Alphas suck at apologies."

"Besides we always do this as a group," Willa said. "It's our thing."

"How?" Archer asked. "How is this our thing?"

"Remember Finn groveling to Pru on the roof?" she asked. "We were all there. And then when Willa had to grovel to Keane at his house on Christmas Eve? We were there too. See? It's *our thing*."

Too tired to argue, Archer sank gratefully onto the passenger seat and let out a careful breath.

"You need a nap first, old man?" Spence asked.

He could nap when he was dead. He slid a long look at Spence, who grinned.

"Just saying, you look a little rough. Maybe you want to wait until—"

"No," Archer said. "Elle's waited long enough for me to get my head out of my ass."

From the backseat, Willa clapped her hands and bounced up and down. "Are you going to grovel? You're going to, right? I want to see it!"

"Do you need some groveling tips?" Kylie asked.

Since it hurt like hell to crane his neck, he had to be happy with sending them both dirty looks via the rearview mirror.

Kylie held up a sleeping Vinnie. "Look," she said. "A puppy."

Willa snorted at this attempt at distraction and took Vinnie to cuddle him close.

"Where to?" Spence asked.

They all stared at each other, making Archer realize that they actually really *didn't* know where Elle was.

"She's not at her office," Spence said.

"Nor at home," Kylie said. "I went by there."

Archer leaned back and closed his eyes to think. Clearly she'd wanted to be alone. Why? To lick her wounds. She'd never liked an audience when she was hurting or feeling vulnerable. He had no doubt that wherever she was, she was holed up by herself, thinking too hard. Which would lead to bad memories from the past, *their* past, probably all the way back to when this whole thing had started, and just like that he knew. "I know where she is," he said, straightening in his seat. "But I've got a detour to make first."

Half an hour later, just as the sun was setting, Archer directed Spence to the park where he'd first met Elle that long ago fateful night.

"There," Willa said as they parked, pointing to the battered playground that included monkey bars, a swing set, and a slide attached to a jungle gym. The grass had died long ago, if there'd ever been any in the first place, leaving overgrown weeds.

A figure sat on one of those two swings, a curvy, beautiful blonde overdressed for the neighborhood.

Possibly the first person to ever sit on one of those swings in four-inch heels.

It was almost funny to him that he'd warned himself not to fall for her because his life was so dangerous, when the truth was that her life had sometimes been much more dangerous than his.

His heart had been sitting heavily in his gut ever since he'd realized she'd taken off on him and it didn't go back to its designated spot in his chest now either. She'd had a messed-up childhood but in spite of that, or maybe because of it, she'd become the most amazing woman he'd ever met. He'd tried to tell himself that she wasn't for him, that she deserved far better, and that was all still true.

But he didn't want to let her go.

He got out of the truck and turned back when he heard everyone else shift to get out as well. "Stay," he said.

"But—"

"But—"

"But—"

He held up his good hand. "I've got this."

"You sure?" Willa asked doubtfully.

No. And actually, he'd never been less sure of anything in his life. "I have to do this alone."

They all nodded reluctantly.

"I'll call you when I need a ride back," he said.

"It's kinda cute that he thinks we're leaving, isn't it?" Willa asked Spence.

"Yeah, but is it cute or delusional?" Spence asked.

"Both," Pru said. "With more than a touch of ego."

Taking in a deep breath, Archer turned and walked across the sand pit and grass, heading toward the swings.

Elle saw him coming and braced herself. She'd come out here to remember. To think. To put things in perspective, but although she'd been here a while, she hadn't been succeeding at any of it. Not until Archer had shown up with the cavalry, whom he'd apparently told to stay put.

And of course they had.

They loved him. They'd do anything for him, including—she thought a little darkly—help him find her.

She couldn't be mad. She'd needed this, needed him to come after her.

She had to admit to herself she was impressed that he'd located her. But then again, when Archer wanted something, he was doggedly determined, and against all the odds, he wanted her. She knew that much. Just as she knew she'd run scared. It'd never been about her doubting him. It was her doubting herself. She had no track record at this love game and it terrified her how much power her feelings for Archer held over her.

He didn't attempt to get on the swing next to her but sat on the bench facing her, looking pale and shaky, making her heart squeeze.

"Are you okay?" she asked.

"No. My arm and shoulder are on fire and my balance is shit." He paused and let out a low laugh. "But just the sight of you has me finally breathing again, so there's that. Will you sit with me, Elle? And notice that I asked, because you like to be asked, not told. See? Learning new tricks."

She smiled at that, but he didn't. "We need to talk, Elle."

Her smile faded. Nothing good had ever come from those four words. "I don't have anything to say."

"That's okay, I do." He patted the bench with his good hand.

She hesitated but she did move to the bench. Not within touching distance though. She wouldn't be able to think if he touched her. She met his gaze. His color was really off and so was his breathing. "You shouldn't be out here, Archer, you should be resting."

"I needed to see you."

She shook her head, throat tight. "You watched over me for eleven years. Your duty is done."

"This wasn't about duty. I meant everything I said to you, everything, even when I didn't know I was saying it. But when I asked you to leave my hospital room, it was because I was embarrassed for you to see me and my dad go at each other. I meant for you to leave the room, not my life."

"I figured that out," she said. "But it occurred to me that I was in deep with you, that I wanted to be in even deeper, and that scared me. I'm still not sure what you really want from me."

"A lot," he said. "But I'll start with a promise to stop saying stupid shit to you if you promise to toss out all the stupid shit I've already said."

She stared at him. "That's a lot of shit."

He choked out a laugh and then winced. "Yeah, I know. Think you can do it?"

"Did you know that Joe actually bought us tickets to Vegas?" she blurted out.

"Yes," he said. "I was serious about it." He cocked his head. "Is that why you ran?"

She looked away and her eyes landed on Archer's truck at the curb. Pru was holding up a piece of paper with the number five on it. Willa had four fingers up. Spence had used his iPad, showing a big, fat two. "What in the world?"

"I think they're grading my effort to get you back, and apparently I could do better. So about my promise . . ."

"If I've learned anything from life," she said, "it's that promises don't work."

"They do if they aren't broken. And I don't break my promises, Elle. Ever." He scooted closer, grinding his back teeth as he did, probably from the pain the movement caused. "You asked what I want. In all seriousness, I want to be yours. I want you to be mine. We could fly to Vegas, or go home to my place because I have the better shower. Whatever you want as long as we do it together."

"But we irritate each other."

"Yes," he said, "but I've discovered that I want to spend every irritated moment with you."

Her insides went mushy and she scooted closer.

The back window of his truck rolled down and Kylie stuck her face out. "It's the fountain," she called out. "It's working! The legend is working! You can't fight the legend!"

Elle shook her head. "The peanut gallery's crazy."

"You're just now figuring that out?" Archer took her hand and tugged her even closer.

"Hey, can we come out yet?" Willa yelled.

"No!" Archer yelled back without looking. He didn't take his eyes off Elle. "Kylie might be onto something about the fountain and true love thing."

She blinked. "You're not serious."

"I am. I want a life, Elle, with *you*. I want *everything* with you, including having a—"

"Whoa," she said quickly. "You heard I'm not pregnant, right? And I don't know if I'm ever going to be ready—"

"Dog," he said. "I want a dog with you, Elle."

She choked out a low laugh. Okay, so yeah, he got her, all the way got her, and she loved that. "But what if I don't ever want a big house with a high chair in my kitchen?"

His eyes were warm with affection and honesty. "I can go either way on kids, babe. What I can't go either way on is you. Did you forget? I love you. You."

"No, I didn't forget," she whispered. "But I thought maybe you did, or that it was just the drugs talking."

He grimaced. "Yeah, I'm a lightweight on drugs but that doesn't change anything. I'm ridiculously, deeply in love with you, Elle."

Oh. Oh, that was good to know, really good. "So you're not scared of being tied to me?"

"Oh, I'm terrified," he said. "You should hold me, Elle."

This got a real laugh out of her. "You're not terrified of a single thing. Not even nearly dying for me."

"You're wrong," he said seriously. "I'm afraid of plenty. Mostly of being without you." He gently squeezed her fingers in his. "You're it for me, Elle. From that long ago night when you looked at me like I was something special to you to when you reamed me out after the squirrels ate the wires to when you so fiercely went to protect your sister, even knowing you could get hurt. You're it for me, Elle. It's always been you. Only you."

She let out a breath she hadn't realized she'd been holding. "I feel things for you that I can't even name."

"Glad to hear it." He pulled her into him, carefully, slowly. "But it's your turn to say it."

She hesitated and the smile left his face and he became very serious again. Very serious, very intent, as he withdrew his arm from around her and closed his eyes.

"No, no, you don't understand," she whispered,

entwining their hands again. "It's hard because those words . . . I don't say them lightly." She paused. "Actually, I've never said them at all," she admitted and watched as he opened his eyes. "But I do love you, Archer. Always have, always will."

For a long moment they sat there in mutual surprise. After all the time they'd waited, they'd both finally come to the table with their feelings.

Feeling freer and lighter than she had in a long time, Elle smiled up into his serious face and watched his answering smile start at the corner of his lips and spread into his eyes. Then he began to awkwardly and one-handedly fumble through his pockets for something.

"You deserve better," he said, "but until I got my hands on you, I couldn't concentrate on anything else. *Shit*." He turned toward her a little, gesturing with his chin to his right front pocket, which he couldn't get into because of the sling. "Pull it out for me."

"Are you kidding me? We have an audience."

He flashed a grin. "I mean the box."

She blinked. "Oh." She reached in and retrieved a small clear plastic box. With a fake ring in it. The kind that came from a bubble gum machine. She stared at it, heart pounding. "Is that—"

"Yeah," he said. The band was painted gold with a gaudy green fake stone and she felt her throat tighten as he slipped off the bench to his knees, nearly falling over in the process. "Will you marry me, Elle?"

She gulped air. "You took too many pain meds, right?"

"No." He laughed a little. "You're killing me here, Elle. Yes or no."

"You're serious."

"Very. My knees are gone."

She dropped to her knees in front of him and stared into his beautiful warm, slightly impatient hazel eyes. Then she kissed him and pressed her forehead to his. "Yes." Her eyes filled as the horror of the last day overcame her, the horror *and* her overwhelming love for this man, and she sniffed. *"Yes."*

He cupped her face. "Don't cry. I promise to get you a better ring. There weren't any jewelry stores open."

Now she was both crying and laughing. "The ring's perfect. *You're* perfect." She ran her fingers over his scruffy, unshaved jaw. "I love that you couldn't wait until the stores opened. That's how I know how much you want this."

"You better believe I want this. We fought like hell for it. So let's stop wasting time and spend the rest of it together."

"Yes, please."

"Great. I can't get up."

Laughing, she helped him back to the bench, where she snuggled into his chest and held out her hand to admire the wildly gaudy ring ten sizes too big on her finger. "Where did you get it?"

"There's a lineup of candy machines at the pizza joint on Divisadero," he said. "And trust me, it wasn't easy. It took twenty-five bucks in quarters to get the one I wanted. Those fuckers are totally rigged. Spence was ready to buy all of the machines just so I'd sit down. Pru and Willa spent the whole time laughing their asses off and Kylie missed the whole thing because she was flirting with some guy who worked there."

"Never tell me you're not romantic," she said, and he smiled his trouble-filled smile.

"Well, you do inspire me," he said.

Epilogue

#HappyEverAfter

Two weeks later Archer woke up first. Since he was still on light duty, he hadn't had to get up at the crack of dawn to work out and then get to the job. He'd have gone ape-shit stir-crazy days ago except for Elle. She'd insisted that he, being incapacitated, needed someone to watch over him. She'd appointed herself the boss, demanding he rest and recuperate and recover by sitting on his ass until the doctor said otherwise.

There weren't many who'd ever been able to tell Archer what to do. Actually, there'd been no one.

Until her.

And the only reason he let her was because when she bossed him around in that sassy tone of hers, eyes flashing, it turned him on, enough that he sometimes gave her trouble just so she'd give him 'tude. She wasn't onto him, yet, although she'd been practically sitting on him every day, to keep him quiet and still.

There'd been some noteworthy exceptions of the naked variety. They'd had to be inventive to work around his limitations, but it turned out that, on top of being smart and amazing, Elle was also creative as hell.

But today was to be his first day back into the office. And yet with Elle wrapped around him like a pretzel, suddenly he wasn't in a rush to get back to real life at all.

Unable to wait any longer for her to wake up, he shifted against her. She stirred, smiling without opening her eyes as he gently rolled her onto her back. Covering her body with his, he spread featherlight kisses along her throat, heading south.

"Don't you have to go soon?" she murmured, still smiling. Her eyelids fluttered open and her baby blues focused on his.

He ran his hand across the naked curve of her hip before burying his face in her hair. "I'm calling in sick."

She froze and then struggled to sit up, trying to fight his hands to get a look at his shoulder. "I knew it, you pushed yourself too hard and you're hurting—"

"Not even a little bit," he promised, capturing her hands. "I just want you to myself for one more day."

She met his gaze and gave the slow smile that never failed to rev his heartrate. "Did you have something specific in mind?" she asked.

In fact, he did, and he reached for the remote on his nightstand and hit a switch.

Instantly a fire came to life in the hearth.

"That's kind of cheating, don't you think?" Elle asked.

He paused, looking over his shoulder at the flames dancing in the hearth, then back to Elle. "It's a gas fireplace."

"I know. But I'd have loved to watch you build a fire with your bare hands." Her eyes were dancing with humor. "Shirtless."

He laughed. "And I suppose I should've chopped the wood shirtless too?"

She let out a little whimper that had him grinning. "Yeah?" he asked.

"Oh yeah."

"Well, you're the boss."

She grinned and kissed him, a really great kiss, a deep, soul searching, body tingly, brain cell destroying kiss. "Say it again," she whispered.

He rolled to his back, pulling her over top of him, tugging her face to his. "You're the boss." He grinned. "For this one last day."

This made her laugh. "Just one more day? That's it? Then you're going to take a turn?"

"Yeah, then I'm taking my turn. Make it count, Elle."

She kissed him with such tenderness it made his heart feel like it might burst from his chest. Fisting a hand in her hair, he kissed her back with everything he had, adding a little nip of his teeth and then a glide of his tongue to soothe the ache.

She laughed softly as she straddled him and rubbed up against him until he couldn't laugh. Hell, he couldn't breathe. All he could do was hold on and try to show her with his body how much he loved her. He reached into the nightstand drawer and grabbed a condom. "We'll double up for now, at least until we figure out the high-chair dilemma," he said, lifting up to press a kiss over her heart. Then he turned his head slightly and kissed her breast, lingering until she sucked in a breath.

"I love you, Archer," she whispered and sank over him until he was deep inside her.

Flooded with intense pleasure as he rocked up into her, he gripped her tight, almost unable to believe they were finally here, in this very spot, doing what he'd dreamed about every night for years. "Fuck, Elle."

"Yes, please."

With a choked groan, he slid his hands into her hair, holding her head so that she couldn't look away as they began to move against each other. He began to drown in her eyes and he reared up to nip at her full bottom lip, taking control, making her melt into him as he buried himself into her over and over, holding her gaze in his, seeing everything she felt for him. He groaned her name, which sent her into a shattering orgasm. She was still shuddering when he thrust into her one last time and followed her over.

When she caught her breath she lifted her face from the crook of his neck. "I do have one last demand."

"Anything," he said, and he meant it. At that moment he'd have signed over everything he had to her, every-thing he would ever have.

"Love me," she whispered.

"Forever, Elle."

Did you love Arthur and Effie?
If so, be sure to check out the other books
in the Heartfelt Bay series:

SWEET LITTLE LIES

THE TROUBLE WITH MRS. LLOYD

and the special holiday novella

ONE SNOWY NIGHT

available now from Reading Hearsall

And read on for an exclusive sneak peek
at Jilly's next novel

LOST AND FOUND SISTERS

Coming summer 2021

Chapter 1

I walk around like everything is fine, but deep down,
inside my shoe, my sock is sliding off.
—From the mixed-up files of Tilly Adams's journal

Here was the thing: Life sucked if you let it. Quinn
Wellers worked really hard to not let it. Caffeine
helped. For up to thirty-eight blissful minutes it could
sometimes even trick her into thinking she was in a
good mood. She knew this because it took forty-eight
minutes to get from her favorite coffee shop through
LA rush hour traffic to work and those last ten minutes
were never good.

That afternoon, she got into line for her fix as always
and studied the menu on the wall even though in the
past two years she'd never strayed from her usual.

A woman got in line behind her. "Now *that's* a nice
look on you," she said.

Quinn looked at her. It was Carolyn, a woman she'd
seen maybe three times in her life, all right here in line
at the coffee shop. "Excuse me?"

"The smile," Carolyn said. "I like it."

Quinn didn't know whether to be insulted or flattered.

She smiled all the time. Didn't she? Okay, so maybe she forgot to smile lately. "I'm pretty desperate for the caffeine today," she said.

"Nectar of the gods," Carolyn said conversationally. Something about her reminded Quinn of an elementary school teacher with her gray streaked hair pulled back in a messy bun, the glasses perpetually slipping down her nose, expression dialed into sweet but slightly harried. "You're up," she told Quinn, gesturing to the front counter.

Trev, the carefully tousled barista behind the counter winked at her. "Hey, darlin'," he said warmly, hands working at the speed of light while the rest of him seemed chilled and relaxed. The LA beach bum slash aspiring actor forced to work to support his surfing habit. "How you doing?"

"Good," Quinn said automatically. And hey, she didn't like to brag but she'd totally gotten out of bed today. "How did your audition go?"

"Got the part." Trev beamed. "You're looking at the best fake Thai delivery guy who ever lived. I think you're my good luck charm. Say you'll finally go out with me."

Quinn smiled—see, she totally *did* smile!—and shook her head. "I'm off dating right now."

He said the words in perfect sync along with her and shook his head. "You're too young to be in a rut, you know that, right?"

She wasn't in a rut. She was . . . not feeling life right

now, that was all. "Hey," she said, realizing he was already working on her coffee. "I didn't give you my order."

He kept moving. "Has it changed? Ever?"

Well that made her want to order something crazy just to throw him off. Hell, it would throw *her* off too, but she held her silence because she wanted her damn regular.

And shit. Okay, she was in a rut. But routine made life simpler, and after the complications she'd been through, simple was the key to getting out of bed and putting one foot in front of the other every day.

"You should go out with him," Carolyn whispered. She smiled kindly when Quinn looked at her. "You only live once," she said.

"Not true," Quinn said, beginning to lose her sense of humor. "You live every day. You only die once."

Carolyn's smile slowly faded in understanding. "Then make it count, Quinn. Go hog wild."

Hog wild, huh? Quinn turned to Trev, who got a hopeful look on his face.

"An extra shot and whip," she said.

Trev blinked and then sighed. "Yeah, we need to work on your idea of hog wild."

When Quinn got to Amuse Bouche, the trendy, up-scale restaurant where she worked, it was to find her fellow sous chef Marcel already in the kitchen.

He glanced over at her, sniffed disdainfully, and

went back to yelling at Sky, the new hire, who was chopping onions the way Quinn had shown her.

"Leave her alone, Marcel."

He slid her a glacial stare. "Excuse me?"

Sky backed away from them both as if they were a live grenade. Quinn squared her shoulders and faced down Marcel the Tyrant, as the staff called him.

Behind his back, of course.

"I showed Sky how to chop," she told him. "She was doing it correctly."

"Yes," he agreed, dropping his fake German accent. "If you work at a place flipping burgers and asking what size fry you want with your order."

Here was the thing. Some days Quinn surprised herself with her agility, and other days she put her keys in the fridge. But she was good at this job. And yes, she understood that at twenty-nine years old and quickly rounding the corner kicking and screaming into thirty, that she was young and very lucky to have landed the sous chef position in such a wildly popular place. But she'd worked her ass off, going to a top notch culinary school in San Francisco, spending several years practicing cutting and or burning her fingers to the bone. She knew what she was doing—and had the tuition debt to prove it.

Oddly, Marcel wasn't that much older than her—late thirties, maybe. He'd come up the hard way, starting at the age of twelve washing dishes in his uncle's restaurant not all that far from here, but light-years away in style and prestige. He was good, excellent actually, but he was hardcore old school and as far as she could tell, he resented a woman being his equal.

Quinn did her best to let it all bead off, telling herself that she believed in karma. What went around came back around. But near as she could tell, nothing had kicked Marcel in the ass yet.

"You," he said, pointing at her. "Go order our food for the week. And don't forget the pork like last time. Also your cheese supplier? She's shit, utter shit."

Quinn bit her tongue as Marcel turned away to browbeat Sky's dicing of some red peppers. He jerked the bowl away to prove his point and ended up with red pepper all over the front of his carefully starched white uniform shirt.

Karma had finally shown up, fashionably late, but better than never.

On Sunday, Quinn got into the fancy Lexus her parents had given her for her last birthday in spite of her insistence that she wanted a cheaper, more affordable car, and headed to their place for brunch. A command performance since she'd managed to skip out on the past two weekends in a row due to working overtime.

She hoped like hell it wasn't an ambush birthday party. Her birthday was still two weeks away but her mom couldn't keep a secret to save her own life and had let the possibility of a party slip several times in spite of the fact that Quinn didn't like birthdays.

Or surprises.

She parked in front of the two-story Tutor cottage that had been her childhood home and felt her heart contract. She'd learned to ride a bike on the long driveway, alongside her sister who'd been a far superior bike rider, so much so that Quinn had often ridden on Beth's handlebars instead of riding her own bike. They'd stolen flowers from their mom's beloved flower garden lining the walkway. Years later as teens, they'd also sneaked out one of the second story windows, climbing down the oak tree to go to parties they'd been grounded from attending—only getting caught when Quinn slipped and broke her arm.

Beth hadn't spoken to her for weeks.

Coming here alone never failed to make Quinn feel hollow and empty. And cold.

And deep down, she was afraid nothing would or could ever warm her again.

It'll get easier.

Time is your friend.

She'll stay in your heart.

Quinn had heard every possible well-meaning condolence over the past two years and every single one of them was shit.

It hadn't gotten easier. Time wasn't her friend. And as much as she tried to hold on to every single memory she had of Beth, it was all fading. Even now she couldn't quite summon up the soft, musical sound of Beth's laugh and it killed her.

Shaking it off the best she could, she slid out of her car and forced a smile on her face. Sometimes you had to fake it to make it.

Actually, more than sometimes.

June in southern California could mean hot or hotter, but today was actually a mild eighty degrees and her mom's flowers were in full, glorious bloom. She ducked a wayward bee—she was allergic—and turned to watch a flashy BMW pull in next to her, relieved to not have to go inside alone.

Brock Holbrook slid out of his car looking camera ready and she couldn't help but both smile and roll her eyes. "Suck up," she said gesturing to his suit and tie.

Brock flashed a grin. "I just know where my bread's buttered."

He worked for her father's finance company and no one could deny that Brock knew how to work a room. He was good-looking, charismatic, and when he looked at her appreciatively, she waited for the zing she used to get from that very look.

But it'd been two years almost to the day since she'd felt a zing for anything. She sighed and Brock tilted his head at her, eyes softer now, understanding.

He knew. He'd been there when she'd found out about her sister Beth's death. But his understanding didn't help.

She'd rather feel again, dammit.

The front door opened behind them and Quinn glanced over. Both her parents and Brock's stood in the doorway, all four of them smiling a greeting at the chickens coming home to the nest, where they'd be pecked at for all the details of their lives.

Quinn loved her parents madly and they loved her, but brunch was going to be more invasive than a gyno exam on the 405 South at peak traffic hours.

Brock grabbed Quinn's hand, tugged her into him and planted a kiss on her lips. It wasn't a hardship. He also looked good, and he knew it. He kissed good as well and he knew that too.

But though they'd slept together occasionally over the years, it'd been a while. Two, to be exact. Still, the kiss was nice, and normally she'd try to enjoy it— except he was only doing it for the show.

So she nipped at his bottom lip. Hard.

Laughing, he pulled back only very slightly. "Feeling feisty?"

"I'm not sleeping with you."

"You should."

"Pray tell why."

"It's been so long, I'm worried you're depressed."

This was just uncomfortably close enough to the truth to have her defenses slam down. "I'm not depressed."

"Not you," he said. "Your vagina."

She snorted and pulled free. "Shut up."

"Just keep it in mind," he said, a smile in his voice. He took her hand back and held it as he led her up the front path, clearly having already accessed that she was a fight risk.

"I should've bitten you harder," she murmured, smiling at the parentals.

"Next time," he murmured back, also smiling. "Feeling vicious today, I take it?"

"*Annoyed*," she corrected.

"Ah. I guess turning old does that to a person."

He was nine months younger than her and for just about all their lives—they'd met in kindergarten when he'd socked a boy for pushing her—he'd been smug about their age difference. She nudged him with her hip and knocked him off balance. He merely hauled her along with him, wrapping both his arms around her so that by all appearances *he'd* just saved *her* from a fall. His face close to hers, he gave her a wink.

And suddenly it occurred to her that this wasn't about her at all, but him. His parents must be on him again about giving them grandbabies. The truth was everyone expected them to marry. And she got it, she did. Brock had been her middle *and* high school boyfriend, and they'd gone off to college together until they'd had a wildly dramatic and traumatic breakup their first year involving his inability to be monogamous. Oh, he loved her. She had no doubt. But he also loved anyone who batted their eyes and smiled at him.

It'd taken a few years, but eventually they'd found their way back to being friends. Best friends at times, and had gotten into the habit of being each other's plus one. They even had a promise that if they were still single at age forty, they'd put a ring on it, but it was more a joke than a real vow.

"You're only making it worse for both of us," she whispered as they got close to the front door.

"If they think we're working on things," Brock said out the side of his mouth, "they'll leave me the hell alone."

She shrugged, conceding the point. There were hugs of greeting and airy almost-but-not-quite cheek kisses. "Still not used to it," Lucinda murmured to Quinn, clinging for an extra minute. "It never feels right, you here without her . . ."

She didn't mean it hurtfully, Quinn knew it. Her mom wouldn't hurt a fly, but as always, a lump the size of Texas stuck in her throat. "I know, Mom."

"I miss her so much. You're so strong, Quinn, the way you've moved on."

Had she? Moved on? Or was she treading water, staying in place, just managing to keep her head above the surface? One thing for certain, she'd buried her feelings, deep. It'd been the only way to survive the all-encompassing grief, which sat like a big fat elephant on her chest. She'd locked it away in a dark corner of her heart and built a wall around it, brick by painstaking brick to contain the emotions that had nearly taken her down.

But she knew she was lucky. She had a job she loved, parents who cared, and a best friend slash fall-back husband if it ever came to that. Yes, she was turning thirty soon and that surprise party still lay in wait regardless of the fact that she didn't want it. And while she'd like to pretend that wasn't happening, it wouldn't derail her because compared to what she'd been through, there was nothing scary ahead of her.

Famous last words.

A week later, Quinn was in line for her usual afternoon before-work latte when she felt the weight of someone's gaze on her. Turning, she found a guy around her age with black tousled hair and black rimmed glasses, who looked a lot like a grown-up Harry Potter.

He was staring at her with an intensity that had her blinking and then craning her neck to peek behind her. No one, which meant he was staring at her. She turned away and did her best to ignore him. The women in line in front of her were chatting . . .

"Orgasms after the age of fifty suck," one said to the other. "No one tells you that but they do."

Her friend agreed with an emphatic head bob. "I know. It's like sand paper down there in Lady Town. Takes an entire tube of lube and a bottle of gin."

The first woman snorted. "Don't get me started. Alan can't give me ten minutes to find the G-spot but he'll spend thirty minutes looking for a golf ball . . ."

Quinn must have made some sound because they both turned to her with apologetic laughs. "Sorry," Dry Vagina said. "But it's just one of the many, many things coming your way, along with hot flashes and murderous urges."

Yay. Something to look forward to.

"Excuse me," someone said behind her.

Harry Potter, her stalker.

"I need to speak to you," he said.

Oh boy. "Sorry," she said but before she could finish her polite excuse, one of her new friends spoke up.

"No need to make a hasty decision, honey. He might be suitably employed with no baggage."

"Impossible," Dry Vagina said. "That'd be like finding a unicorn."

"Are you a unicorn?" the first woman asked him.

Harry Potter blinked at her and then looked at Quinn with more than a little desperation. "Can I please talk to you . . . alone?"

"Not alone," the first woman said. "That sounds like stranger danger. You can do your pickup line magic right here in the crowd, or better yet do it online like the rest of the world."

The guy never took his gaze off Quinn. "You're Quinn Weller, right?"

How did he know her name? "You're going to need to go first," Quinn said.

"I'm Cliff Porter. I'm an attorney and I really need a word with you. Privately."

She stared at him, trying to come up with a reason why an attorney would be looking for her.

"Porter or Potter?" Dry Vagina asked. "Because Potter would make more sense."

He looked pained. "I get that a lot but it's Porter."

"How do you know my name?" Quinn asked.

"Look, can we just . . ." He gestured to a small table off to the side of the line.

Torn between curiosity and a healthy sense of survival, Quinn hesitated. "I'm late for work."

"This will only take a minute."

Reluctantly, she stepped out of line and moved to the table. "You've got one minute."

He took a deep breath. "As I said, I'm an attorney. I'm from Wildstone, a small town about two hundred miles north. I'm here to give you news of an inheritance."

Quinn blinked. "Okay first, I've never heard of Wildstone. And second, I certainly don't know anyone from there."

"We're a small ranching town that sits in a bowl between the Pacific Coast and wine country," he said. "Would you like to sit?" he asked quietly, and also very kindly she had to admit. "Because the rest of this is going to be a surprise."

"I don't like surprises," she said, "and you have thirty seconds left."

It was clear from his expression that he wasn't happy about having to go into the details in public, but as he was a stranger and maybe also a crackpot, too damn bad.

He drew a deep breath. "The person who left you some property was your birth mother."

She stared at him and then slowly sank into the before-offered chair without looking, grateful it was right behind her. "You're mistaken," she finally said, shaking her head. "I wasn't adopted."

He gave her a wan smile. "I'm really sorry to have to be the one to tell you, but you were."

"I have parents. Lucinda and James Weller."

"They adopted you when you were two days old."

The shock of that reverberated through her body. "No," she whispered. Heart suddenly racing, palms clammy, she shook her head. "They would've told me. There's absolutely no way . . ."

"I'm very sorry," Cliff said quietly. "But it's true. They adopted you from Carolyn Adams." He pulled a picture from his briefcase and pushed it across the table toward her.

And Quinn's heart stopped. Because it was Carolyn, the woman who she'd met here in this very coffee shop.

Chapter 2

Quinn blinked, shocked to find herself sitting on the curb outside the coffee shop staring blindly at the Lexus her parents had given her.

Her parents. Who might not really be her parents.

"Here," Cliff said, pushing a cup of cold water into her hands as he sat next to her. "Drink this."

She took the cup in two shaking hands and gulped down the water, wishing a little bit that it was vodka. "You're mistaken," she said again. "Carolyn was just a woman I met here. We spoke only a few times."

"Three." Cliff gazed at her sympathetically. "She told me about the visits. She drove down here to get a peek at you, borne out of a desperate curiosity."

"I don't understand," Quinn whispered.

"She knew she was terminal and had set a trust in place," Cliff said. "She had every intention of telling you herself, but she had a seizure driving back to Wildstone the last day you saw her. She died in the accident."

"Oh my God."

Cliff took the cup of water from her before she could drop it. "The funeral was five days ago," he said.

Quinn let out a sound that might have been a

mirthless laugh or a half sob, she wasn't sure. She shook her head for what felt like the hundredth time in the past few minutes, but it still didn't clear.

It wasn't true, she told herself. Not any of it. Harry Potter here was just a stalker, a good one. Or maybe a scammer. She hated to think that the nice woman she knew as Carolyn could be a part of something so seedy, but she simply couldn't accept that her parents wouldn't have told her such a crucial thing such as being adopted. For God's sake, she'd seen infant pictures of herself in the hospital with them.

"Look," she said, standing up. "I don't want any part of this."

"There's an inheritance."

"Especially that," she said. "I don't want it or any part of this game you're playing. I wasn't adopted and your minute is up and I'm leaving."

"Wait." He stood up too, and looked at her with nothing but kindness and understanding in his gaze. "Take my wand."

She blinked, expecting to see a lightning bolt scar appear on his forehead. "What?"

"My card," he said, his gaze turning to concern. "Give yourself some time to think about it. Contact me when you're ready. Are you going to be alright?"

There was only one answer to that. "Of course."

Always.

She drove to work on auto-pilot, Cliff Potter, er Porter's, tale eating at her. She was clumsy in the kitchen, dropping and spilling things, plating the wrong entrees, mistaking shallots for onions, forgetful . . .

"What the hell is wrong with you?" Marcel had lost his temper with her somewhere around the time she'd dropped a platter of stuffed peppers. "Get out of my kitchen, you *schlampe*."

She wasn't positive of the exact translation on that one, but she was pretty sure it was something along the lines of grungy or dirty woman. She carefully and purposely set down her knife so she didn't run it through him.

"You're clumsy, forgetful, and making more work than food!"

For once he was right. Because all she could think about was Cliff Porter's visit.

They adopted you when you were two days old . . .

"Are you listening to me?" Marcel yelled up at her. Up, because he was five-foot-two to her five-foot-seven, something that normally gave her great pleasure.

"*Du flittchen*," he muttered in disgust beneath his breath, and the entire staff froze in the kitchen like dear in the headlights.

Slut. She turned to him. "*Schiebe es*," she said, which meant *shove it*. It was the best she could do, at least in German. Pushing past him, she walked out of the kitchen.

"Where are you going?" he yelled after her. "You can't just leave!"

But leaving was exactly what she was doing. Outside, she pulled out her cell phone to call her boss, Chef Wade.

"Everything okay?" he asked.

"I have to leave early," she said. "I'm sorry for the short notice but Marcel is here. He's got things under control." By being a tyrannical asshole, but that was another story.

After she disconnected, she drove on autopilot to her parents' house. She needed to straighten out this stupid adoption story and she needed to do so before her life imploded.

Her mom and dad were in the living room in front of their lit gas fireplace, sharing a drink. It was June in LA and the air conditioner was on full blast, but her mother liked a nightcap with ambience.

"Darling," her mom said, smiling as she stood in welcome. "Such a lovely surprise. Where's Brock?"

"I'm alone," Quinn said, not bothering to address the fact that she didn't spend nearly as much time with Brock as they seemed to believe. "I met someone today."

Her mom blinked. "Other than Brock? What will people think?"

"Mom . . ." Quinn pressed her fingertips into her eye sockets to ward off an eye twitch. "I keep telling you, Brock and I aren't going to get married."

"Right *now* you mean," she said. "Right?"

A conversation she didn't have the strength for. "I met someone who told me an interesting story. Do either of you want to guess what that was?"

Her mom shook her head and looked at her dad, who did the same.

"The story is that I'm adopted."

And at the twin looks of shock and guilt on her parents' faces, she knew it was true. "Oh my God." She staggered to the couch opposite them and sank to it, staring at them. "Oh my God, it's not a story at all."

There was an awkward beat of utter silence and Quinn stood up and headed straight to the kitchen. She needed alcohol or sugar, stat. Thank Toll House, she found some ready-made cookie dough in the fridge.

She was stuffing spoonfuls into her mouth when her parents appeared in the doorway. "It's day one of my new raw food diet," she said around a mouthful.

"Quinn," her dad said. "We need to talk."

Ya think? "I just have one question," she said.

In unison, they came up to the opposite side of the island as she chewed and swallowed cookie dough with enthusiasm. "Honey," her mom said quietly, earnestly. "Me first, okay?"

Quinn nodded.

"If you eat that whole thing, it's the equivalent of forty-eight cookies."

Quinn stared at her. "*That's* the something you wanted to say? Really?"

Her dad sighed and leaned onto the island. "Quinn . . ." He paused to nudge the block of knives out of her reach. "We never expected you to find out."

She felt her mouth fall open. She scooped up the last of the dough with her bare fingers and shoved it into her mouth.

"Quinn," her mom said but stopped when Quinn held up a finger.

She chewed. Swallowed. Took a deep breath. "Why?" she asked. "Why didn't you tell me? What possible reason do you have for keeping it a secret?"

"Because I wanted you to be mine," her mom said softly, her eyes soft and dammit, a little damp.

Her dad slid an arm to her mom's waist. "It wasn't important *how* we got you," he said. "We wanted a baby, and we couldn't have our own."

Quinn sucked in a breath as something occurred to her. "Beth. Was she adopted too?"

"No," her mom said. "We'd tried for years and were told we couldn't have our own. So we set an adoption in motion. When you came along, we were so grateful, but then the unbelievable happened. I got pregnant when you were two months old."

Quinn's heart squeezed hard.

"I'm more grateful to Carolyn than you could ever know," her mom said. "But she signed a confidentiality agreement. We could sue her for talking about the adoption."

"Too late," Quinn said. "She's dead too. And apparently she left me an inheritance."

"What? She had nothing to speak of."

"I don't know. I was so shocked I didn't ask." She drew a careful breath. "Why didn't you tell me? Were you sorry you'd adopted after Beth came along?"

"No." Her mom came around the island and took

Quinn's hands in her own. "No," she said again more firmly. "It was a happy accident. The truth is, we didn't want to take away from either of you so we just kept it quiet. It didn't matter to us, and I know this is asking a lot, but I wish it didn't matter to you."

Her dad nodded.

Quinn let out a breath and took a step away from them. "I need to think."

"But why?" her mom asked. "It doesn't matter, none of this matters. Let's just look forward to you marrying Brock and getting on with your lovely life."

"Mom—" Quinn broke off and closed her eyes. "I'm not getting married. How can I? I don't even know who I am."

"Okay," her dad said. "That's a little dramatic, don't you think?"

Quinn let out a low laugh. "You know what, Dad? You're right. It is. And now I'm going to take my dramatic ass home. I need some time."

"Time?" her mom asked. "But you're still coming over next week for dinner, right?"

Quinn had gotten to the door. She turned around to find them standing in the same position at the island, looking shocked at her little temper tantrum. "Let me get this straight," she said. "You can't keep my surprise party a secret, but you were able to keep my adoption one?"

Her mom bit her lower lip. "There's no party."

With another low, mirthless laugh, Quinn left. She drove home to her cute, quiet, comfortable condo and stared at herself in the bathroom mirror. She was in shock, adrift, sad, angry . . . so many, many things.

It was more emotion than she'd felt in two years.

She'd meant it when she'd told Cliff that she didn't want anything to do with any inheritance, especially not from someone who'd apparently thrown her away without so much as looking back.

Not that she was happy with her parents right now, either. They should have told her the truth a long time ago. Instead they'd hidden it, and even now had tried to underplay it, encouraging her to get on with her nice, comfortable life.

But it suddenly didn't feel so nice or comfortable anymore.

Feeling shockingly . . . alone, she looked at her phone. She wanted to call her sister. God, how she wanted that, but instead she called Brock.

"Hey," he said when he picked up, his voice brisk and rushed. "I'm in a meeting. Can I get back to you?"

Disappointment washed over her. "Yes, but—"

"Great, thanks."

And then he disconnected. She tried to let that short connection be enough, tried to tell herself that just hearing his voice helped. But her heart was racing and it didn't seem to fit in her ribcage. *Everything* felt tight and she couldn't breathe because she had no one else to call.

Well, except one person.

Harry Potter, a.k.a. Cliff Porter.